"Joe, I'd be indebted to you forever if you could tell me what's wrong with me. Maybe I can fix it before I put myself out there again."

Rebecca shook her head. Now that the question was out, she wished she'd kept it to herself.

She started to tell him not to answer.

Catching her hand, Joe froze the words in her throat as he turned her to face him. For a moment, he said nothing. He just stood there while the breeze blew her hair across her neck and his eyes moved slowly over her face.

He lifted his hand again to tuck her hair behind her ear. "There's nothing to fix. There's nothing wrong with you, Rebecca." The temptation was to let his touch linger. Her hair felt like silk, her skin like warm satin.

"You just haven't met the right man yet."

The City Girl and the Country Doctor

CHRISTINE FLYNN

MILLS & BOON

Pure reading pleasure

*First published in Great Britain 2007
by Harlequin Mills & Boon Limited,
Eton House, 18-24 Paradise Road, Richmond, Surrey TW9 1SR*

© Harlequin Books S.A. 2006

*Special thanks and acknowledgement are given to Christine Flynn for her
contribution to the TALK OF THE NEIGHBOURHOOD mini-series.*

ISBN: 978 0 263 85660 6

23-1107

*Harlequin Mills & Boon policy is to use papers that are
natural, renewable and recyclable products and made from
wood grown in sustainable forests. The logging and
manufacturing processes conform to the legal environmental
regulations of the country of origin.*

*Printed and bound in Spain
by Litografía Rosés S.A., Barcelona*

For my wonderful editor,
Susan Litman,
with thanks for her insights –
and for asking me to be part of the
crowd on Danbury Way

Prologue

Every black skirt Rebecca Peters owned lay spread out on her bed as she stood in the closet trying to decide between a sexy little camisole and a more conservative sweater. She was seriously leaning toward conservative when the phone rang.

Still clutching the tops, she glanced at the caller ID on the phone on the nightstand a second before she snatched up the handset.

"Jack. Hi," she said, holding the phone with her shoulder while she held up her two choices for her date with him. "I was just thinking about you. Did you decide where you want to go for dinner?

"Jack?" she asked after five seconds of dead silence.

"I'm here," Jack Lever finally replied, hesitation heavy in his tone. "I came by to see you a while ago, but you weren't home."

"I was at the printer's. They didn't have my copies ready, so I had to wait."

"Yeah, well, it's probably better this way, anyhow."

It was her turn to hesitate. "What's better?

The faint rushing sound on the other end of the line sounded suspiciously like an uneasy expulsion of breath.

"Jack. You're a lawyer." He was also the stepson of the man she thought was her father, which was why she'd wanted to get to know him in the first place. Jack didn't know that, though. No one did. But her reason for having come to Rosewood was beside the point at the moment. "Words are your business." Now uneasy herself, she sank to the edge of the bed. "What are you trying to say?"

"That I don't think it's fair of me to waste your time," he finally admitted. "You're a great girl, Rebecca. But I've got a lot going on with work and my kids—"

"—and you don't have time for a relationship," she concluded for him. At least, not a relationship with her.

She heard him draw a breath. "Yeah," came his relieved reply.

She couldn't believe this was happening. She had only asked the other women on Danbury Way about the widowed father of two because she'd wanted to confirm his background. Never had she intended for Jack to misconstrue her interest and ask her out. Not on a *date* date, anyway. But one dinner had led to another and now here he was breaking up with her when she hadn't planned on being attracted to him that way to begin with. All she'd wanted was to get to know him to seek his help meeting Russell Lever, his stepfather. Russell was the reason she'd come to Rosewood. He was *her* father. At least, she thought he was. Yet, not only had she not met Russell, she was being dumped. Again.

She was back on her feet. "Not a problem." She absolutely refused to let him know that what he was doing mattered to her in any way. If she possessed any talent at all, it was her ability to appear unfazed by what wounded her. "You take care. Okay?"

"Yeah. Sure. You, too."

"'Bye, Jack."

Punching End Call before he could say goodbye himself, she stuck the handset back in its base and turned to gather her clothes.

She didn't head for her closet, though. Once she'd snatched up everything, she simply stood there, hugging her skirts while hurt slowly spread through her.

For all her bravado, she didn't feel unfazed at all.

Chapter One

In the front yard of her leased house on Danbury Way, Rebecca took another swipe at the leaves with her rake. She had no idea how many leaves an oak tree could produce, but the one gracing this particular patch of lawn was shedding them by the ton.

She was *so* not into yard work, but the job had to be done. It also gave her something to do while she forced herself to accept that she, Rebecca Anne Peters, a still-single, twenty-eight-year-old freelance fashion writer who possessed excellent taste in clothes and hideous taste in men, was never going to find the security and happiness all of her friends had found. Most of them, anyway. Angela Schumacher's life was a bit of a struggle. But her best friends in New York were all now married, engaged or seriously involved and none of those options was ever going to be available to her. What had happened with Jack a few days ago had proved that in spades.

It wasn't as if she'd fallen in love with the guy, she reminded herself as she attacked the leaves. She'd only liked him. So at least she'd been spared having her heart ripped out and handed back to her. Still, she'd been left feeling totally embarrassed and rejected.

The awful sensation seemed all too familiar. It also brought back the numb, hurt and sick feeling she'd been left to cope with after Jason Cargill had broken up with her six months ago. She'd spent two years dreaming of a future with that man only to have him inform her on their way home from a movie that they were over. Two months to the day he'd said he had never really loved her, he had married someone else.

She hated that she could still feel the painful sting of their ugly split. She hated even more that the awful sense of rejection she'd been living with was once again so acute.

Golden leaves scattered and crunched as she waded through them in her Ralph Lauren riding boots—the only boots she owned with a heel that wouldn't sink into the grass—to start another pile. Rake in hand, she loosened the pumpkin cashmere scarf that matched her V-necked sweater and the warp thread in the brown plaid Burberry jacket she wore with her designer jeans and attacked the dead vegetation with renewed vigor.

The breakup with Jason had been like the starting bell of a downhill race into a single woman's worst nightmare. Right on the heels of his betrayal had come the gorgeous weddings of two of her best friends and the birth of another friend's beautiful baby girl. She'd been thrilled for them all. At least, she'd wanted to be, but each event had been an in-her-face reminder of all that she had always wanted so badly herself.

She figured she'd hit bottom when her apartment had been broken into and her CD player and television had been stolen. With her insurance about to go up again and her personal life going nowhere, she'd taken the break-in as a sign to get the heck out of Dodge—or midtown Manhattan, anyway—and make a new beginning for herself.

Finding her father had seemed the perfect place to start. If she could just meet him, she might finally have the family and security she'd never had growing up with just her mom. Then, she'd found herself actually getting interested in his stepson….

She forced her mental mutterings to an abrupt halt. She would not go there again. The only thing that mattered was that she had now been dumped twice in a row. Next time, if there ever was a next time, she would be the dumper. Not the dumpee.

Her determination gave way to a disheartened sigh as she looked from the charming two-story colonial she'd leased to the other impeccably neat homes in the cul-de-sac. Resolving to take the upper hand was all well and good. In the meantime, however, she was stuck alone in the suburbs in a too-big house with two hairy cats who hated her, two months left on her lease and not a clue what to do next. Unlike her neighbors, she had no kids, no husband and no interest in the state of her lawn. With so little in common with them, it was as clear as the early November sky that she didn't belong here, either.

The sharp bark of a dog had her jerking around to look behind her. That excited sound also put an end to her little pity party when she noticed one of the little fur balls in her charge atop one of the brick columns flanking Carly Alderson's long driveway.

She'd had no idea that the cat had escaped. Whenever she left the house, she always checked to make sure the little monsters, who'd come as a condition of the lease, weren't anywhere near the door. Obviously, as preoccupied as she'd been with her totally messed-up life, she'd overlooked that precaution when she'd come out a while ago.

Of more concern than her lapse, however, was the cat's behavior. It had its back arched and was hissing at Molly and Adam Shibb's young black Labrador. Elmer, the dog, kept barking, his tail wagging as if he thought the racket might somehow convince the cat to come down and play.

It occurred to Rebecca that with Adam at work and Molly at her new prenatal yoga class, the puppy shouldn't be out, either. Aware of his newly discovered talent for digging, and thinking he must have dug himself right out of the backyard, she turned to prop her rake against the trunk of the oak. Even as she did, she heard the dog's bark change pitch and the cat screech.

She had no idea what had happened, but she'd no sooner turned back than she noticed that the cat was no longer atop its perch. It was part of the yipping, screeching tangle of fur at its base.

Adrenaline had barely turned the beat of her heart into sickening thuds when Elmer gave a shake that somehow sent the cat flying. As if landing on the run, the tabby raced in a streak of black-and-silver fur through the piles of leaves and up the rose trellis at the other end of the house.

Elmer had already turned tail and scrambled for home, the house on the other side of Carly's mansionlike place. She could see his little butt wiggling as he shimmied himself under the fence near the front gate and back into the safety of his yard.

The breath she'd held had barely left her lungs before she darted through the leaves herself to peer up at the frightened feline clinging to the top of the latticework.

Her stomach gave a sick little lurch. On a good day, animals of any variety simply made her uneasy. One hissing at her with blood leaking down the side of its face flat-out frightened her.

Reminding herself that she was bigger than he was didn't make her any braver.

She eyed the cat. The cat eyed her back. She couldn't tell if this one was Columbus or if it was Magellan. Since she'd never been able to tell the cats apart, she also didn't know which of the two had peed in one of her pink Prada pumps. But even if this one was the culprit, she couldn't let him stay there and bleed.

The viney vegetation had turned brown with the frosts. Gingerly pushing the crackling foliage back so she wouldn't get stuck on its thorns, she hooked one foot on the bottom rung of the wrought iron trellis and inched herself up. The cat inched exactly that much higher.

"You are not dying on my watch." You *little brat,* she would have added, but she was too busy avoiding rose thorns to bother.

The cat ran out of trellis. He had nowhere else to go that didn't involve a leap.

Rebecca had no desire to chase him all over the neighborhood. Catching him around the middle before he could spring over her head, she slammed the ten pounds of struggling fur against her chest, jumped at his indignant screech and promptly lost her balance. Had she not still had hold of the trellis with her other hand and somehow managed to turn and come to a stop with her back against the house, she would have landed with him in a heap in the flower bed.

Her reward for the rescue was the sharp sting of claws as they scraped the side of her neck.

Sucking in a breath, she flipped the cat around paws-out to avoid getting slashed again and hurried through the open garage and into the house.

Multitasking came as naturally to Rebecca as breathing. She'd been known to conduct a phone interview while scanning photo proofs for another article and still manage to slip a note with her sandwich preference to whoever was making a deli run for lunch. In an animal emergency, however, she was a tad out of her element.

Having no clue what she could do for the mewling cat on her own, she stuffed him and a towel into the carrier she'd noticed in the laundry room, made sure the other cat was inside and hurried into the garage. After shoving the carrier onto the passenger seat of her sporty little leased coupe, she backed onto the street and parked in front of Molly and Adam's place.

A ten-inch pot of mums sat on the corner of their porch. Leaving the engine running, she grabbed the pot and ran to where the dog had dug the hole under the fence, shoved the pot into the hole to thwart another escape and hurried back to her car.

The Turners, who owned the house she currently resided in, had left a list of emergency numbers pinned to the kitchen bulletin board. At the top of the list had been the name, number and address of their veterinarian in the strip mall across from Fulton's Hardware Store. Having ripped the list from the board on her way out, she headed for the animal clinic, using her cell phone on the way to tell them she was bringing in a cat that had been in a fight with a dog and was bleeding all over the place.

Within minutes she'd pulled into one of the three empty

spaces near the All Creatures Animal Clinic, pushed her way through the door with the carrier and been ushered into an exam room by an abnormally calm, middle-aged veterinarian's assistant wearing a pastel paw-print scrub top.

Rebecca was afraid she'd sounded every bit as panicked as she felt on the phone. That panic fed a high-energy state that was pretty much normal for her, anyway, but she didn't know if it was her anxiety or because she'd mentioned blood that the woman immediately took the carrier from her. She barely had a chance to tell the kind-looking, copper-haired woman that she'd gotten there as quickly as she could before the assistant removed the still-displeased animal from the carrier and set him and the crimson-spattered towel on the exam table protruding from the middle of the wall.

"I didn't see exactly what happened. I mean, I saw the cat on the column and the dog barking at it," she explained to the woman as someone else entered the room behind her. "But I turned away for barely a second and all of sudden there was all this noise, then the cat was flying one way and the dog ran the other."

"The dog had the cat in its mouth?"

The rich, deep voice had her glancing toward the man who'd stopped on the other side of the table. Seeing nothing but a white lab coat, she jerked her eyes past his broad shoulders to the lean, carved lines of his face. Dark, neatly trimmed hair brushed his broad brow. Intense blue eyes barely met hers before returning to his patient.

She was definitely upset. She barely noticed that Joe Hudson, DVM, according to the embroidery above his pocket, was drop-dead gorgeous. All that really registered was how gentle he was as his assistant held the animal and he ran his hands over the cat's little body.

"I don't know," Rebecca replied, watching his long, lean fingers move expertly over fur. He wasn't wearing a ring. She didn't notice a tan line, either. "I guess he must have, to toss him like that." She crossed her arms, tightened her hold. "It all happened so fast."

"So the dog shook it," he concluded, holding the cat's head between his hands to look at its eyes. "How big was the dog?"

"Three times the size of the cat. Maybe four. Elmer's a puppy, but he's big already. Can you save him? The cat, I mean? Please?" she begged, struck by his incredible gentleness with the animal. "Like I told the woman I talked to on the phone, he's not mine. He's the Turners'. I don't even know if it's Columbus or Magellan," she admitted, her agitation rising in direct proportion to how much the cat had calmed. It was getting too weak to move. She was sure of it. "I can never tell them apart. They're the same color and the same size and their markings all look the same, so it's impossible to tell which is which."

"Why do you have the Turners' cats?"

"Because I'm leasing their house while they're in Europe. They've been gone for four months and have two to go. Taking care of the cats was part of the deal because they thought they'd be happier in their own environment. They said that as long as I kept their litter box clean and their food and water dishes filled they'd practically take care of themselves, so I've been doing that, but I really don't know anything about animals at all because I've never had a pet," she explained without taking a breath. "The buildings I've lived in wouldn't have allowed them anyway," she went on, uncrossing her arms, crossing them again. "I've only seen cats in alleys before and the only dogs I've ever been exposed to are the ones I've seen with dog-walkers in Manhattan."

Joe's first concern was to identify the source of the blood. Next was to check for telltale signs of internal injury or broken bones. The cursory skim of his hands over the cat's body revealed nothing alarming. The feline's eyes were bright and clear, the color of his tongue good. The majority, if not all, of the bleeding also seemed to be coming from its head, specifically the ear missing its tip.

His second order of business was to calm the incredibly attractive and stylish brunette who reminded him of a gnat on caffeine. She talked a mile a minute and her body language was all over the place. What it said—even more than how anxious she was about the cat—was that she was not at all comfortable in her present surroundings. Given what she'd just admitted about her nearly nonexistent experience with animals, he'd be willing to bet his veterinary degree that she wasn't comfortable with the cat, either.

Not quite sure what to make of her, he spoke in the same easy tone he used to calm agitated animals. "Are you afraid of this little guy?"

She wore her shining, coffee-brown hair skimmed back in a low, tight ponytail. Her skin looked flawless. Subtle shades of gray eye shadow darkened her deep blue eyes. But it was her mouth that had his attention. Glossy and full, her lips fairly begged to be kissed.

Her mouth had opened to respond to his question, only to snap closed. Looking as if she didn't want to admit to fearing anything, she lifted one slender shoulder in a shrug. "I don't trust anything I can't reason with."

"Does that include small children?"

"Those I can handle. I think. I haven't spent much time with the under-two set, but I hope for the opportunity someday. After I find a husband," she qualified. If that ever happens, she added to herself. "In the meantime, what about the cat? He's not going into shock or anything, is he?"

Joe stifled a smile. "He'll be fine," he assured her. "I'll check him more thoroughly, but I really think he just needs his ear cauterized. And probably a couple of stitches. He may have nicked a vein." That would be where most of the blood was coming from. Cartilage didn't bleed much.

"Take him in and get him ready, will you, Tracy?" he asked the redhead wearing the paw prints. "I'll be right there."

With the efficiency of someone accustomed to dealing with anxious, agitated or otherwise unhappy animals, his assistant wrapped the towel around the cat to keep him immobile and tucked him under her arm like a football.

"He really will be fine," she assured Rebecca with a smile, and hurried through the door with the squeak of athletic shoes on the shiny beige tiles.

"By the way," came the deep voice from behind her, "that one is Columbus. With half of his ear gone, it should be easier now to tell him from Magellan."

The vet had moved to the sink behind him and turned on the water. "It won't take long to take care of him. But before that," he continued, washing his hands, "let's take a look at you."

"Me?"

"Your neck. He got you good."

Rebecca blinked at the strong lines of his profile as she touched the scratch.

"How did you catch him? Just curious," he explained, drying his hands on paper towels. The open shelves above him held a small array of supplies. Grabbing a couple of items, he set them on the table between them. "Cats can be pretty quick."

"I caught him at the top of the rose trellis. There was nowhere else for him to go."

She had the impression of powerful muscles beneath his lab coat as she watched him walk over to her. Lean, hard muscle that came from hours pumping iron in a gym. Or working outdoors. She couldn't honestly say she'd ever known a man who'd worked out that way, but the thought seemed more suited to him as he stopped in front of her.

She figured him to be a little over five feet, ten inches. At five feet six herself, and with the two-inch heels on her boots, she barely had to look up at him.

Catching her chin with his fingers, he tipped her head. "This definitely looks more like cat claws than thorns. Did he get you anywhere else?"

She swallowed. Hard. He smelled of antiseptic soap and a decidedly male aftershave she couldn't begin to identify. All she knew was that it was something masculine. And warm. Like the amazingly gentle feel of his fingers as he touched them to the side of her neck.

"It was. Is." She breathed out. "And no."

Dropping his hand, he reached for a small white packet. "What's your name?"

"Rebecca. Peters," she added, in case he needed it for his records or something.

"Okay, Rebecca Peters. This is going to sting."

The scent of antiseptic had barely reached her nostrils when she felt something cold touch just under her ear and curve toward her collarbone. An instant later, the sensation turned to burning.

She sucked in a breath.

"Ow!"

"Sorry," he murmured, only to quickly repeat the process. "But I warned you."

"Barely." The burning sensation suddenly didn't seem so acute. Or, maybe, she was just more aware of his fingers on her neck as he narrowed his eyes at the three parallel scratches. "Isn't that for animals?"

"Not necessarily."

Apparently satisfied with what he saw, he tossed the pad to the table. Without another word, he picked up a tube of antibiotic cream and dabbed it over the five-inch-long scratch.

"Here," he said, handing the tube to her when he was finished. The little lines at the corners of his eyes deepened with his smile. "Put that on a couple of times a day. I'm going to go save the Turners' cat. You can either wait or come back in an hour."

He didn't stick around to see what she decided to do. Leaving her staring at the tube in her palm, he simply walked out the open door.

Rebecca dropped the tube into her purse. She would come back, she decided, partly because, if she stayed, she'd have to wait in the waiting room with a huge Saint Bernard and some sort of rodent in a cage. But mostly because she didn't want to sit there thinking about Joe Hudson's incredible gentleness, the heat she'd felt when he'd touched her and, now that she knew the cat wasn't hurt all that badly, how helpless he must think her for panicking when panicking wasn't really like her at all. At least, it hadn't been.

Hating how inept she felt on top of everything else, she decided she needed a latte, anyway.

Exactly one hour and one tall, double, skinny, sugar-free vanilla latte later, she walked back into the clinic to find the previous occupants of the reception area no longer there. They had been replaced by an elderly gentleman with a cat who was conversing with a woman who bore a strong resemblance to the Pekingese in her lap.

The veterinarian's assistants apparently doubled as receptionists. This one, a perky blonde wearing a wide wedding band and a scrub top sporting kittens stood behind the counter looking up something on the computer. The moment the woman saw Rebecca, her glance skimmed from her scarf to her boots. An instant later, she smiled.

Apparently, she already knew who she was.

"Columbus did fine," she said, over the ring of the phone. "But Doctor is with another patient. It will be a few minutes."

With her smile still in place, she answered the call, leaving Rebecca to turn to the small waiting room.

Sitting wasn't something Rebecca did well when she felt anxious or uncertain. Caught between a vague unease at the prospect of seeing Joe Hudson again and a more pronounced uncertainty over what nursing skills would be required to tend the injured cat, she was feeling a little of both.

Having already let alarm get the better of her that day, she wasn't about to let anyone around her know she now felt anything less than in total control. She couldn't remember how old she'd been when her mom had first started pounding in the lesson, but having grown up in the city, she'd learned early on that the key to survival was to mask any sign of weakness.

That didn't mean she never felt vulnerable. She just rarely let the world know it. Especially on the street. Or when it came to her work, cutthroat as the fashion business could be. Or to men. With her self-confidence with that particular species in the subbasement at the moment, she

"I'm not much for dangling over cliffs," she admitted, managing not to sound totally horrified at the thought. "Actually, I'm not much of a nature person at all. The closest I've come to the wilds was a rock concert in Central Park."

"So you're into photography, then?"

"Not that, either. Not me, personally, I mean. I've just worked with a lot of photographers and recognize quality when I see it."

"You're a model."

She couldn't help but smile at his conclusion. Feeling flattered, she also felt a funny flutter in her stomach when he smiled back. "No, but thank you. I worked at a fashion magazine in New York, so I've worked with a lot of photographers. Still do, actually. I'm just freelancing now."

His glance fell to her mouth. Her own faltered as her heart bumped her ribs.

The ringing of the phone had stopped. So had the conversation taking place between the Pekingese lady and the elderly man with the cat.

It was only then that Rebecca realized how close she and the doctor were standing, and that everyone but the animals was staring at them.

Clearing her throat, she took a step back.

"You should put the cat in the carrier," he said, sounding far less self-conscious than she felt having been so totally absorbed in their conversation. "Here."

While he held open the flap of the soft-sided carrier for her, she slipped the decidedly docile cat inside. He was zipping it for her when his assistant held up two white plastic bags, one large, one small and each bearing the name of the clinic in royal blue.

"It's your towel," the clearly curious woman explained. "And Columbus's antibiotic."

"Give it to him twice a day in his food," the doctor added, back to business. "Like I said, he has a couple of stitches. They'll dissolve on their own, but I'd like to see him next week to make sure he's healing all right. In the meantime, call if he won't eat or drink or if you have any questions."

Looking vaguely distracted, he gave her one last smile and headed for the hallway. Rebecca promptly turned back to the assistant, made an appointment for next week, thanked the woman and walked out wondering what on earth all that had been about.

Joe Hudson was definitely not the urbane and sophisticated sort of man she was usually drawn to. He made his living taking care of animals. He was into the outdoors. He actually climbed mountains, and apparently enjoyed it. He had also somehow calmed her heart rate with his touch—and accelerated it all over again with his smile.

She ran her fingers alongside the scratch he'd tended, then promptly dropped her hand. Considering that she was only six months from a major breakup and seventy-two hours out on a minor one, she had no business thinking about him at all. Or anyone else, for that matter. The only man she should spare any mental energy on was the one she'd come to Rosewood to find. Given that her access to personal information about her father had been cut off, thanks to Jack, she needed to focus on some other way to meet the man who was proving to be as elusive as the emotional security she feared she'd never know.

If there was anything Rebecca could do it was focus. Once she set her mind to a task, nothing short of the Second Coming could stop her.

Or so she'd thought until a little after nine o'clock that night.

Chapter Two

Rebecca sat in the middle of the blue toile print sofa in the family room of her leased house. Across from her, the television in the carved country French armoire was off. So was the overhead light. The only illumination came from the brass candlestick lamp on the end table beside her and the glow of the laptop computer screen on the long maple cocktail table.

On the wall behind her hung a huge replica of a European railroad station clock and, as in the entryway, several framed photos of the Turner family she'd left up to keep her company. The quiet tick of that clock merged with the soft purr of the bandaged cat she had nestled beside her on one of the sofa's blue-and-cream-checked throw pillows.

Columbus had now stirred a time or two, but he'd yet to waken for long. Whatever the vet had given him still hadn't completely worn off. Or, maybe, he was just exhausted from his ordeal. Whichever it was, as docile and dependent as he was on her at the moment, she actually found him rather sweet.

Absently stroking his soft fur so he would know he wasn't alone, she told herself she should turn off the computer. Or, at least, sign off the Internet. As rejected as she felt, and the more she considered what little she'd learned from Jack about his stepfather, she no longer felt as certain about wanting to meet the man as she once had.

That unexpected realization left its own kind of emptiness.

She had wanted to know her father since she'd first noticed in kindergarten that, unlike her, most of the kids had a mom and a dad. She'd been fascinated by the sight of a couple walking down the street with a child, or a dad skating with his son or daughter at the rink at Rockefeller Center, or a man holding the hand of a child. Those kids always looked so happy to her, so protected, so... complete.

She'd wanted a dad of her own. She'd told her mom that, too, but her mom had said she didn't need one. Her mom had also refused to talk about the man who'd fathered her, so after a couple of tries, Rebecca stopped asking who he was.

She hadn't stopped daydreaming about him, though. Or about being part of his family. In her mind, that family was huge and happy and everyone welcomed her with open arms. Other than through the state's birth records, which she'd checked, futilely, years ago, she'd had no hint of where to start looking for him—until just before her ten-year high school reunion last May.

She'd been in the recesses of her mom's storage closet

looking for her yearbooks so she'd be sure to recognize everyone when she'd come across an old diary of her mother's. It hadn't been the sort with a lock and, at first, she'd absently flipped through it, thinking to show it to her mom and ask if she even remembered having it.

Then, the dates had caught her attention. So had the names and initials entwined in hearts on some of the pages.

Quickly calculating back, she realized that her mom would have been nineteen and in college when she'd poured her heart onto the neatly written pages. She also realized that she'd been madly in love with a business major named Russell Lever—and that the entries had been made around the time she would have been conceived.

She'd put the diary back and never mentioned having found it. The next day, though, she'd been online to adoption sites checking to see if anyone named Russell Lever was looking for his daughter.

She'd found nothing, but the need to track him down had led her to hire an attorney who had located a Russell Lever in the appropriate age range and tracked him to Rosewood. All the attorney had been able to tell her at that point was that the man was married and that he had a stepson named Jack.

It was right about then that her apartment had been broken into. Since she couldn't afford to have the attorney gather more information for her and because she wanted out of the city anyway, she'd contacted a real estate agent in Rosewood to find her an apartment.

The agent had come back with several apartments, and the house on Danbury Way. The woman had admitted that the only reason she even mentioned the large house to her was because the lease was a spectacular deal—even less than what Rebecca had been willing to spend on far less space. The problem was that the lease came with cats, which was proving a challenge for the owners since they couldn't find a lessee willing to pet sit.

Rebecca would have turned it down flat herself, had the agent not mentioned that her sister-in-law lived on the street and that there was a very attractive widower just a few doors down. A local attorney, she told her. Jack Lever.

The Fates were clearly watching out for her. Despite the cats, learning that a man who might well be Russell's stepson lived on that very street removed any possibility of not leasing the house.

She'd had no intention, however, of waiting around for the Fates to dump either man in her lap. She'd been in Rosewood less than twenty-four hours when, armed with her map, she'd set out to drive by the address her attorney had given her for Russell Lever—only to discover that the address was inside a gated residential community.

She'd returned to her leased house to look him up herself. There had been no residential listing but she'd found Russell Lever Consulting Services in the yellow pages. The address was the one she already had.

Though she'd had no idea what sort of consulting he did, she decided that his office must be in his home. A quick check on the Internet proved him to be "an international management consultant specializing in maximizing profit potential in the purchase and liquidation of businesses and their assets."

In other words, she'd thought, he helped companies buy up the competition and strip them bare.

She hadn't been sure how she'd felt when she'd realized that. But she wouldn't let herself judge the man she thought was her father. It had taken her nearly a week after that, though, to work up the courage to call his phone number.

She'd been informed by a recording that Mr. Lever would return her call if she would leave her name, number and the purpose of her call.

She'd been nowhere near ready to do any such thing. She wanted to see him first, just catch a glimpse of him if that was all she could manage. Uncertainty and nerves had become totally tangled up in the need for their first meeting to be perfect and she wanted whatever advantage she could get to make it that way. But advantages of any sort had been hard to come by.

Since she couldn't get into the exclusive, gated development to catch a glimpse of him outside what had to be a gorgeous home, judging from those visible from the street, she'd decided to see if she could find out what kind of car he drove so she could spot him driving through those gates.

It took her a week and another fee to the attorney to come up with the make of his cars and their license numbers.

It took another week of sitting outside the gate for an hour or so at different times of the day to see one of the two Mercedes sedans he apparently owned drive past the guard and head toward town.

She didn't follow.

The driver was a nicely coifed middle-aged blonde who might well have been Russell's secretary. Or his wife.

It took another week for one of the guards to call the police on her because he finally noticed how often she'd been parked down the street. She told the female officer that the guard must have her confused with someone else. The officer said she didn't think so and asked for her driver's license, the papers on her car and wrote down her license plate number before citing her for parking too close to a fire hydrant.

That was when she decided she really did need to get to know Jack. Yet, despite the time they'd spent during their dinners together, he hadn't told her much about his stepfather. As she'd found with most men, he'd been more than willing to discuss his own views and interests, which basically included politics and his own work. He'd also distracted her with truly fascinating stories about his cases, but he'd been reluctant to talk at all about the man who had raised him. He had, in fact, pretty pointedly changed the subject the only two times she'd managed to bring up his childhood. All she'd been able to gather was that his relationship with the senior Lever was strained at best and that the man had never had time for anything or anyone that didn't involve work—including Jack.

She listened to the slow tick of the clock, stroked the cat every third beat. She had already concluded that having Jack for a stepbrother could prove a little awkward. Infinitely more important had been the realization that if Russell didn't have time for the son he'd raised, the odds of the happy reunion she'd envisioned with him welcoming her into his family weren't looking good at all. That was why she'd thought it might help her chances with the man if she learned something about the business he was in—which was why she'd starting researching on the Internet again.

There was just something about having to try that hard to gain acceptance or affection that made her feel even more lost and dejected than she already did.

Leaning forward, she reached for the mouse, clicked Close and shut the computer down.

The action did nothing to alleviate the huge void inside her.

Oddly, what helped a little was petting the cat.

* * *

Restlessness drove Rebecca out into the chilly air early the next morning—right through the newly fallen leaves that totally mocked the time she'd spent raking yesterday afternoon. It was barely eight in the morning, but she'd been up since five checking on Columbus and waiting for the newspaper. It seemed to be some sort of unwritten law that the newspaper always arrived late on the morning a person was up early.

Thinking it might have been delivered while she'd been in the shower and getting dressed, she hugged her arms over the black turtleneck sweater she wore with her slim black slacks and searched all the usual places it might be hiding. The paper rarely landed in the driveway or the front walk, and never on the porch.

She found it in the hydrangea bushes by the front window. She only knew the plants were hydrangeas because elderly Mrs. Fulton across the street had told her how beautiful they usually were when properly watered and cared for. The sweet, silver-haired woman with the unfortunate bouffant also mentioned something about adding iron sulfate or aluminum something-or-other to the soil to keep the blooms blue. Rebecca figured that for someone whose only exposure to plants had been to those tended by a plant service in the offices of *Vogue*, keeping them watered—and not killing them—was accomplishment enough.

Newspaper in hand, she backed out of the bushes and glanced down the street. The way her house was situated near the top of the cul-de-sac, she could see all of her neighbors' driveways. Two doors down, she could see Angela Schumacher backing her van out of her drive. Thinking of how much that poor woman had on her plate, what with being a single mom to three children and working two jobs, she lifted her hand and waved. Angela, hurried as always, tossed a wave back. Directly across from Angela's house was Jack's. Since his garage door could open any moment, she was about to head back inside when she saw Molly Jackson-Shibb come out her front door and cut past Carly's driveway toward her.

"I got your message," she called, hurrying across the street in slacks and a long blue sweater that hid much of her basketball belly. "Elmer's fine. And thanks so much for plugging that hole. Adam is going to fill it in before he leaves for work. How's the cat?" she asked, meeting Rebecca in the street. "I would have called last night, but I had a meeting in the city that ran late and your lights were out when I got home."

"Everything's okay. Columbus is fine."

Molly's expression went from concerned to surprised. "You know which one it was?"

"The vet told me." She hadn't a clue how he'd known him from his brother, though. "He's just missing part of his ear. The cat," she explained, trying desperately not to be envious of the woman's glow. At eight months pregnant, Molly looked absolutely fabulous. "Not the vet."

Concern was back. "Elmer bit off his ear?"

"Only part of it. He probably thought he was a chew toy. Don't worry," she assured the woman who was as close to being a friend as anyone on Danbury Way, "it's not good for the baby."

Or so she'd heard, she thought. She'd probably have to be a single mom herself to know for certain. Only, Molly wasn't single anymore. She and Adam had been married for a couple of months now and seemed more in love than ever.

Rebecca's smile was genuine enough. Molly, though, seemed to catch the bittersweet edge behind it.

The mom-to-be tipped her head, pushed back her long, curly brown hair. "How are you doing?" she asked, sympathy heavy in her voice. "You did great at the party the other night, but it was kind of rough, huh?"

The infamous Halloween party, Rebecca thought. Jack's nanny, Zooey, had thrown it for his two children. The week before, Zooey had invited everyone on Danbury Way, including her. Knowing she would have to see Jack, Rebecca had toyed with the idea of not going after he'd called off their date, but it was a neighborhood function and, trying to fit in, she hadn't missed one yet.

Everyone on Danbury Way had been there. Just about everyone had known that she'd been interested in Jack, too—though not a single one of them had a clue why that interest had originally been there. Not even the slowly reforming workaholic waiting for her reply.

The really awkward part was that everyone had also seemed to know that Jack wasn't seeing her anymore.

"It was a little uncomfortable," she had to admit. "But not going to the party would have made a bigger deal out of the situation than it is. Jack and I only had a couple of dates," she reminded her. "And there really wasn't a lot of real chemistry there."

"Not like there is between him and Zooey?"

Jack's new nanny definitely had his eye.

"Nothing like that." The easy little laugh she gave made it clear that she was far more embarrassed than hurt by the public's knowledge of his lack of interest in her. "Most women would kill to have a man look at her that way. Except me," she insisted, wishing the lost feeling she couldn't shake would go away. "I've decided I'm swearing off men for a while."

Including my father, she insisted to herself, only to have the thought interrupted by a silver, bull-nosed pickup truck coming up the street.

The unfamiliar vehicle had both women glancing toward it. Suddenly sidetracked, Molly's brow pinched. "Who's that?"

Rebecca narrowed her eyes at the approaching vehicle. "Dr. Hudson?"

She'd barely recognized Joe Hudson's undeniably attractive features through his windshield before he swung the vehicle into her driveway and killed the engine. A moment later, the dark-haired vet in khakis and a leather bomber jacket stepped out and started toward them.

"Morning, ladies. Mrs. Shibb," he called, nodding to Molly as he walked to where they watched him from the middle of the street. "How's Elmer?"

Joe Hudson was apparently their vet, too.

"Generally?" Molly asked, smiling back. "Or in relation to yesterday's fight?"

"Both."

"He's fine. Thank you."

"Glad to hear it." His easy smile shifted to Rebecca as he pushed his hands into the pockets of his pants. "I hope I'm not interrupting. I just came by to check on my patient."

Rebecca wasn't sure which had the greater hold at the moment, surprise at his unexpected visit, or dismay at the way her heart had jerked at the sight of him. Preferring to ignore the latter, she indulged puzzlement.

"I didn't know veterinarians made house calls."

His response was the shrug of his broad shoulders.

Molly lowered her head, whispered, "They don't," and stepped back to check her watch. When she glanced back up, speculation fairly danced in her eyes, but her voice returned to normal.

"Well, I have to go," she announced. "Good to see you," she said to the vet. "I'll talk to you later," she promised Rebecca.

The woman was clearly intent on getting details of the good doctor's visit. Rebecca hated to disappoint her, but there would be none. She'd meant what she'd said. She truly was swearing off men. In the romantic, physical and emotional sense, anyway. The platonic friendship she'd formed with Molly's husband was okay. And for support services, they were allowed. But those were her ground rules.

"Sure," she murmured to Molly, pretty sure she'd covered her bases, and watched her clearly curious friend head back across the cul-de-sac.

"If this isn't a good time, I can come by later. I was just on my way to the clinic—"

"It's fine," she said quickly. The man was there to check on the cat. That fell squarely into the service category. The least she could do was be gracious to him. "I put on another pot of coffee a while ago. It should be ready if you want some."

Another pot? Joe thought. "That would be great."

Joe watched the beautiful brunette in the black turtle-neck sweater, slim black slacks and high black heels give him a cautious smile before she led him up the walkway of the rather large, two-story colonial-style house that looked pretty much like all the nicely tended homes in the upper-middle-class cul-de-sac—except for the mansion-like structure taking up two lots next door, anyway. But his attention wasn't on the house or the neighborhood so much as it was on this particular resident.

He honestly did want to know how the cat was doing. He knew he could have one of his assistants make the usual follow-up call to make sure everything was going all right. But he wanted to know how she was coping, too. There had been no mistaking her uneasiness with the little guy yesterday. Between what he suspected was a fear in general of animals and her total lack of knowledge about the care of an injured one, stopping by to check on both seemed like the most practical thing to do.

Rebecca opened the storm screen and the front door, only to immediately bend in a graceful stoop and hold her hand low as if to intercept a potential escapee. Apparently, finding no cat waiting to run out, she straightened to hold the door for him and closed it when he'd stepped inside.

"The Turners have unique taste," she said, to explain the eclectic collection of Asian and Mediterranean objets d'art mixed among the chintz prints and colonial Williamsburg furnishings. She preferred a sleeker, more urban style herself. Less clutter, cleaner lines. "They travel a lot.

"Columbus has been hiding out in one of the guest rooms," she continued, leading him past the entry wall of Turner family photos and into a short hallway. Turning into the last door, she knelt beside the high four-poster bed and lifted the edge of the frilly rosebud print bed skirt. "I don't know how he jams himself under there with that collar, but he's still under here if you want to try to get him."

Joe's glance moved over her slender, incredibly appealing shape. She had the lithe body of a dancer, all gentle, feminine curves and long, long legs. She was also dressed like a cat burglar. Even the wide and intricate black belt snugged low on her hips was the color of coal.

"Has he been there since yesterday?"

"Only since about midnight. That's when the tran-quilizer or whatever it was you gave him wore off and he jumped down. Before that, I had him on the sofa with me."

It sounded as if she'd slept on the sofa to keep an eye on the cat. Or, maybe, he thought, to keep the cat company. Either way, it seemed she wasn't as uncomfortable with the animal as he'd thought she was. Or, maybe, he thought, dead certain he hadn't misread her fear, her sympathy for its injuries had outweighed that unease.

The other gray cat wandered in. Striped silver and black like its sibling, Magellan held up his tail in a high, slow wave and did a lazy figure eight around Joe's legs before poking his nose under the skirt to see what had his keeper's attention.

Noting the other cat beside her, Rebecca eased back as if she didn't trust what it might do and rose to her feet.

"You're welcome to get him out if you can," she said, leaving behind the subtle scent of coconut shampoo as she passed him at the door. "He'll just run off if I try."

Ignoring the faint tightening low in his gut, he nodded toward the bed. "Has he been eating or drinking?"

"Both. He turned up his nose at the cat food, but polished off half a can of tuna. I'll get your coffee. How do you take it?"

"Black."

"I'll be in the kitchen, then. When you're through, just turn left at the end of the hall."

Rebecca watched him acknowledge her with a nod before she closed the door in case the cat decided to make a run for it. Despite Molly's insistence that vets didn't make house calls, she was truly relieved that this particular one had decided to make an exception. The cats hid from her all the time, and seemed to take particular delight in pouncing out and scaring her witless. Yet, regardless of the way they terrorized her, she needed to know the injured one was okay.

Two minutes later, coffee poured and waiting on the counter that divided the big colonial kitchen from the sunny breakfast nook, Joe walked in with both cats bouncing at his heels.

Her first thought was of the Pied Piper. The animals never followed her around that way. But, then, the man filling the room with his reassuring presence had a definite knack with the four-legged set. Yesterday, she'd actually seen Columbus visibly calm at his touch.

He seemed to have that gift with two-legged species, too. When he had touched her, she'd felt that calming gentleness herself.

Preferring not to think about that odd phenomenon, she focused on his patient. "How is he?"

"He's doing fine. How about you? How are you doing with him?"

"He's really doing okay?"

"He really is, " he assured, echoing her phrasing.

"Then, I'll be better now." She had checked on the cat every half an hour since she'd awakened at five to make sure he was still breathing. Apparently, she wouldn't need to do that anymore. "Thanks.

"Tell me," she hurried on, watching Columbus paw at the cone collar he clearly hated. "When I brought him in, how did you know which one he was?"

"We have a picture of each patient in their file," he explained. "Tracy pulled the Turners' files right after you called. I knew this one because the two darker gray marks above his eyes remind me of horns. The marks on Magellan look more like exclamation points." He glanced toward the piles of papers on the table in the breakfast bay, then to the coffee cooling on the counter. "Mind if I have that?"

She was still dwelling on the markings. "Of course, Dr. Hudson," she murmured, handing the mug to him. Horns. How appropriate, she thought, now eyeing the cat. The little devil probably was the one who'd ruined her shoe.

"It's Joe."

Her glance jerked from the cat who'd just curled up near the other in a sunbeam.

"My name," he said, since she looked so preoccupied. "Call me Joe." Without waiting for a reply, he turned his attention to the table with its stacks of photographs, envelopes and papers. "You were already working."

"I was just getting ready to."

"You said you're freelancing?"

"For the magazine I used to work for," she explained. "I have proposals out to a couple of others, too. I wrote for accessories and American fashion. Still do. But I like doing research pieces."

Mug in hand, looking curious, he nodded his dark head toward the stacks. "May I?"

She lifted her hand toward the table, told him to go ahead. Even as she did, her glance darted from the blue chambray shirt visible beneath the open brown leather jacket that looked more comfortably worn than fashionably distressed, down the length of his neat khakis and landed on his brown, tasseled boaters.

Her mental wheels spinning, she watched him sip his coffee as he frowned at a collection of glossy photos.

He was exactly the sort of man she was writing about in her make-over-your-mate project; intelligent, handsome and sexy, but, she suspected, clueless about fashion beyond denim and khaki.

"Would you be interested in helping me?"

One dark eyebrow rose as she moved beside him.

"One of the articles I'm working on requires men's opinions. It'll be really easy," she hurried to assure him, since he was already looking skeptical. "I have a questionnaire that's multiple choice and photos that just need to be listed in order of preference.

"Not those," she muttered, seeing his skepticism grow as he glanced back at the photos of brooding and gaunt males. From his frown, it seemed glaringly obvious that the runway look was something he just didn't get. But, then, some designers did go a tad over the top. "Those are for a menswear article and are a little…"

"Bizarre?"

Her expression held tolerance. She would be the first to admit that she knew nothing about animals. It was only fair to cut him some slack on the fashion front. "I was going to say cutting-edge. It's like any of the runway fashions," she pointed out, warming to her subject. "Everything from hair and makeup on down is exaggerated. The designer is going for a statement. A theme, if you will. You rarely see exact copies on the street, but elements show up on the racks the next season. Or the next," she hurried to explain, "depending on which part of the country you're in. Buyers buy differently for different markets. But that's not the article I need help with.

"I have photos of other designers and more mainstream lines, too," she said, reaching across the table to pluck a manila envelope off a stack. "Calvin Klein, Ralph Lauren, Versace. Issey Miyake. Armani. He's my personal favorite." She turned with a smile. "Levi Strauss."

She'd already put those photos in each of the five hundred manila envelopes stacked across the back of the table. This morning's project was to add the last of the photos to the questionnaires already in them and start making her rounds of men's clothing stores and the men on Danbury Way—with the exception of Jack. That was one man's opinion her article would have to go without.

"Is this why you came to Rosewood?" Joe asked, watching her punch the metal tab on the envelope through the hole in its flap. "To outfit the suburban male?"

"My job is merely to enlighten."

His glance skimmed from the animation in her lovely blue eyes to her slicked-back hair. She was truly, classically beautiful, yet nearly everything about her confused his idea of what he usually found attractive in a woman. The severely restrained hair said "don't touch." The stiletto heels that put her nearly eye level with most men, including him, seemed to say "don't mess with me, I'm not vulnerable to you." She wasn't soft, yet she was indisputably feminine. The black clothes that covered her from neck to pointed toe weren't provocative at all by themselves, yet on her, they were as sexy as hell.

"That wasn't my question," he said mildly.

Her animation slipped with the quick blink of her lush lashes. "I came here because it's where I thought I needed to be." Purposefully looking back to hold his glance, she tipped the envelope toward him. "So," she continued, clearly intent on sticking to what she felt comfortable with, "are you game?"

He didn't know what intrigued him more; her contradictions or the effect of her scent, her smile. Seeing no need to figure it out now, he gave her a shrug. "I have no idea how much help I'd be, but sure. I'll be glad to. You'll just have to explain all of what you just said. Only not right now," he continued, taking one last sip of his coffee. "I have to get to the clinic. How about Saturday afternoon?" he asked, setting the mug on the counter. "I'm hiking near the meadow where I took some of the pictures you were looking at. Hang on to that," he said with a nod to the envelope she held, "and if you want, you can come with me and we can talk on the way."

"Hike?"

She wasn't sure if it was the activity she questioned or the invitation itself. Either way, there was no masking her incredulity.

"It's not much of one," he assured her. "There's absolutely no dangling from cliffs involved. It's more of a walk in the park. Do you have other plans?"

She hesitated. "Not exactly…"

"Then I'll pick you up at one thirty. The clinic doesn't close until one." She was vacillating. He could see it. Not wanting to give her a chance to point out that she hadn't actually accepted the invitation, he glanced to the pointed toes of her heels. "Wear sturdy shoes. And thanks for the coffee." He backed toward the door. "I'll see myself out."

Joe turned then, checking to make sure he didn't have cats at his feet as he left the house. As candid as she seemed to be, he felt certain that if Rebecca hadn't wanted to go with him, she'd have been fast on his heels with a reason or an excuse for not being able to join him. All she'd done was stay where she was, looking temporarily speechless.

He had the feeling she wasn't often at a loss for words.

He climbed into his truck and immediately frowned at the file folders on the passenger seat. He had no business taking Saturday afternoon off to go hiking. He had a mountain of paperwork to fill out for a small business loan to expand his clinic. With any luck, and the kind of hard work that kept him from second-guessing the decisions he'd made, this time next year, he would have started construction on a bigger clinic that would include an animal hospital so he could offer his clients round-the-clock care.

He should also run up north and help his dad and brother finish weather-stripping the barn before the snows set in. But that would take more than an afternoon. Aside from that, nearly every time he'd gone back home lately, his mom had managed to have her latest candidate for her future daughter-in-law stop by.

It had taken his mom a while to forgive him for breaking up with Sara Jennings after he'd graduated from veterinary school, but ever since then she'd been on an on-again, off-again mission to find him a spouse. But he wasn't in the market for a wife. He had too much he needed to accomplish before he even thought about taking on the responsibility of a committed relationship.

That didn't stop him from wondering about Rebecca Peters, though. He couldn't help being drawn by her attempts to care for animals that clearly made her uneasy, and the compassion that somehow pushed her past the worst of her discomfort. She was dealing with them, and her fear, far better than he had anticipated. There was no denying the physical pull he felt toward her, either, but he hadn't been with a woman in months, so that chemistry was easy enough to explain. What had him most curious as he left Danbury Way, though, was the suspicion that she wasn't all that happy with the reason she was in Rosewood.

There had been no mistaking the unease that had slipped into her expression when he'd asked what had brought her there, or how quickly she'd shied from the subject. Since she was still doing the same type of work she'd done in the city, he didn't think the move was job-related, though he'd be the first to admit that he knew zip to squat about what it was she did for a living. Or why. All he knew for sure was that it had been a long time since he'd met a woman who so thoroughly intrigued him. He also knew for a fact that he'd never met one who seemed so clearly out of her element.

He just had no idea how totally out of her element she was until two mornings later when he picked her up for their day in the Catskills.

Chapter Three

He really shouldn't be taking the afternoon off.

That thought had occurred to Joe more than once in the past couple of days. On any given weekend, the only spare time he had was Saturday afternoon. His Sundays were committed to chores around the house he was slowly renovating, and maintaining the five acres of property that provided elbow room for him and his pets. Sunday afternoon, weather permitting, he also tried to squeeze in an hour or so at Rosewood Park with his dogs to keep them socialized, before heading back home to finish whatever he'd left undone or clean up the mess he'd made doing it.

His weekday evenings inevitably seemed just as crowded.

With his current time constraints, he'd thought about calling Rebecca and asking her to just drop the questionnaire by the office so he could work on his loan application. The only reason he hadn't was because he wasn't in the habit of backing out on any sort of commit-ment—unless an emergency arose and he had no choice.

Poor planning on his part did not constitute an emer-gency. The good news, however, was that he'd only be gone for a few hours.

It was with that mental concession that he pulled onto Danbury Way.

The moment he did, he noticed the guy in front of the house on the corner stop mulching leaves with his lawn mower and follow his progress into Rebecca's driveway. On the other side of the street, an older woman leaned on her rake, peering at him from beneath the rim of her purple gardening hat. Two trim, middle-aged gals in matching jogging suits pulled their attention from the *Gone With the Wind*-like mansion at the end of the street to check out his truck, him and the stylish woman emerging from the door of the Turners' house on their way by.

He had the distinct feeling that not much got past the residents in this particular neighborhood as he headed to where Rebecca stepped off the low porch. The joggers had already continued on, their pace uninterrupted but their necks cranked back so they wouldn't miss anything. He had no idea who else still watched them, though. His concerns were with more practical matters as he watched Rebecca tuck her keys into a small, backpack-style leather purse while trying not to drop the manila envelope that probably held her questionnaire.

Between the quilted, rust velvet, elaborately embroi-dered vest she wore with her matching scarf, mustard-colored turtleneck and slim, embellished jeans, she looked more like an ad for trendy autumn wear than someone actually planning to hike.

"Hi," she called, walking toward him.

"Hi, yourself." He forced himself not to frown at her boots. They looked very much like those she'd worn the first day they'd met, sturdy enough but with heels way too high and totally impractical for a walk in the wilderness.

Thinking she looked a little preoccupied, he decided to deal with first things first. "How's the patient?"

"He hates me. They both do."

"That good, huh?"

"I don't know why else they leap out at me the way they do. I was getting out of the shower and Columbus jumped at me from behind the toilet." The little monster had startled her so badly, she'd screamed. It had served him right that his cone collar had gotten him jammed between the cabinet and the wastebasket. "Magellan did it last night when I got up to turn off the TV."

To keep an image of her body, naked and dripping, from forming, he kept his focus on her face. "Did they hiss at you?" he asked, his forehead furrowing with the effort. "Or swipe at you with their paws?"

"No," she replied, as if scaring her were quite enough.

"Then, they're probably just playing. 'Pounce' is like a game with cats."

"Playing? I thought they were trying to stop my heart."

He tipped his head, nodded toward his truck. "Why don't you tell me what else they do while we're driving. Maybe I can explain the behavior so you can deal with it better."

"Would you?"

The phenomenon was interesting. He'd never felt gut-punched when a woman simply smiled at him. But that was what he felt when he saw the gratitude in her beautiful blue eyes. "Be glad to."

As if aware that she'd just betrayed some vulnerability,

she quickly looked away. He couldn't begin to imagine why she should be uncomfortable needing help with something she didn't understand. He just knew she did in the moments before he nodded to her boots.

"Can you walk any distance in those?"

Rebecca glanced at her feet, then to the rugged, lug-soled hiking boots Joe wore with his comfortably worn jeans and a gray fleece shirt. Her chunky heels were barely two inches high, practically flat as far as she was concerned. Thinking it couldn't possibly be that difficult to walk through a meadow, she gave a shrug. "I can run in stilettos if I have to."

Pure doubt creased his features. "You can?"

"I did it all the time in New York. Chasing down cabs," she explained. "But you know, Joe, I never actually agreed to do this hike thing," she reminded him, wanting to keep the record straight. "If you want, we can just go for a latte while I explain what I'm looking for on my question-naire."

"It's too nice a day to be cooped up inside."

"We can sit at a table outside, then. Latte and Lunch has café—"

"I don't care for stuff in my coffee." His eyes narrowed on hers. Like every other time he'd seen her, she had her hair smoothed back from her face and clipped tightly at her nape. On any other woman, he would have given little thought to the simple style. On her, it seemed to enhance that don't-touch-me sophistication—and made him want to set it free.

Minutes ago, he would have taken her up on her offer to stay in town, simply because of the time it would save. Seeing her again, listening to her logic, the hike became something he wouldn't miss for the world.

"You're not nervous about hiking, are you?"

Joe watched her open her mouth, only to see her close it again. Like the other day in his office when she wouldn't directly admit to being afraid of Columbus, he sensed now that she didn't like to admit that there was something she couldn't handle.

"Of course not," she finally said.

"Good." He didn't know if it was stubbornness, determination or simple obstinacy that pushed the woman. All he knew was that he wanted to see how far it would take her. "Because I promised Bailey he could go for a run."

"Bailey?"

They'd reached his truck. With the patterns of leaves reflecting off the windows, it was hard to see inside—which was why Rebecca hadn't noticed that Joe wasn't alone until he opened the driver's door.

"He's a sweetheart. I promise. Come on, boy."

The simple command had barely followed his assurance before seventy pounds of blissfully panting German shepherd leaped to the ground and planted himself on his haunches by the open door.

From the corner of his eye, Joe saw Rebecca stiffen. "He's totally harmless. Honest." He curled his fingers around her wrist, drawing her attention from the dog to him. Aware of how skittish she was about animals, he wouldn't have brought the dog had Bailey not been the most gentle canine on the planet. "He's just going to say hi. Okay?"

Rebecca couldn't have imagined anything that would have made her tear her eyes from the large amount of tan-and-black fur sitting six feet away. But Joe's touch had done just that. She wasn't sure, either, if it was the odd, calming effect that touch had on her or the quiet reassurance in his deep voice that had her giving him a barely discernible nod.

"Okay, Bailey," she heard him say, "come meet Rebecca."

As if pulled by a string, the dog immediately popped up on all fours, walked over to her and sat back down again. She'd barely felt Joe's hand slip away before the dog held up its paw and, tongue lolling, blinked his bright eyes at her.

"He wants to shake."

This was a bit more than she'd bargained far. There was only one reason that she hadn't already backed out of this nondate with the man standing almost protectively beside her. And it was a nondate as far as she was concerned. Joe was her support system for the cats. Even before he'd offered to explain their behavior, she'd figured that as long as she had to be with them for another two months, it would be infinitely easier on her if she would ask him to do just that. As far as subjecting herself to the wilds was concerned, her less-than-enthusiastic willingness to face the experience was strictly for self—and job—improvement.

Those who knew her would say that if she was inspired by anyone, it would be some iconic fashion designer such as Coco Chanel or Yves St. Laurent. But the bit of inspiration she'd always remembered had come from a quote Mrs. Morretti, who owned a little Italian restaurant not far from where Rebecca had grown up, kept taped to the mirror above her cash register.

You must do the thing you think you cannot do.
Eleanor Roosevelt.

Regardless of the fact that both Mrs. Morretti and Mrs. Roosevelt could have used some major style advice with their respective wardrobes, Rebecca had found the challenge pushing her off and on over the years. It pushed her now.

A hike held all the appeal of a root canal for her. Going would be the self-improvement part of the program. As for the job perspective, she figured the hike might help her better understand the suburban male, and thus better understand his apathy toward fashion. If she could find an angle, she might even be able to get another article out of it.

Trying not to look as tentative as she felt, remembering that Eleanor's advice applied to the dog, too, she swallowed hard, reached down and when he didn't bare his teeth, shook his paw.

"Nice...dog." Not sure what else one said to a canine, she straightened as Bailey pulled back his paw and watched him look to his owner.

Joe gave him a pat on the head and motioned him back into the truck.

"It won't take long to get to the trailhead," he said, walking her around the blunt nose of the vehicle to the passenger's door. "Less than half an hour or so. I brought granola bars, trail mix and water. If you want anything else, we can stop at the market on the way out of town."

Not wanting to alter the experience with a request for a bagel and a latte, Rebecca told him that whatever he normally took with him was fine. Waving to Mrs. Fulton across the street, she climbed into the cab of the truck and promptly stiffened again.

Bailey, looking expectant, had claimed the console in the middle. The dog also apparently knew he couldn't stay there. The moment Joe climbed in on the other side, the dog turned in the confined space, brushing her forehead with his long tail and settled on one of the small jump seats behind them.

She hugged the door. "You seem to be good with them. Animals, I mean."

His deep chuckle sounded easy and oddly relaxing. "I hope so. I'd starve if I wasn't. You never had *any* pets growing up?"

She couldn't tell if he'd asked because he couldn't imagine such a possibility, or because he didn't want to talk about himself. Having never met a man who didn't consider himself his favorite subject, she decided he simply found her lack of animal companionship as a child somewhat incomprehensible. Or, maybe, unfortunate.

Having been under a bit of stress when she'd first met him, she couldn't quite recall if she'd mentioned the impracticalities of pet ownership in the city, or if having one had simply never occurred to her or her mom. If she had, he didn't seem to mind if she repeated herself as they left Danbury Way with her neighbors still watching and headed for the Catskills.

Except to go shopping in Albany, Rebecca hadn't been outside Rosewood since she'd arrived. She had also never in her life set foot in a national or state park. She knew there were people in the city who kept summer homes or lodges in New England where they "escaped" during the summer or skied in the winter. She wasn't one of them. Neither were her friends, though Carrie Klein, her onetime roommate and unfortunately no relation to Calvin or Anne, had dated a stockbroker with a great little place in the Hamptons. Her vacations were always to the fashion meccas of the world. Rome. Milan. Paris. Stateside, she stuck with Chicago, Los Angeles, San Francisco. Or the beach. She liked to be where there was room service, cabs and at least some semblance of nightlife.

She didn't consider herself spoiled. Heaven knew there had been times that the only reason she could afford to go out with her girlfriends from work was because the happy hour hors d'oeuvres were free so she didn't have to pay for a meal. The designer clothes she wore came from sample sales, or sales at Barneys or Saks, but mostly from the Vogue clothes closet, which housed cast-off items from photo shoots.

Roughing it meant having to walk thirty blocks in the rain because she couldn't get a cab. Though she wasn't about to mention it, within five minutes of leaving Joe's truck to follow a narrow dirt path through the woods, she would have preferred a walk in a downpour from Union Square to East 59th to the trek she was on now.

The trail was too narrow to walk side by side, so she followed Joe into the forest with bushes brushing her on either side. She kept shifting her focus between the bright orange day pack slung across his strong back to the vegetation attacking her legs and snapping beneath her feet. The dog had run ahead. He returned now with a short piece of tree branch in his mouth. Obviously, he didn't mind the taste of dirt.

"How far is it to the meadow?" she asked.

She watched Joe take the limb from the dog and toss it ahead of them. With the dog making the bushes rustle as he took off after his new toy, she glanced down in time to avoid tripping over a skinny tree root sticking up through the leaves and pine needles. Seeing bits of bush clinging to her jeans, she brushed them off.

Joe glanced at her over his shoulder, waited for her to catch up. "Only a couple of miles."

"Miles?" They were going *miles?*

"Only a couple," he repeated. "It's an easy walk."

Easy was a relative term. In the interests of job research and self-improvement, however, she trudged on.

"Why do you do this?" she asked, falling into step beside him as the trail mercifully widened.

"I like being outside."

"Why?"

"Because I'm cooped up inside most of the week."

"Why else?"

Joe adjusted the weight of his day pack. "Because it's a great way to unwind. It puts you back to basics." Her inquisitiveness reminded him of his four-year-old nephew. *Why* was his favorite word.

"So it's a primitive thing? Like you're feeding your inner pioneer or something. You know," she coaxed, when a frown creased his face, "like your inner child."

He knew all about the inner child. His little sister was a psychologist who'd blithely informed him after a family dinner last year that his lack of a serious romantic interest was probably his inner child's fear to commit. That remark had only fed his mother's fears that, unlike his married siblings, he was going to wind up old and alone, which was no doubt why she'd resumed her efforts to find him a suitable mate.

He loved his family. He just wished they'd stay out of his love life.

"It's not that complicated," he assured her. "I just like being where you can hear the wind in the trees and get some exercise."

"Wouldn't it be easier to join a gym?"

"Why pay to run on a treadmill when you can do this for free?"

She swiped at something small and pesky buzzing past her ear. "Because there are no bugs?"

"These aren't bad at all. You should be out here during mosquito season."

"Thanks, but I think I'll pass. I'm not crazy about things that suck blood."

"So you don't date lawyers?"

"Not anymore," she muttered.

From the corner of her eye, she saw Joe glance toward her. The smile that deepened the vertical lines carved in his cheeks faded with his curiosity.

"Burned bad?"

The only lawyer she'd ever dated had been Jack. "Barely singed," she murmured, though the experience had definitely contributed to the void that didn't feel quite so awful at the moment. Marveling at that, she started to smile at the man beside her, only to notice that the path had turned— and that there were no longer any trees on their left.

They were now parallel to a ravine. With Joe between her and the edge of that rocky drop-off and a wall of trees to her right, she deliberately edged toward the foliage.

"Do heights bother you?"

Clutching the insulated water bottle he'd given her, she quickly shook her head. Heights normally didn't bother her at all. "I used to work on the thirty-second floor. My apartment was on the tenth." There had also been glass or a guardrail between her and all that space.

It only looked to be about ten feet to the bottom. A single story. Still, with all the rocks down there, a fall would hurt. Joe, however, seemed totally unfazed by how close he was to the edge as he told her that this section of the trail was short, only an eighth of a mile or so. Short or not, she needed to pay less attention to how he actually enjoyed being so far from civilization and more attention to where she was putting her feet.

Narrowing her focus to the path, she concentrated on where she stepped while he pointed out a squirrel darting up a tree and Bailey trotted ahead of him. It was only when the trail curved again, trees once more hugging both sides of it, and the path angled what seemed like straight up that she let herself be distracted by the scream of her thigh muscles and the rustling in the bushes.

She wanted to know if there was anything carnivorous in these woods. He told her there probably was, but that on the carnivore side, he'd personally never encountered anything bigger than a fox. What she'd heard was probably just a rabbit.

A few hundred yards later, a raccoon streaked across her path. She didn't scream. The hand she clamped over her mouth after she gasped prevented it. It was the same way she usually reacted to the cats.

Joe said nothing to minimize, patronize or otherwise imply that she was acting like a girl. He just identified the little masked beast, stuck a little closer to her and called Bailey back to walk with them since the dog had been responsible for flushing out the critter to begin with.

His attitude remained patient, almost…relaxed, she thought. Still, she had the feeling when he glanced toward her at times, that he was mentally shaking his head at her. Or, most likely, having second thoughts about having brought her along. Even if he wasn't, she was.

With her heart rate finally back to racing only from exertion and not from fright, and with Joe within grabbing distance, she reminded herself of her purpose for subjecting herself to his little slice of heaven and let herself be distracted by the crumbly-looking silver-green stuff growing on some of the trees and fallen logs.

"What is that?" she asked, pointing to a patch lit by a sunbeam.

"Lichen."

Whatever that is, she thought. "It's a great color. Perfect for a shimmery fabric like dupioni or charmeuse."

"It's made up of an alga and a fungus."

"Algae?"

"That's plural. Alga is singular. The plant is thallophytic."

She eyed him evenly. "I have no idea what thallophytic is."

He eyed her back. "I have no idea what you just said, either."

His mouth wasn't smiling. Only his eyes were. But any thought of explaining silk fabrics to him evaporated with her next heartbeat.

"It means it's a plant with a single-cell sex organ. There's another explanation, but then we'd have to get into gametes and haploid chromosomes."

His glance had slipped to her mouth, causing her pulse to jerk and pick up speed all over again.

She absolutely did not want him to know that he affected her. Not wanting him to have any effect on her at all, she simply turned away and moved on, slapping at bugs as she went.

"What's dupioni?" he called after her.

She kept going. "It's a silk fabric, woven with slubbed yarns. You'd get a nice drape in the ten momme range."

"What's mummy?"

"It's a Japanese unit of weight used to measure and describe silk cloth. That's not how other fabrics are assessed, but then we'd have to get into weight grades and thread counts."

Joe hung back. Watching her go, his attention moved

from the totally impractical little purse strapped to her back to the sweet curve of her backside, to the long length of her legs. His glance had barely reached the heels he couldn't believe had carried her this far when she gave a little jump to the side and frowned at a stick she must have thought was a snake.

He couldn't help wondering when she was going to tell him she was done, that she'd had enough of the nature thing and that he could take her home now. She wasn't having a good time. But when he caught up with her, she didn't say a word other than to remark about the intensity of the fall colors and the crystal-blue sky. She did, however, look visibly relieved when they finally entered the wide meadow and he led her to a spot by the wide stream cutting through it.

Surrounded by green pines and sugar maples the color of fire, he watched her sink to a flat boulder. Beside her, the water bubbled white as it tumbled over a dam of rocks.

"Who'd have thought," she murmured, over the water's burble and splash. "A spa." Watching the bubbles, she casually slipped off her boots to reveal socks that matched her rust-colored vest and rubbed one arch. "You have no idea how I miss massages and seaweed wraps."

He hadn't a clue what a seaweed wrap was. Some kind of sushi, maybe. Massage, however, he definitely understood.

Slipping off his backpack, he lowered himself to the rock across from her. With his boots planted a yard apart he pulled the pack to him and took out two granola bars.

He handed her one. "What else do you miss?"

Thanking him, she peeled the wrapper back halfway, took a bite and continued rubbing. "Thai takeout at two in the morning," she said as soon as she'd swallowed.

"There's this place around the corner from where I used to live that makes the most amazing shrimp soup with lemongrass, and their Pad Thai is to die for. And shopping the sample sales. And all the theaters and the clubs and my friends." She lifted the granola bar, started to take a bite, stopped. "I think I even miss the sirens."

She'd never known quiet could be so...silent...until she'd moved to Rosewood. She glanced around her. Out here, it was quieter still.

"What about you?" she asked, not wanting to taunt herself with anything else she could have mentioned. "If you were to move from Rosewood, what would you miss?"

Two-thirds of his bar was already gone. As he considered her question, the last third disappeared.

With his forearms on his spread knees, he watched her work at her arch.

His expression thoughtful, he nodded to what surrounded them. "Access to this. My friends. My practice."

Leaning forward, he reached out and circled his hand around her ankle.

"Let me do that," he said, and propped her sock-covered foot up on his knee. Pushing his thumbs into her heel, he rotated them in tiny circles to the middle of her arch.

Rebecca slowly slid to the ground to lean against the rock. If she'd intended to protest, she forgot all about it as her toes curled.

"My patients' pets," he continued as if he'd had no break at all in his thoughts. "The lakes where I boat. High-school football games in the fall. Basketball in the winter. Baseball in the spring. We have some pretty good teams," he informed her, still rubbing. "We could use some new turf on the football field, though. It's going to be a mud bog when it starts to rain."

She'd thought his touch calming before. Now, with even the muscles in her shoulders going limp, she thought it purely...magic.

"Did you play sports in high school yourself?"

"Some. Basketball mostly because the season didn't interfere with my chores at home."

"In Rosewood."

He shook his head. "Peterboro. It's a little farming town north of here. When I went to college, I played a little in undergrad," he continued before she could ask anything about his home, "but I gave it up in graduate school."

"Where did you go to college?"

"Ithaca. Cornell," he clarified. "Excellent veterinary school." He switched feet, started rubbing the other one. "Where did you go?"

"Fashion Institute of Technology. Excellent bachelors' and graduate programs. You've probably never heard of our basketball team."

He kneaded her toes. "Can't say that I have."

"Do you miss it?" she asked, praying he wouldn't stop. "Playing, I mean."

"I still play a little. I help coach sometimes at South Rosewood," he said, speaking of the youth center in what was considered the poor side of town. "The director there is a client. And a few of us have a pickup game once a week at the community center. Anyone who wants to play can come in and start playing on either team. Adam Shibb plays with us."

Adam was Molly's husband. It sounded very much as if Joe was friends with him in addition to being their dog's vet. What struck her more at the moment was the way he'd so easily glossed over his occasional work with under-privileged kids. She was just wondering which to ask him about first when he rubbed over a sore spot on her heel that drew a quick intake of breath instead.

His hand immediately went still. Before she could say a word, the dark slashes of his eyebrows merged and he slipped off her sock.

Bailey, who'd been sitting beside him, rose, shook, then walked over to plop down beside her. She'd barely felt her shoulders stiffen at him being so close when her stomach tightened at the feel of Joe's fingers on her bare skin.

The dog plopped his head on her thigh.

"You have a blister."

She had a dog in her lap.

She glanced up from the huge furry head to see Joe's eyes narrow first on Bailey, then on her. As if he thought nothing at all of his dog using her for a pillow, or maybe waiting to see what she would do, he totally ignored the apprehension that had to be visible in her face and reached into his backpack. He clearly trusted the dog. The jury was out on her.

"Are you okay?" he asked, seeming far more conscious of her wariness than she'd first thought. "I'll call him back over here if you're not."

Bailey blinked up at her, emitted a soft insistent sound that almost seemed like a whine and laid his paw across her knee.

"He wants a pat," Joe explained, over the crackle of paper as he tore the wrapper from an adhesive strip.

With her foot still propped on his knee, Joe ducked his dark head to see where to apply the bandage and curved the strip over the back of her heel.

Rebecca was rarely at a loss for words. It was even more

seldom that she found herself disarmed. At the moment, she was both. She'd had men open doors for her and carry packages. She had doormen hold an umbrella over her while she dashed from awning to cab. But she couldn't remember any man ever making her feel as if he was taking care of her. Yet, that was exactly what Joe was doing as he made sure the bandage was flat against her skin, slid her sock back on, then lifted her other foot to pull that sock off and make sure she didn't have a blister on her other heel.

She wasn't at all sure how she felt about that totally unfamiliar phenomenon. Part of her balked at the feeling. She was perfectly capable of taking care of herself, had been doing so for years. But part of her couldn't deny how that feeling seemed to soothe something inside her that felt a little too tender and bruised.

"This one looks fine," he murmured and reached for her sock to put it back on.

She was so focused on him she'd barely noticed that her hand had settled on the top of Bailey's smooth head.

Feeling less threatened by his dog than what Joe made her feel just then, she leaned forward and tugged the sock from his hand.

"I can do that. Thanks," she murmured, not wanting to sound ungrateful for what he'd done. "It's your day off," she reminded him, giving him a smile to distract from her abruptness. "You're not supposed to be working." She glanced at the dog. "You're going to have to move, sport. I can't reach my boots."

"Here, boy," she heard Joe say quietly as he sat back.

Aware of him watching her, she pulled on her sock and the boots that really would have been fine had they done all their walking on the flat.

"Where do you usually go from here?" she asked him.

"To the fire tower. Great views."

"Where is it?"

He pointed to the top of the mountain behind him. "Up there."

The look she gave him said he had to be kidding.

"But I don't plan on going there today."

She couldn't begin to tell him how grateful she was for that. As soon as she got through this one, her hiking days were over.

Rising in front of her, he held out his hand. Hesitating only slightly, she took it. She was instantly aware of its warmth and his strength as he pulled her to her feet. Finding herself within inches of his lean, solid-looking body, she was also more aware than she wanted to be of the curiosity carved in the compelling lines of his face.

He didn't release her hand. Or, maybe, it was more that she didn't let go of his. With the heat of his palm seeping into hers, she simply stood there while she watched that curiosity turn to something less definable when his glance grazed her lips, then slowly lifted to meet her eyes.

Her heart bumped her ribs. She had absolutely nothing in common with this man. Yet, he and his nearness disturbed her in ways she couldn't begin to describe— which made no sense at all when she considered how easy he was to talk with.

Refusing to consider that dichotomy, or the strength of the pull she felt toward him, she deliberately slipped her hand from his.

"Thanks for the assist," she murmured, and turned to brush bits of grass from her jeans. "Were you going to take pictures of anything while we're here?"

Either he hadn't felt the heat that still singed her nerves, or he was as intent as she was on ignoring it as he picked up his backpack.

"I thought about getting some of Bailey and the foliage for next year's clinic calendar. We send them out to our clients," he explained. "I use different pets for each month. He can be next November."

"Good advertising," she murmured. Planting her hands on her hips, she turned to survey the setting. "Where are you going to set up your shot?"

He checked out the scenery himself, finally decided to start near a copse of birch trees. On the way, she asked if he'd mind taking a few shots of the lichen they'd seen. And maybe the stones in the stream because the speckled patterns on them were kind of interesting. So were the shades of gold in the birches. And the plum and scarlet in the bushes. She was thinking of doing an article on men's clothing based on the outdoors. Maybe men would wear more and brighter hues if they realized that color was simply part of nature.

He told her he doubted it. Turquoise was part of nature, too, but no guy he knew would wear it. Guys didn't like to wear bright stuff.

She told him there were degrees of brightness and, pointing to a red bush, told him he'd looked rather good himself in the scarlet.

He told her that was poison sumac and hid a smile as he handed her a light meter and turned away to set up his tripod.

Rebecca couldn't help but smile at his broad back. Except for the bugs and the itchy grass that had somehow worked its way up her pant leg, and the blister she absolutely refused to complain about because she didn't want to hear him say I-told-you-so about her boots, she enjoyed being with him. If she could just overlook the effects of his touch and his smile, he had great potential as a friend. For now, a friend was all she wanted.

She wasn't sure what he wanted, though. She thought for certain that he'd been about to make some sort of move in those unnerving moments after he'd helped her to her feet. Yet, he made no other attempt to get close. His dog, however, seemed to have adopted her.

She would never have imagined being friends with something so furry and large. But by the time they'd made their way back to the truck, stopped at the first gas station they'd come to to use its facilities and pulled back into her driveway late that afternoon, she had to admit feeling a certain affection for Bailey.

Part of that was because the dog had retrieved her water bottle when she'd dropped it down the ravine on their way back and she hadn't had to go get it herself. But mostly she figured she liked him because Joe hadn't given her a chance to let her naiveté about animals get in the way. And naive she'd been. She hadn't realized that the cats might have been trying to play with her and, as he'd later explained, that their misbehavior was probably related to them missing their owners, and to her fear of them, which made them fear her.

Bailey wasn't afraid of her, though. Every time she'd sat down, he'd stretched out beside her and shamelessly plopped his head onto her lap for a pat.

As Joe cut the engine now, Bailey poked his big head between the seats.

She'd just reached to pet him when Joe noticed the manila envelope sticking up between her seat and the console.

Glancing at his watch, he winced. He was already over an hour later than he'd thought he'd be.

"We didn't get to your questions."

"We can do it now," she offered, stroking soft black fur.

"Actually, I can't. I didn't realize it was getting so late." He'd be up until midnight filling out forms. And that was only on the first section.

"How about we give it another shot tomorrow?" he asked, fully aware that it was more than her questionnaire he was interested in. "I'm taking Bailey to Rosewood Park tomorrow to play Frisbee. I'll be there around three."

Chapter Four

Rebecca hadn't been sure if Joe had meant she should meet him at the park at three o'clock, or if she should just show up sometime after that. As it was, she hadn't told him she would meet him, anyway. She'd simply acknowledged his statement that he and Bailey would be there, which meant that if she did show up, it would just be a casual thing and nothing even remotely resembling a date.

The fact that she was going to such lengths to justify her appearance at the park without it implying interest in a romantic involvement with the man told her she was probably already more interested in him than she should be.

Assuring herself that the only reason she wanted to see him was because she really did want his input on her project, she arrived at the park at three fifteen—then spent another five minutes in her car looking around to see if she could see him from where she'd parked along the curb.

Rosewood's main public recreation area was a postage stamp compared to the park she'd known all her life in New York. Unlike Central Park, it had no ponds, lakes, bridges or wide walkways lined with benches. No statues, elaborate carousel, or old men in tams playing boccie ball. The tree-lined blocks were large enough, though, to contain a baseball diamond, an open field, picnic areas and a playground that seemed to fill the locals' needs just fine.

Unable to spot either Joe or his truck from where she was, she finally headed past a large expanse of grass where a couple of teenage boys tossed a ball to a dog of indeterminate pedigree and an older couple strolled by with one resembling a white mop on a leash.

Trees blocked her view of the other side of the park. Thinking he might be over there, she followed the winding sidewalk to another meadowlike area where kids were kicking around a soccer ball.

She didn't see Joe, though. Not anywhere.

The gleeful shouts of children at play carried in the crisp autumn air. It was a gorgeous fall day. Too nice to spend inside, as Joe would say, she thought, only to promptly frown at the thought. It was never a good sign when a woman started quoting a man to herself. If she started quoting him to her friends, she'd know she was in trouble.

The sounds of the children came from the play area ahead of her. They hung from monkey bars, swung on swings and took turns making each other dizzy pushing the little metal merry-go-round. A couple of the kids looked familiar to her. Specifically, the two blond seven-year-old girls at the freestanding water fountain. One was Angela Schumacher's daughter, Olivia. The other was Emily, Jack's little girl.

"Rebecca?" a woman's voice called. "Over here!"

Angela waved to her from one of the picnic tables near the swings. Having caught Rebecca's attention, the slender woman with the chic, chin-length blond bob lifted her five-year-old son, Michael, from where she'd perched him on the table to tie his shoe.

With her little boy running off to join the girls, she glanced to where her nine-year-old sat at an empty picnic table twenty yards away, playing somewhat sullenly with his Game Boy.

Everyone knew that Anthony wasn't dealing well with his father's absence from his life. Rumor had it, too, that Angela was having even more difficulty with the boy lately.

Despite that challenge to the woman's parenting skills, Rebecca was actually a little in awe of the divorced mother of three. Angela worked full-time as an office manager for a pediatric dentist and part-time at a cute little boutique that carried the most adorable clothes and accessories for tween-aged girls. Yet, even with what seemed like no time left in her day, Angela's children always looked as nearly perfect as she did, she was an excellent cook, her yard looked fabulous and she threw the best parties on the block.

Rebecca couldn't cook anything that didn't need simply to be thawed and microwaved. Or, better yet, reheated in its deli container. And her disabilities where yard work was concerned were legendary on Danbury Way. Entertaining involved takeout or a caterer. She could multitask with the best of them, but domestic, she was not.

She still felt awkward about her lack of skills in that department, too. Her only attempt at entertaining since she'd arrived in Rosewood had been the baby shower she'd thrown for Molly a couple of months ago. She'd used the best caterer and baker in town for the buffet and the cake, and served the best champagne she could afford. Sparkling cider for Molly, of course. Everyone had told her they thought the event a success, but she'd been a wreck. She was afraid she'd been overly exuberant so no one would notice the lack of home-prepared fare. But people apparently just thought she was an enthusiastic hostess. Or so Rebecca had heard from Molly, who'd heard the comment from Angela's sister, Megan, who'd heard it from Zooey, who was now avoiding Rebecca like the proverbial plague.

"I'm surprised to see you here." Smiling as Rebecca approached, Angela wearily pushed her hand through her hair and sat down on the bench. "I didn't think anyone over the age of emancipation ever came here without a book, a child or a pet."

At the mention of children, Rebecca's glance darted uneasily to the little girl with Olivia. Jack's daughter looked exactly like him.

"Neither Jack nor Zooey is here, if that's what you're thinking about." A touch of sympathy came with Angela's astute observation. Like everyone else on the cul-de-sac, she'd known about her dates with Jack—and about his no-longer-latent attraction to his children's nanny. "I brought Emily with us to play with Olivia. Those girls are practically joined at the hip."

Assured that she wouldn't have to make awkward small talk with Emily's dad or nanny, Rebecca smiled back. "A girl needs a best friend. Or a good girlfriend, anyway. There are things guys just don't get."

Angela had barely murmured, "Amen," before Rebecca glanced around once more.

"Is Megan here, too? I'd like to ask a favor of her.

Actually, of Greg," she explained, thinking of her current work project. "I'm working on a make-over-your-mate article and could use his input if he wouldn't mind filling out a questionnaire. I don't have an extra one with me, but I can drop one by if he's willing."

"Megan is working on a killer deadline. Why don't I ask Greg to call you?"

"Would you? That would be great. Thanks."

Angela's sister, Megan, was a freelance graphic artist who lived above Angela's garage and babysat for her while she was away at work herself. It was expected any day that she and Greg Banning, Carly Alderson's ex, would announce their engagement. Megan and Greg were going to wind up married and making a whole new life for themselves—which would leave Angela without anyone to help her care for her kids.

Wondering if that was why Angela seemed a bit discouraged at the moment, Rebecca sat down beside her.

"How are Megan and Greg doing?"

To her surprise, that discouragement faded. "I've never seen my sister so happy. Or, Greg, either, for that matter." Her smile softened. "I really hope things work out as well for them as they did for Carly and Bo."

So much for her powers of perception, Rebecca thought. She didn't seem down about Megan at all. "It's hard to believe that Carly and Greg were once married. It wouldn't be for you," she hurried to explain, "because you lived on the same street with them for so long, but they hadn't been divorced long at all when I came here. I thought I'd seen just about everything in New York, but this is all so…"

"Soap-opera-esque?"

"I was thinking more like…civilized."

"That, too. So," Angela murmured, casually checking out Rebecca's faux fur vest and tweed slacks. "What brings you to the park?"

Rebecca wished she hadn't asked that—especially since her reason for being there had apparently had a change of plans. As she had so emphatically pointed out to herself, she didn't have a date with Joe, so it wasn't as if he'd stood her up. The odd empty spot inside her just made it feel that way.

She bent to take the manila envelope out of her purse, thinking to somehow explain that she was there because of work. Her focus was still in the vicinity of her caramel-colored stack-heeled boots and matching bag when a bright pink plastic disk and a large amount of tan-and-black fur appeared in front of her.

Bailey plopped down on his haunches in front of her and dropped his Frisbee at her feet.

"Oh, my." Angela didn't seem to share Rebecca's inherent, though admittedly waning, sense of discomfort with animals. She was already holding out her hand for the big, bright-eyed German shepherd to sniff. "Aren't you beautiful?"

"I think he'd prefer handsome."

From the corner of her eye, Rebecca caught a glimpse of large running shoes, denim and blue fleece.

"Joe."

He had another dog on a leash. This one was all gray fur and wiggles and couldn't have weighed ten pounds.

"I thought that was you over here." Moving his easy smile from her to the woman staring up at his undeniably attractive face, he held out his free hand. "Joe Hudson," he said, introducing himself. "And that's Bailey," he added with a nod toward the dog who'd just put his paw on Rebecca's knee.

Knowing Bailey wanted a pat, and scrambling to avoid the quick speculation in her neighbor's eyes, she obliged. "Joe is the cats' veterinarian," she explained, eyeing the dog wriggling by his feet. "Joe, this is Angela. She lives down the street from me. Whose dog is that?"

"Mine. This is Rex. He wanted to come, too."

"You have two dogs?"

"And an iguana, but he's not crazy about his leash. You ready to play Frisbee?"

Her eyebrows shot up. He had a lizard? "You want me to play?" After yesterday, he had to know she wasn't into things that involved the outdoors and exertion. She definitely wasn't into anything that involved the outdoors and sweat. "I don't know how."

"Trust me. It's not complicated. You toss the Frisbee. They get it and bring it back. You do it again."

Joining him on the field had never occurred to her. She'd thought she'd watch for a while, then they could sit at one of the tables and she could guide him through the questionnaire. She was saved having to explain that, however, by the dogs.

Olivia and Michael were suddenly there asking Angela if they could pat them. Emily was right behind, wanting to know if she could, too.

"Take it easy. All of you," Angela said to the excited children. "They're mine," she explained to Joe. "These two, anyway." She put a hand atop Michael's blond head, smoothed Olivia's hair with the other. With a nod toward the lanky child now watching them from his self-imposed exile, she added, "So is the one by himself over there. Emily here is a neighbor."

It occurred to Rebecca just then that most of the men she'd met, including Emily's father, would not be terribly comfortable to find themselves the focus of three animated and chattering kids they didn't know.

Joe didn't seem to mind at all. He simply hunkered down in front of them, told the children to reach for the animals slowly and let them take turns stroking his dogs' shiny fur.

Apparently aware of the older boy watching them from where he'd distanced himself from his family, Joe looked to Angela. "Does your other son like dogs?"

"Anthony loves them. We're just not home enough to have any pets ourselves."

"Bailey's gentle. Rebecca can vouch for that," he said, the blue of his eyes seeming more intense as he considered the situation. "Rex is okay, too," he assured her. "He's just noisier. They have room to run at home, but I bring them here to keep them socialized. Would he want to play with them?"

Angela glanced toward her oldest son, looked quickly back to Joe. "Normally, I'd say yes." Resignation tinged her tone. "Today, your guess is as good as mine."

It was already apparent to Rebecca that this wasn't one of Anthony's better days. It seemed equally clear now that his attitude was the reason the woman everyone thought of as Supermom seemed a bit disheartened today. She'd obviously brought the kids to the park so they could enjoy their Sunday afternoon together, but Anthony was having no part of that plan.

It was Joe who had most of her attention, though.

There was no denying the aura of quiet strength that surrounded him. Or the sense of compassion that ran as deep as his kindness.

"If you want," Joe said to Angela, "I'll take all the kids. We can toss the Frisbee right over there." Pointing behind him, he indicated the open field on the other side of the walkway. "You two won't even have to lose your bench."

Grinning, Olivia and Emily started jumping up and down.

"Can we, Mom? Please?"

"Can we, Mrs. Schumacher?"

"Please, please, please," little Michael begged.

Pure skepticism slashed their mother's face. "Are you sure you want to do that?"

With Rex on the ground beside him, Rebecca watched Joe plant his hands on his powerful thighs. Rising with an easy, athletic grace to tower over them all, he gave her a wink and glanced back to her neighbor.

"No choice." He dipped his head toward Rebecca. "She doesn't want to play with me," he concluded and walked away with the kids and dogs fast on his heels.

"He's the guy you went out with yesterday."

Rebecca jerked her thoughtful frown from his retreating back. "How did you know that?"

"The whole neighborhood knows. Sylvia saw you leave with him yesterday afternoon. When she described the truck to Molly, Molly knew exactly who it was. She said she had a feeling he had a thing for you."

"Sylvia did?"

"Molly. She didn't know you'd had a date with him, though."

"It wasn't a date. It was more like an…appointment."

It was as clear as the woman's curiosity that she wanted to know if today was an appointment, too. But Angela wasn't the sort to put another person on the spot.

"Your Joe Hudson seems to be a very perceptive man," was all she said.

"He's not mine," Rebecca insisted, intent on nipping

further gossip in the bud. "And, yes, he certainly seems to be."

He had appeared to instinctively know that if he got the other kids involved, it would be easier for the one holding himself back to join them. How he'd known that, she had no idea. She was just impressed by the fact that he'd even noticed the situation—and cared enough to offer his help—as she watched Anthony catch his mom's eye.

The boy nodded to where his siblings were running with the dogs.

Giving him a smile of permission, Angela watched him go.

Rebecca's attention was back on the intriguing man with the easy manner and even easier smile. What he'd done for Angela and Anthony wasn't something most people would consider doing for strangers. It also spoke volumes about the sort of man Dr. Joe Hudson was.

"Molly said he's a great vet."

"I think he is. But, then," she qualified, hurrying to cover her totally unguarded response, "he's the only one I've ever met."

"Well, he seems to be as good with kids as he is with animals."

Rebecca had just thought of that herself. But she refused to let her mind go there. It didn't matter that everything about him spoke of a man who seemed decent, responsible, kind and caring. Noticing such things would only lead to wishes and dreams and she was not about to consider any sort of a dream involving any man right now—no matter how perfect he was starting to seem.

"I can't do this."

"Do what?" Rebecca asked.

"Leave him out there to cope with all of them alone.

We should go help." Rising, Angela's glance slid to Rebecca's short boots. "Don't you own any flats?"

"Not really."

"Sneakers?"

"One pair," she admitted, but she only wore them with her velveteen sweatpants and hoodie. They didn't go with anything else she owned.

Angela shook her head. "Well, you might want to wear them," she suggested. "That guy has real potential."

"Then you go out with him."

"I'm not the one he's interested in. Aside from that, I don't want a relationship. I have enough to deal with."

"You've sworn off men?"

"You might say that."

With a sigh, Rebecca stood, hiked up the strap of her purse and straightened her shoulders. "Me, too."

The days were growing progressively shorter. By four thirty, the sun had moved below the treetops, fading the daylight and taking the temperature down with it. Most everyone in the park was heading for home to start supper, including Angela and the kids now that the children had given the dogs one last hug. Except for Anthony. He'd been all smiles playing Frisbee with their canine companions, but he'd withdrawn again the moment his mother had said it was time to go.

Having nothing to offer the beleaguered mom but a sympathetic smile, Rebecca waved to Angela as the woman gathered her charges and hustled them to her van.

With the dogs trotting beside him, and Bailey carrying the pink disk in his mouth, Joe walked over to where she'd watched from the sidelines.

"I take it Anthony is going through a hard time."

"His dad has started blowing off his visitations. At least, that's what I hear." Looking from the retreating family and their little friend, an unexpected softness entered her voice. "What you did for him was really nice, Joe. I know Angela appreciated it. A lot."

"Boys and dogs. The combination is a natural."

He didn't seem to think he'd done anything extraordinary at all. He was also suddenly sidetracked when he noticed the manila envelope tucked under her arm.

Apology pinched his expression.

"We didn't get to your questions." Again, he might have said. "Look." He glanced at his watch, back to her. "It's getting too dark to work on them now. Just give that to me and I'll take it home. I'll fill out the questionnaire as best I can and give it back to you when you bring Columbus in for me to check his ear."

The quick stab of disappointment she felt just then caught her completely off guard. While the light had faded too much to work at one of the picnic tables, there was plenty of light to be had in a restaurant. There were several casual places in town and they both had to eat. She just hadn't realized how much she'd hoped he would suggest they have dinner together until he'd removed the possibility.

Cramming that disappointment behind her smile, she held the envelope out to him. "Not a problem," she insisted, her tone as light as she could make it. "Just call if anything isn't clear. Otherwise, I'll see you Thursday."

Joe quietly studied her as he took the envelope. As sexist as it was, he would freely admit that her beautiful face and knockout body were the first things he noticed about her—a split second before her animated agitation had registered. In her defense, she had been a little stressed about the cat that morning.

Yet, now, as his glance shifted over her in the gray evening light, it wasn't her flawless skin or her lush mouth that held his interest. It wasn't even the thick fall of glossy hair spilling in layers below her shoulders. Today was the first time he'd seen it down, and the urge to touch it was stronger than he'd ever known such a desire to be. What kept him so still was what he'd seen in her eyes.

He was intimately familiar with how animals tried to hide their wounds so their predators wouldn't know they were vulnerable. In the wild, that trait was key to their survival. Even in pain, some creatures could mask an injury so well that it wouldn't be apparent at all, until the animal went into shock and died.

That sort of protectiveness was what he was beginning to sense in the woman deliberately pulling her glance from his scrutiny now. There was a little-girl-lost quality about her that she would hate to know was visible, given how street-smart and savvy she was. Her urbane, confident attitude went a long way to cover any outward signs of wounds or weakness. But the sadness he sensed beneath her breezy exterior told him that something really wasn't right with her world.

Without questioning why it felt so important, he wanted to know what that something was.

"Where did you park your car?"

"By the other field."

"Come on. I'll walk you to it. On the way you can tell me whether or not I'm right."

Looking totally puzzled, she fell into step beside him, Bailey at her side, Rex at his.

"Right about what?"

"You never really did say why you came to Rosewood," he reminded her. "But if I had to guess, I'd say you came here to get away from something."

Rebecca had admired his sense of perception earlier. With it turned on her, it simply gave her pause.

"Are you in some sort of trouble?"

The concern in his voice had her glance darting to his. That same concern was carved in the strong lines of his face.

"Trouble?"

"Are you in some kind of witness protection program or something?"

She couldn't tell if he was serious or simply teasing her. All she knew for certain was that he wasn't smiling.

"Do I seem that out of place here?"

"I didn't say that," he murmured, though he was clearly thinking it.

One dark eyebrow arched. "So?"

"I'm not in trouble," she assured him. Certainly not the kind that required a change of identity. "I'm just…" *Lost,* she thought, only to frown at the silent admission. She hated how the feeling rested so close to the surface.

"Running?" he suggested.

She shook her head. "It not like that."

"Then tell me what it is like. What are you trying to get away from?"

"I never said I was trying to get away from anything."

He stopped in the middle of the walkway. Catching her arm, he stopped her, too.

As if wanting to make sure he had her full attention, he caught her chin with his fingers and tipped her head toward him. "Unless you're just inherently stubborn, I don't think you'd be this evasive unless something was wrong. For what it's worth, if there is something wrong, maybe I can help. Just keep that in mind," he murmured, and let his hand fall.

He wanted to help. For a moment, the thought brought confusion. Mostly because he didn't seem to have an agenda with her. He wasn't asking anything of her, other than that she talk to him. As she'd discovered yesterday, talking to him was incredibly easy to do.

He had more questions, that was as apparent to her as the way her heart had squeezed at his touch. Yet, as they continued on, he said nothing else while he waited for her to decide whether or not to let him in.

All she cared about just then was that she needed him to know she wasn't running. Not exactly, anyway.

"Getting away was part of it," she finally admitted over the even beat of their footsteps. She hadn't come to get away from a man. She'd come to find one: her father. But she hadn't talked about Russell Lever with anyone. Feeling totally ambivalent about meeting him now, she wasn't ready to talk about him with Joe, either.

"Things weren't going all that great in New York," she explained. "My girlfriends were all getting married and having babies and my apartment was robbed," she told him, though she doubted he would understand the emotional impact that girlfriends' milestones had on a woman. "Then, there was this guy." Having been burglarized seemed almost incidental now. "But that was over six months ago."

That still didn't explain why she'd chosen Rosewood. Yet, that wasn't what disturbed Joe at the moment. It was the way she'd hugged her arms around her waist when she'd mentioned her ex-boyfriend. The self-protective gesture spoke volumes.

"Whose call was that? His or yours?"

"His," she muttered. "I made the mistake of asking him if we were ever going to get married. He said he didn't want to talk about it, but I did, so I pushed. You know that saying, 'be careful what you ask for'? Well, I got what I asked for when I asked him why he didn't want to talk about it and he said he'd never considered marriage an option with me."

Realizing what she'd just admitted, she shoved her fingers through her hair, slowly shook her head. "I can't believe I just told you that."

Joe felt himself hesitate. Part of him was glad that she had told him. For the first time since he'd met her, he had the feeling he was beginning to understand the woman behind the perfect makeup and designer clothes. The one behind the beautiful, protective mask. But another part of him felt as if the Fates had just tossed a bit of his own past in his face.

The man Rebecca had hoped to marry had pulled her dreams right out from under her.

He had done that very same thing to Sara Jennings.

That had been a lifetime ago. Still, despite the fact that it had been best for both of them, he hated knowing that he'd hurt her. Especially since he was presently faced with the aftermath of what both Sara and Rebecca undoubtedly regarded as total betrayal.

Though he reminded himself it wasn't Rebecca that he'd hurt, caution entered his tone. "I take it he wasn't into marriage."

"It wasn't that," she murmured. "According to him, our problem was that he didn't love me enough. Two months to the day we broke up, he married someone else."

"Had he been seeing her while you were together?"

"For about a month."

With her trust having been betrayed on a number of levels, his hand moved to his heart. "Ouch."

"Yeah," she murmured, unable to help smiling at his reaction. "Ouch."

She didn't want the lingering hurt to matter. She didn't want it to be there at all. More than anything, she didn't want that awful sense of not belonging anywhere. Incredibly, though, when she was talking with Joe those unwanted feelings didn't feel quite so threatening. She wasn't sure why that was. She wasn't sure it even mattered. All that did matter to her just then was the friendship he seemed to be offering, and the fact that he wanted to help. Because he did, and because she didn't know who else to ask, there was something she rather desperately needed to know.

"I'm afraid I've started a trend," she confided, her tone deceptively breezy. "A few weeks ago, I finally started going out with this guy here. It wasn't anything serious. Just a few dinners," she explained, because she didn't want him to think her heart had been battered all over again. "But he broke up with me for someone else, too." She gave a wry little laugh. "I'd be indebted to you forever if you could tell me what's wrong with me. Maybe I can fix it before I put myself out there again."

She shook her head, jammed her fingers through her hair. Now that the question was out, she wished she'd kept it to herself. She didn't mind if he thought her out of place, out of her depth or outlandish. She just didn't want him to think her pathetic.

Feeling that way just then, hating it, she held up her palm, started to tell him not to answer that.

Catching her hand, he froze the words in her throat as he turned her to face him. For a moment, he said nothing. He just stood there while the breeze blew her hair across her cheek and his eyes moved slowly over her face.

Joe knew he wasn't a man who spent much time

analyzing his personal relationships. He had always simply known what felt right and what didn't. He knew what attracted him, what turned him off and what he wanted for the long haul, when that time came.

He also knew he had no desire to rush into a relationship with someone on the rebound. This woman had been hurt enough. Since he had no interest in anything serious or complicated, he didn't want to start anything that might leave her hurt all over again—and him with regrets.

Despite the fact that he had other things he needed to do, he had toyed with the idea of asking her if she wanted to grab a pizza with him after he dropped off his dogs at his place. Considering the need he suddenly felt to keep things casual, a little distance seemed like a better plan all the way around.

Easing her hand to her side, he lifted his again to tuck her hair behind her ear. "There's nothing to fix. There's nothing wrong with you, Rebecca." The temptation was to let his touch linger. Her hair felt like silk, her skin like warm satin. But the desire to keep things uncomplicated prevailed. "You just haven't met the right man yet."

She tipped her head, studying him as he stepped back while her mind absorbed the quiet certainty in his words that wrapped like a balm around her battered heart. She was more grateful than she wanted to be for his kindness, and more touched than she could have imagined by that simple show of faith.

Afraid he could see both, she ducked her head, hiding that too-vulnerable expression from him. Helping and making things better was simply what he did. He did it every day when people brought their animals to him. He did it with small children, and with a frazzled mom he'd never met before. What he'd done probably meant nothing special to him at all.

They'd stopped beside her car. Bending, she ruffled Bailey's fur, then bent lower to give the adorable and energetic little Rex a pat, too. Now that she was beginning to realize that her attitude toward animals could have a direct effect on theirs toward her, the edge seemed to have come off the worst of her discomfort with them. With the cats and Joe's dogs, anyway. She felt a little grateful to his companions at the moment, too. By focusing on them, she could ignore the empty feeling that had already started to return.

"What time is your appointment Thursday?"

"At ten, I think," she replied, straightening.

"I'll make sure I have this done by then." With his easy smile, he lifted the manila envelope.

"Call me. If you have any questions about that," she quickly explained.

"Will do. You have a good week."

"You, too," she murmured, and watched him motion to his dogs before they all walked away through the blowing leaves.

Hugging her arms against the deepening chill in the air, she turned to her car. There was no way he could possibly be as good as he seemed.

That was exactly what she told Molly, too, when Molly called that evening to find out what was going on because Angela had told Megan, who'd told her that they'd been together at the park that afternoon.

"There's nothing going on," she assured her neighbor. "He said he'd help with my menswear article, so I met him there with my questionnaire. I have one for Adam, too. He won't mind filling it out, will he?"

"Probably. His idea of coordinating an outfit is to make sure his socks match. But he'll do it, anyway." A hint of disappointment shaded her tone. "There's nothing going on?"

"Nothing. Honest. Unless he has a problem with the questions, he probably won't even call."

Despite her claim, she truly hoped he would.

But he didn't call that week. Not once. He didn't call while she worked on a filler piece her editor asked for on sexy summer feet where she waxed poetic about pedicures, toe rings, ankle bracelets and the importance of exfoliating and moisturizing. Or while she pored over the latest editions of all the current fashion magazines she could find to make sure her approach to her pending articles was still fresh, and to get ideas for new ones. He didn't even call and hang up without leaving a message while she was out distributing her questionnaires to department and men's clothing stores for their customers to fill out. She knew that because she checked her caller ID every evening when she returned—which was why she was feeling totally ambivalent about taking Columbus in for his appointment when the phone rang Thursday morning an hour before she was due at the clinic.

Chapter Five

"Mom, hi." In a hurry because she'd already changed her clothes twice, Rebecca switched her phone to the other ear and finished pulling her final choice of sweater over her head. "You sound terrible. What's the matter?"

"It's just a cold," Lillian Peters replied from her fourth-floor apartment around the corner from Macy's. The rent-controlled unit had been Rebecca's home for years. With its proximity to everything her mom needed and only blocks from the subway that could get her to JFK and LaGuardia for her frequent buying trips, it would remain her mom's home until the building was condemned or Lillian departed the planet.

Though decades from her demise, the woman sounded truly awful. Her consonants were muddled and her *l*'s were nonexistent.

"I just wanted to see how you were holding up in the

suburbs." She coughed, sniffed. "I still don't understand why you gave up a perfectly fabulous job to move up there. Your office had a window."

Her office hadn't had a window. It had only had a view of one, but that point was moot. Rebecca knew her mom didn't understand what she'd done because her mom didn't know what had driven her to make the decision. She also knew the only reason her mother would call at this hour on a workday was because she was home alone with a miserable cold and feeling lonesome.

Rebecca loved her mom. And she greatly admired her killer instincts when it came to predicting the hot items for the next season and her go-for-the-jugular approach negotiating the best buys for her employer. But her mom had a fragile, almost needy side that surfaced only when she felt too lousy to keep up her defenses. When that happened, she holed up until she had her edge back.

Having inherited that particular trait from her, rather wishing she'd inherited her mother's talent for blocking what she didn't want to think about instead, she sat on the edge of the bed and reached for a boot. "I told you, I wanted to try my hand at freelancing. Are you sure it's just a cold? You've worked with a cold before. It's not like you to stay home."

"You can't freelance from Manhattan? And, yes, I'm sure it's just a cold. I'm in bed with NyQuil."

Rebecca smiled. "Do I know him?"

Her mom laughed, then started coughing and excused herself to take a sip of tea.

"That reminds me," Rebecca continued, pulling on her other boot, "are you still seeing that guy from the ad agency? Arnold?"

"Armand. And no. He had too much baggage. All he

talked about was how much his ex-wife was costing him. I hate it when men do that," she mumbled. She coughed again, then blew her nose. "Especially before the waiter brings the menu. Makes you feel as if you should only order salad."

Her mom's luck with men had been no better than hers. Lillian was still young at forty-seven, and incredibly attractive. But she had never married. To Rebecca's knowledge, she'd never even had a relationship that went past the third date. But then, Lillian had been beyond circumspect with her love life. No man had ever spent the night in their apartment. No man had ever even set foot in it, other than to come in to collect her mom to take her out—or to repair the plumbing.

Yet, Rebecca now knew from what she'd read in her diary that she had once been madly in love. Her mother had never admitted that, though. The few times she had asked about the man who had fathered her, her mom had closed up like a storefront at six o'clock on a Saturday night. Only once had she received a response other than to be told she didn't need a dad.

He was a good man, but it was a complicated situation. He's not part of our lives and we don't need him to be. Just leave it alone.

That was when Rebecca had finally stopped asking about him. She'd been fourteen at the time. Her questions, though, had lingered. They still did. Only now she was trying to reconcile her mom's description of him as a good man with the impression Jack had given her of Russell being a distant, self-focused father who cared about nothing but his work.

She wasn't about to mention her search for Russell Lever to her mom. Once she met him, if she ever did, she would tell her. Until then, there was no point in upsetting her.

"Chicken," she repeated, heading for the mirror in her bathroom. "Sorry about the guy," she added, because she really did wish her mom could find someone special, "but you need chicken soup. Why don't you call Mrs. Morretti and see if she can send some up?"

"Goldberg's deli makes better."

Rebecca suggested that, in that case, she should call the deli, which lead to a discussion about the medicinal value of chicken soup while she brushed her hair and touched up her makeup. That conversation then reminded her mother to tell her about a new restaurant she wanted to try if she ever got her taste buds back.

Ordinarily, her mom never went on about such things. She was usually off the phone in the time it took to make sure her daughter hadn't up and moved somewhere else inexplicable and to tell her where in the country, or the world, she would be in case she needed to reach her. The fact that she was going on about the ordinary would have had Rebecca feeling a tad impatient, too, since she was due at the vet's in twenty minutes. But her mom wouldn't have called now had she not been lonely.

Totally understanding the feeling because she'd been there herself so much lately, Rebecca didn't have the heart to cut the conversation short.

That was why eighteen minutes later, after her mom finally said she was going to take a nap, Rebecca practically flew out the door with the cat and carrier in one hand and her cell phone in the other as she told whoever answered at the clinic that she was going to be late.

Running late had distinct advantages. It robbed her of the time she would have spent feeling anxious about seeing Joe again. It also kept her from worrying about why that ambivalent feeling was there. As she finally hurried into the clinic schlepping the cat carrier and her large shoulder bag, her only thought was that she'd made it.

She recognized the late-thirtysomething woman behind the reception counter immediately. Tracy was the assistant who'd helped with Columbus last week. Today, the paw-print top she wore was in primary colors.

"Come on back, Miss Peters. How's Columbus doing?" the smiling woman asked, rounding the counter to lead her down the hall.

There were only two people in the waiting room. A worried-looking woman and the teary-eyed little girl holding her hand.

Not sure what was going on with them, certain only that it wasn't good, Rebecca followed the assistant into the same room Columbus had been tended in before. As she had been instructed, she'd removed the larger bandage days ago, but left the smaller one and the cone collar on. "I think he'll be glad to get this collar off," she replied, setting the carrier on the waist-high examination table. Apology entered her tone. "I hope I didn't throw the doctor's schedule off by being late."

"Actually, he's in surgery. We had an emergency," Tracy explained, expertly sliding the cat out of his carrier. Her voice dropped. "A puppy got hit by a car. The little girl saw it."

"Is it hers?"

"It is.

"So," she continued, having just explained why the people in the waiting room looked so upset, "he asked me to look at his ear. Don't worry," she said, apparently sensing Rebecca's hesitation. "I do this all the time. I'll just need you to hold him for me."

Before Rebecca could say a word, the pleasant woman handed her the wriggling ball of silver-and-black striped fur. It wasn't the woman's level of expertise that had made her go still, though. She didn't doubt for a moment that the woman knew what she was doing. She just felt bad for the puppy and the little girl. She'd also thought for certain that Joe would walk in any minute. Her heart actually felt as if it had sunk a little knowing he would not.

Once the assistant showed her how to hold Columbus to keep him still, it only took moments for her to remove the bandage and pronounce the cat's wound to be healing nicely. Without the white gauze and the cone, he even looked completely normal and, to her, indistinguishable from Magellan—except for the fact that part of his ear was gone.

"Do I need to make another appointment for him?" she asked.

"Not for this," the pleasant woman replied, only to suddenly turn on her heel. "While you're getting him into his carrier, there's something I'm supposed to give you. I'll be right back." She left.

"The doctor said to be sure you got this," she continued, walking back in seconds later.

She held out a manila envelope. Recognizing it as the one she'd given Joe, Rebecca felt her heart sink even further. Peeking inside, she saw that he'd filled out her questionnaire—the first page, anyway, from what she could tell before she closed the envelope and quickly stuffed it into her oversize bag.

Murmuring, "Thank you," she forced a smile when she didn't feel like smiling at all and turned back to her task. He could have hung on to the envelope and dropped it by her house. Since he'd chosen not to give it to her in person, and since she hadn't heard a word from him all week, it was growing more apparent by the minute that he didn't care to see her anymore. "And thanks for taking care of Columbus," she added, hurrying to get all four paws inside so she could zip the black mesh. "I'll be out in a minute to pay his bill."

The woman told her there was no charge for that day and left to answer the ringing phone. Even as the squeak of her athletic shoes faded, Rebecca could hear the deep tones of Joe's voice. She couldn't make out what was being said, but something about his tone and that of the tiny female voice responding told her he was in the reception area talking with the owners of the puppy he'd been tending.

Not wanting to walk through and disturb them, and preferring to avoid the man who didn't want to see her anyway, she kept her back to the open door and fussed with the carrier until the voices died and she heard his footsteps carrying him toward the back of the clinic.

She thought that was where he was headed anyway—until he walked in.

She never would have thought of scrubs as having even a scrap of fashion potential. But on him they looked amazing. The green drawstring pants hugged his lean hips. The V-necked shirt emphasized his broad shoulders. A green cap covered most of his dark hair. What she noticed most, though, was the preoccupation tightening his features and how the smile he gave her barely curved his mouth

"Everything go okay with Columbus?"

"Your assistant said he's doing great."

He walked past her, unzipped the carrier and checked the cat's ear himself. "Did Tracy give you your envelope?"

"She did."

"Good. I wanted to make sure you got it in case you

were tying up your article. I didn't want to hold you up if you were."

Looking satisfied with the cat's progress, he closed up the carrier again.

"Dr. Hudson?" Tracy appeared in the doorway. "Lily needs you in post-op. And Sylvia Bromley is on her way over with Oscar. He has a thorn in his paw that she can't get out."

"I'm on my way," he replied. "I'm sorry," he said to Rebecca. "I have to go." He nodded to the carrier. "He looks good," he assured her and disappeared out the door.

Rebecca pulled a deep breath. He hadn't said he would call. He hadn't said he'd see her later. Clearly preoccupied with whatever was going on with his emergency, he'd only confirmed what she already suspected. He'd lost interest. Yet, even dealing with the apparently seriously injured animal and its distraught family, he had wanted to make sure she got what he'd filled out for her.

Picking up Columbus, she headed into the reception area. She didn't want him to be thoughtful. She didn't want to think about how fortunate the puppy, the woman and little girl still waiting were to have Joe there for him. As she offered them a sympathetic smile and thanked Tracy on her way out, she wanted only to insist that it didn't matter that he was the second man in two and a half weeks to lose interest in her. But she couldn't. It mattered because he had given her a taste of something she'd never truly experienced before. It had been such a small thing, but she'd yet to shake thoughts of those unsettling moments when he'd tended her sore feet by the stream and he had allowed her to feel what it was like simply to be cared for by a man.

Aware of the funny little ache in her chest, she snatched her to-do list out of her purse as soon as she and the cat were in her car, crossed off the vet appointment at ten o'clock, grabbed a latte at the drive-through at Starbucks, then headed back to the house where Columbus immediately claimed a spot on a windowsill, a position previously denied him by the awkward collar. Having found Magellan curled up in a sunbeam, she headed back out to tackle the second item on the list that would take all day to complete.

She had never in her life set foot in a craft store. But her house was the only one on the block not decorated for fall and the craft store across from the mall was where Molly had bought the orange ribbon for the swag of cattails and fall leaves hanging beneath her porch light. Everyone else had something festive adorning their entries, too. Pots of yellow mums. Pumpkins. Then, there was Carly. Rebecca wasn't about to compete with the corn shock, pumpkin and scarecrow tableau adorning the McMansion's front porch. But the pressure of trying to fit in necessitated some effort in that direction.

Her first thought as she entered the huge store was that the craft industry was as out of sync with the calendar as the clothing market, and that she had missed the fall season. Aisle after aisle was filled with artificial pine trees, boughs and wreaths and the glitter of every imaginable holiday embellishment waiting to be made into decorations for Christmas.

Her thought on the way out with the wreath of faux fall leaves she'd found for fifty percent off on a pre-Thanksgiving clearance display was that the store might actually have some potential. She would never be a craft person. She could barely sew on a button and had no talent at all for creating anything from scratch. But if there was anything she did know how to do, it was accessorize.

That was why she also bought two brass buckets to fill with the yellow mums she hadn't managed to kill in the backyard. She'd also bought Santa hats for Bailey and Rex and a tiny white faux fur collar for Joe's iguana. She had no ulterior motives for the latter purchase. She'd just remembered that on the way back from their hike last week, Joe had said he needed to take a picture of animals for the clinic's Christmas card. She would drop the items off at the clinic in case he wanted to use his own pets. She wasn't sure when she would do that. She just knew she wouldn't do it that day. Not with what he had going on there. She didn't have time, anyway. She had appointments in Albany, forty minutes away.

She wanted several perspectives for her article, so she'd scheduled interviews with the managers of the two largest men's clothing stores there. On her way back, she would swing by the mall and pick up whatever questionnaires had been completed of those she'd left earlier in the week. It had been her experience that store and department managers were more likely to gather feedback for her if she gave them times she would return for the material rather than asking them to mail it.

Being busy was good. Being busy kept her from thinking too much about what she was going to do about Russell Lever. It did not, however, keep her from thinking about Joe, and how difficult his work had to be sometimes.

Joe was still too much on her mind after she returned that evening. Having dined on Lean Cuisine, and wanting badly to stop thinking about him and that puppy, she emptied her briefcase-sized shoulder bag of the notes from her interviews and the questionnaires she'd collected that afternoon. She only had two dozen so far, but was hoping for a better return over the weekend when she pulled out the envelope Joe's assistant had given her.

Sinking into a chair at her breakfast table desk, she slipped out the papers inside.

Joe had completed all three pages of her questionnaire. Neat check marks selected his preferences from the multiple-choice responses. Within a minute, she'd confirmed what she already knew. Their tastes were the polar opposite of each other's. She also now knew that he wouldn't be caught dead in black silk boxers no matter whose name was on them, that L.L.Bean was his designer of choice and that of the five pictures of outfits she'd included for him to put in order of preference, his favorite was her least.

Not that there was anything wrong with corduroy and cable knit, she assured herself. She just liked cashmere and combed wool better. At least, she'd once thought she had.

He'd also put a yellow sticky note on the last page.

Call me at home if you're interested in Thai food Saturday night.

Below that he'd given her his home phone number.

She figured it was probably a mistake to feel such relief, if only because the feeling confirmed how much his friendship was beginning to mean to her. But it was there, front and center, making her smile in the moments before she insisted that there was nothing wrong with feeling pleased that a friend wanted to get together.

She got his answering machine the first couple of times she called. The third time, nearing eight o'clock, she was thinking of just leaving a message when he finally answered with a weary, "Hi. I just got home."

He still sounded preoccupied. Or, maybe, he just sounded tired.

"Then now probably isn't a good time for me to be calling."

"Now is fine. It's just been a long day. Sorry about this morning. I just didn't have time to talk."

"I know." Even rushed, he'd thought of her anyway. "How is the puppy doing? The one you operated on," she asked, protectively reminding herself that he was thoughtful with everyone. "Your assistant said he was hit by a car."

"He's hanging in there." Something clinked on the other end of the line. "We had his owner take him to the animal hospital so he'll have someone with him round the clock. He was pretty banged up, but he was doing good when we checked with the hospital a while ago, so my money's on him pulling through."

She heard the clink again and a muffled thud.

It sounded as if he'd just opened and closed the refrigerator.

"That has to relieve that little girl. The one I saw in your waiting room," she explained on her way into the family room. She'd already turned the volume low on the television. Now, she hit Mute. "It has to be hard dealing with the people who care about your patients."

Over the pop of a can being opened, he told her it was sometimes, which led her to observe as she paced that it had to be equally hard when things went wrong with the animals.

Coming from her, that particular observation probably gave him pause. But with Columbus brushing around her ankles as if to thank her for getting rid of the collar, she was beginning to see how attached people could get to their pets.

"That can be hard, too," he agreed. "But the good days far outweigh the bad."

"That's good to know." She really was glad to hear that. For his sake, she thought, picking up the cat on her way to the sofa. She didn't doubt for a moment that he was the epitome of strength and solace for those who needed him to be. But she also had the feeling that beneath all that compelling, rock-solid stability, there were times his heart broke a little at what he saw or had to do.

Thinking of how strong he truly must be, she couldn't help but wonder what had drawn him to his profession to begin with. Since she had no idea where to even begin speculating, she asked.

At the question, the fatigue seemed to leave his voice. Or, at least, he didn't sound as preoccupied as he had as he told her he'd grown up on a dairy farm in Upstate New York with a menagerie of pets that were as much family as his family was. He and his brother had each had a dog. His sister had a cat, and his mom had raised a potbellied pig with her chickens. They'd had two horses and a few hundred cows that had produced calves every spring. He and his brother had tended animals with their dad pretty much from the time they could walk. Taking care of them for a living just seemed like a natural thing to do.

Rebecca snuggled into the corner of the sofa, absently stroking the purring cat curled up beside her. "So what do your brother and sister do now?"

Sounding as if he'd just made himself more comfortable, too, he told her that his brother, younger, married and the father of two, worked the farm with their dad. His sister, younger, too, was a psychologist married to a pediatrician. They lived in Buffalo, which meant he and his family didn't get together as often as everyone would like. That was probably just as well, he concluded, because when they did, the house was as noisy and chaotic as it had been when he was a kid and no one could hear what the other was saying, anyway.

She could hear the smile in his deep voice as he spoke, and the easy, unapologetic affection he had for his parents and siblings. His childhood sounded utterly idyllic to her. Perfect in ways she could only imagine. Noise. Laughter. A mom and a dad. Siblings.

"When did you last see them?"

"Over the Fourth of July. We always do a big family thing at the farm. Aunts. Uncles. Cousins."

"You have cousins?"

"A ton of them. And they all seem to be doing their best to keep the Hudson genes in the pool."

"So there are lots of little ones around, too?"

A note of wistfulness had crept into her voice. Joe heard it as he lay on his long sofa, across from a wall of state-of-the-art electronics. His head rested on an arm. He'd thrown one leg over the back. With Rex curled up on his chest, and Bailey stretched out in his favorite spot by the gas fireplace, he absently stroked the little guy's soft fur.

"Pushing a dozen," he told her, thinking he'd like to have Rebecca's head on his chest and his fingers in her hair. Just talking with her helped ease the tension that had followed him home. He'd truly had far worse days. Days when no amount of skill could repair injuries and there had been nothing he could do to help. Today, he'd just been behind schedule from the moment the first emergency had come in and he'd been running to catch up ever since.

She had more questions that led to him recalling more incidents he might have forgotten had she not jogged his memory. Busy in his own world, he tended to forget how great it was to get together with the little ones—even when the females did tease or nag him about when he was going to marry and contribute to the brood. But it was the uncharacteristic pensiveness in Rebecca's tone that had his interest, and made him wonder if she might be missing extended family of her own.

"What about you?" he asked. The idea of growing up in the city was as foreign to him as life in the country must have sounded to her. "How many are there of you when your family all gets together?"

For a moment, he thought she wasn't going to answer. The silence on the other end of the phone was that profound. Unable to imagine why, he was about to ask if she was still there when she finally replied.

"Two." Quietly, she added, "It was always just Mom and me."

"Your parents were divorced?"

"They never married." She hesitated again, when hesitation wasn't like her at all. "I don't know my father. And Mom didn't have siblings or much to do with her parents," she continued, hurrying past her admission, "so it was just us.

"There were the Morrettis, though. And Syd and Bea Souder. They're kind of like family. Especially the Souders," she explained, as if to make her childhood sound as crowded as his had been. "I'd stay with them when I was little and share a bedroom with their daughters when Mom was away for work. Before they moved, anyway. Then, I stayed with Rose Etty across the hall."

"How often was that?"

"A couple of weeks a month."

She had been raised by neighbors, and a mother who spent half her time working out of town to support the two of them. Joe couldn't imagine having been raised that way. As she told him about sitting on the fire escape visiting with her friends on summer nights, the street fairs that drew all the neighbors on the block and the hole-in-the-wall restaurants where the owners called their customers by name, it also became clear to him that while she had experienced a certain sense of community, she had never truly experienced family.

The note of pensiveness never left her voice as she spoke. The longer it lingered, the more he began to think of how much she had missed growing up. It also gave him the feeling that either something was still missing in her life, or that, just then, she was missing something in particular.

Thinking she might just be homesick for the city, since she'd told him as much on their hike, he found himself altering what he'd had in mind for Saturday evening. He'd planned to take her to a place a half an hour north. The thought that he might be able to ease that longing for a while turned those plans in an entirely different direction.

"Ohmygosh," he heard her suddenly say. "Have you looked at the time? I had no idea how late it was getting. I should let you go."

"Did you get my note?"

"I did," Rebecca told him. "That's why I called."

"So?"

"So, I'm interested. Since there are no Thai restaurants in Rosewood, are you planning to cook?"

She was prepared to be totally impressed by his myriad talents when she heard him chuckle.

"I don't cook anything I can't pronounce. We're going to a restaurant Adam Shibb recommended. Actually, his wife did. It's in Manhattan. How's four o'clock?"

* * *

"You're spending way too much time on this, Rebecca. It looks fine."

"Maybe I should just do one big pumpkin instead of the three smaller ones. Sometimes less is more."

"The three pumpkins look fine. Especially with the mums. No one would ever guess it was your first attempt at fall decorating."

From where she stood on the walkway in front of her door, Rebecca turned to her pregnant neighbor. She didn't know if the chill in the breeze put the color in Molly cheeks or if she was simply glowing from within, but the woman who'd come over to give her the questionnaire her husband had filled out looked prettier—and her rounded belly bigger—every time she saw her.

Refusing to indulge the longing for motherhood herself, she glanced back at her handiwork. The charcoal-gray door now sported the large wreath of gold and rust leaves. Off to the side of the small porch, three different-sized pumpkins were grouped in front of the two brass buckets she'd filled with yellow mums.

"Come on," Molly muttered. Taking Rebecca by the arm, she tugged her toward the door. "You're finished out here and I'm cold. Make me some tea. I haven't seen you all week and I want to know what's going on with you and Joe Hudson. And don't tell me *nothing*," she warned, as they reached the porch. "Adam said Joe asked him at basketball the other night for the name of the nearest good Thai restaurant, so Adam asked me. I told him there was one in Albany, but the best was Thai Dye in Manhattan. As much as you moaned about there not being any Thai food in town when you first got here, I figured he had you in mind."

"I didn't moan."

"Yes, you did."

Falling uncharacteristically silent, Rebecca led her insistent friend past the gallery of Turner family pictures guarding their home from the entry wall, plucked Magellan off the top of the television, spotted Columbus cleaning his front paw atop a windowsill overlooking the bird feeder in the backyard and headed into the kitchen.

She'd been meaning to talk to Molly. She just hadn't been sure how to go about phrasing the question she needed answered without giving the woman the wrong idea.

"I don't know what's going on with him," she prefaced, because he hadn't made any of the moves nearly every other guy she'd gone out with would have made by now. "But I like his company. He asked me to dinner, so I'm going." She shrugged, opened a cabinet. "There's nothing else to tell."

Settling herself on a stool at the counter dividing the room, Molly pushed back a handful of her long, curly hair. "You could tell me about last Saturday," she suggested. "You were gone all day."

Rebecca turned with a small box in each hand. "Which do you want? Chai or green?"

"Green. So where did you go?"

"Hiking."

Molly nearly choked. "You went hiking? As in on trails through the woods?"

"And a meadow. It was an experience I doubt I'll repeat."

"Angela said you met him last Sunday at the park, too."

"He'd said he'd fill out a questionnaire for me. Like Adam did," she pointed out, filling two mugs with water and setting them in the microwave. "I'm getting all the input I can for my article. Thanks again for that," she said, nodding to the envelope she'd added to the stack on the breakfast table. "And thank Adam for me, too, will you?"

She punched the keypad on the microwave, turned back to see Molly frowning at her. Before her friend could decide whether she should drop or pursue the subject of Joe, Rebecca voiced what concerned her far more.

"What do you know about Jack's father?"

That frown went from perplexed to totally puzzled.

"Jack Lever's?"

"Him."

"Not a thing." Her eyes narrowed. "Why are you asking about his father?"

"I just thought you might have met Jack's family at some point. Maybe at a block party while his wife was still alive."

"Do you still have a thing for Jack?"

"I never had a 'thing' for him. Not a big one, anyway. And I just wondered," she murmured. "Forget I asked."

Concern replaced puzzlement. "Are you okay, Rebecca?"

"Of course I'm okay. Why wouldn't I be?"

"Because your love life is a mess?"

Rebecca smiled. It was good to have a friend.

"Could be," she murmured, and pulled the mugs from the microwave when the timer buzzed. "So," she said, handing Molly a mug and a tea bag. "Do you want to fill me in on whatever's been going on in the neighborhood this week, or help me go through questionnaires to discover what sort of underwear the average American male prefers?"

"Underwear. And show me what you're wearing tomorrow night. Make it something skinny." She splayed her palm over her basketball-belly. "I'll live vicariously."

Skinny, it was.

Chapter Six

Joe knew he had caught Rebecca off guard with his plans. He had caught himself by surprise with them, too. The last-minute change, anyway. But he liked the idea of giving her a taste of what she seemed to be missing.

He'd toyed with the idea of asking her to dinner ever since he'd left her at the park. Just because he wanted to keep things casual didn't mean they couldn't share a meal. Then, there was the curiosity about her that he couldn't seem to shake. Asking her to dinner seemed to be the easiest way to get answers to the questions he hadn't been able to silence—and the new ones that had arisen during their conversation.

He didn't like that she had no one but her mom. He had the feeling she'd hate knowing he felt a little sorry for her because of that circumstance, but he really hadn't expected her to be without relatives.

It seemed that she revealed something unexpected every time he saw or spoke to her. She did it again as he pulled up in front of her house Saturday afternoon and noticed the wreath on the door and the artfully arranged pumpkins and mums beside it. She hadn't struck him at all as the sort of woman who got into the domestic side of the seasons. He wasn't, however, surprised that she'd accessorized his pets. His assistants had proclaimed the Santa hats and fur collar she'd dropped off at the clinic yesterday perfect props for the photo he would shoot sometime that weekend for the clinic Christmas card. As for the whole holiday cooking and baking thing, he really couldn't picture her getting into it the way every other woman he knew did. Something about spike heels and chunky bracelets just didn't jibe with images of flour-covered countertops and lattice piecrusts.

The front door of the Turner house opened before he'd even reached for his seat belt. Rebecca hurried out, then turned to lock it. As she did, her slim black coat swung against the calves of black boots with stiletto heels that could double as weapons.

His first thought when she turned to flip her turquoise scarf around her neck was that she was definitely anxious to get going. Her smile confirmed that conclusion as she climbed into the truck before he could even get out and open her door.

"I wanted to get out before one of the cats did," she said, dropping her keys into what looked like a small black leather flower. Tucking the tiny handbag beside her, she unwrapped the scarf that turned her eyes the color of jewels. "If we had to chase one down, we might be late and lose our reservation."

Looking toward him again, she went still. As her glance

moved from his gray turtleneck to the shoulders of his black jacket and charcoal wool slacks, a question seemed to form behind her smile.

She said nothing, though, other than a quiet, "Great jacket," before she turned her focus to her seat belt.

"Thanks." He still couldn't quite believe he'd bought a leather jacket he couldn't hike or play ball in. Especially one that cost as much as the monthly rent payment on the clinic even on sale. He'd just known that his usual khakis or jeans and a bomber jacket weren't suitable for taking her into the city. Remembering the pictures that had been part of her questionnaire, he'd gone with the look he could live with. "Actually, I moved the reservation back an hour. I'd like to take a detour before we go to the restaurant."

Her curiosity shifted focus. "Where are we going?"

"To your old neighborhood. We don't have to get out or see anyone," he assured her, because it wasn't his intention to put her on the spot. "I've just never known anyone who grew up in Manhattan. As long as we're going to be there, I thought you could show me where a kid would go to school, hang out." Beneath glove-soft leather, one shoulder lifted in a shrug. "That kind of thing."

He kept most of his focus on the road as they left Danbury Way. The rest was on her. Specifically her hesitation at what he had just said. And her legs.

She'd unbuttoned her coat in deference to the warm air circulating from the heater. The way her high collar opened he couldn't see what sort of top she wore, but the black skirt that hit just below the knee had a slit that went halfway up her thigh. The only reason he noticed that was because that slit had split open when she crossed her black-stockinged legs. The tops of her black boots came to her knees.

He wondered if she wore panty hose, or stockings and a garter belt.

"You want to go to my old neighborhood?"

He gave his head a mental shake in an attempt to dislodge the images burning into his brain.

"Do you mind?"

"No. I...no," she repeated, then sent him a frown. "It's just..."

"Just what?"

"The train station is the other way."

"I'd rather drive."

"Have you ever driven in Manhattan before?"

Trying not to let the images in his mind wreck his concentration on the road, he told her he hadn't. He also told her that he hadn't planned to drive in the city tonight, either. He'd heard the stories of bumper-to-bumper traffic and of being cut off by taxi drivers who regarded six inches between two cars as all the space they needed to jam their cab between them. The plan tonight was to drive as far as the train station in Poughkeepsie, take the train in from there and pay a cabbie to put his navigational and assault skills to use for them.

She seemed fine with that strategy, though it led to a slight change when she mentioned that he might want go to a station farther south and catch the subway there if he wanted to see her old neighborhood first. The route would be more direct.

Since she was the one with the expertise, he told her to tell him where to turn off the freeway when they got there, then forced himself to change the subject to the progress she'd made on her article rather than ask anything more about where she'd grown up. He could ask questions when they got there. And, maybe, by seeing where she'd spent her youth, he'd have a better idea of who she was and what he found so intriguing about her.

According to Rebecca, the old neighborhood, with its narrow streets and tall brick buildings separated by narrower alleys, looked pretty much as it always had. Over the years, businesses had come and gone from some of the storefronts that alternated space with single-door entries into the apartments above them, but a few had remained in the same family that had owned them when she'd grown up there.

No Parking signs lined the sidewalk. Another sign designated the hours of delivery for the large department store on the corner. Fifth Avenue was a half a block from the doorway she pointed out as the entry to where her mom still lived. Even with the cab's windows rolled up and its heater rattling, the noise from the traffic was audible and constant.

Surrounded by all that activity and energy, what became immediately clear to Joe was that private space and silence were at a premium. It also became clear that a person had to know where to look in the tightly packed spaces to find a pharmacy, a bookstore, a dry cleaners and a market. It never would have occurred to him that a grocery store would be under a bank building, that a school yard would be a blacktop surrounded by a chain-link fence, or that so much space could have so little elbow room.

Even their restaurant in the decidedly upscale Upper East Side was jammed between two storefronts. An art studio and bakery, actually. Inside the surprisingly austere Thai Dye, the tiny, cloth-draped tables were set just far enough apart to allow a person to get to his or her chair. On either side of them, couples sat with their heads together, creating little islands of imaginary privacy in the middle of everyone else's conversations. The only thing that kept him from thinking it all far too claustrophobic for his tastes was Rebecca herself.

She sat across from him, their knees occasionally bumping under the table that held her steaming bowl of rice noodles with lemongrass and his tiger prawns grilled with a roasted chili sauce so hot his mom could have used it to sear the pinfeathers off a chicken.

He couldn't honestly say he was paying much attention to what he ate, though. The long-sleeved black sweater she wore was even more distracting than the slit skirt that had sidetracked him off and on all evening. It hugged her arms and body like a second skin and left her shoulders and collarbone completely bare.

In the low lighting, her skin looked golden and as soft as her smile when she held up her wineglass for him to refill.

"So once your loan application is approved, then what?"

"Then I break ground. I bought the lot with my share of the money my grandfather left us and hired an architect to draw up the plans. So everything is ready to go. Once the building is up and the equipment in, I'll move the clinic there. I have a friend from veterinary school who wants to relocate his family to Rosewood, so I'll hire him."

"Can two vets handle a clinic and hospital?"

"They can with vet techs and assistants. I've been talking with one of my professors from Cornell. We're thinking of offering an internship program. That would give us more personnel, but interns take time of their own. It would be a while before I could offer that."

He watched her quietly study him over the rim of her

glass. "This is something you've wanted for a long time, isn't it?"

It wasn't a question. Her perception surprised him, too. Even members of his family didn't seem to get how important his goal had become to him. "Since my last year of vet school," he admitted. "Where I grew up, live and working stock got all the attention. That's where the money is. The little guys—the dogs and cats," he explained, "were pretty much left to fend for themselves. Not that they didn't get taken care of," he qualified. "It was just that more often than not, pets weren't a priority. I wanted to make them one."

Her eyes seemed to soften as she tipped her head. "You didn't want to do that in Peterboro?"

"Peterboro is too small and the farms are too spread out for a small animal hospital. People have pets, but the two vets there handle everything in the area. Big animals. Small."

"You didn't want to go to work with one of them?"

He picked up his own glass, studied the open interest in her lovely features. "I had the opportunity. Doc Jennings wanted me to go into practice with him when I graduated. But the job came with…" What? he wondered. An encumbrance? A price tag? "…qualifications," he finally decided.

"Qualifications?"

The murmur of conversations around them rose and fell. Glass clinked against pottery bowls and plates. The last thing he wanted Rebecca to think was that he'd done to Sara what the guy she'd hoped to marry had done to her. Led her on for a couple of years, then let her go. He'd never led Sara on. At least, that hadn't been his intention, even though she'd accused him of it. He had seriously considered marriage. The end result, however, had been the same.

"He expected me to marry his daughter."

He saw her eyebrows slowly arch.

"Pretty much everyone did," he told her. "We'd gone together off and on since high school. When I finally had my degree, they assumed I'd propose."

"Why didn't you?"

"I almost did."

She reached for the wine bottle herself. "So what happened?" she asked, adding another splash to her glass.

"It would have been a mistake. For both of us," he said simply. "We had everything in the world in common. And I liked her. I just can't honestly say I loved her. I couldn't take the job with her dad without making a commitment to her. And I didn't want to give up the idea of having a practice of my own someday." He hadn't given real thought to that unsettled and difficult time in years. "It was just time for me to go."

Something that looked suspiciously like sympathy shadowed Rebecca's face. He couldn't tell if that sympathy was for him, or for the woman he'd left behind as she took another sip of her wine.

She lowered the goblet, toyed with its stem.

"What was she like?"

"She was…sweet," he said, because everyone had said that about Sara. And she had been. She still was, he imagined. "And kind of unassuming."

That part was an understatement, actually. That was also, ultimately, the root of their problem. Sara had deferred to him on everything, and challenged him on nothing and in no way. She'd never seemed to have an opinion of her own. If she did happen to form one, she changed it if she thought it was different from his. His younger brother had said that at the end of a long hard day, having a docile wife could be a blessing. To Joe, the more he realized that Sara's whole life would be him, the more suffocating the relationship had become.

"How did your family take it? You not marrying her, I mean."

"They weren't too happy with me for a while. My parents were in a difficult situation because they'd been friends with Sara's family for years. The community is small, too, so there was talk. But Dad said he understood." His dad had been the voice of reason in the midst of a whole lot of hurt and hard feelings, and female dreams that had gotten even further out of hand than Joe had thought. "He agreed that marrying her just because others expected it wouldn't be right. Mom came around after Sara married and started having babies."

"How long ago was that? That she married, I mean."

He had to think. "Seven, maybe eight years ago."

"So all is forgiven?"

"I can't speak for Sara. But she's seemed really happy the few times I've seen her since."

"And your family?"

"All is forgiven," he echoed. "On that score, anyway," he had to qualify, more than willing to move past the true confessions portion of the program. He'd wanted her to know about Sara. He wasn't totally sure why. It had just felt like something he needed to get off his chest ever since she'd told him how the guy she'd wanted to marry had so unceremoniously dumped her. "My mom would be a whole lot happier with me if I were married myself. Last summer she went back on her campaign to find me a suitable woman."

Rebecca was trying hard not to let herself imagine how devastated his Sara must have been when he'd left her. All too easily, she could see how a woman could weave hopes and dreams around this man. She knew exactly what those dreams were: home, husband, children, sharing. She also knew in intimate detail how it felt to have a future like that disappear right before her eyes.

Joe, though, had obviously known what he wanted, and he'd let nothing and no one stand in the way. He'd simply bucked the tide of public opinion and moved on.

Moved on, she thought, feeling oddly more pensive than she would have imagined given that Joe had just proved himself to be totally capable of typical guy behavior. He hadn't exactly left the girl standing at the altar, but he'd…

…done the right thing, she reluctantly concluded and took another sip of her wine. She doubted there had been anything "simple" about what he'd felt he had to do. She couldn't imagine the man she was coming to know being anywhere near as heartless as Jason had been. Joe knew what was fair, and what wasn't. Above all, he was not a man without compassion. Knowing what she did of him, she suspected that his integrity and his own dreams simply hadn't allowed him to compromise himself or his almost fiancée—and he'd probably saved them both a lot of heartache in the long run.

Though she couldn't have imagined thinking such a thing until now, it was quite possible that Jason had done her an enormous favor by not wanting to marry her.

Her forehead furrowed.

"What?" Joe asked, swallowing his last bite of shrimp.

She didn't want to think about hurts anymore. She was so desperately tired of their presence. "What constitutes suitable?"

"Childbearing age. Breathing."

"She thinks you can't find your own wife?"

"She knows I'm not looking for one."

"Too much else to do?"

At her perception, he hesitated. A moment later, he gave her a smile.

"For a city girl, you're pretty astute."

For a country boy, he was seriously messing with her head. Wanting to ignore that, too, she nudged their appetizer plate toward him. The waiter had tried twice to take it. "Pia Muk Tod?"

He glanced at the fried squid. It wasn't half-bad, but he knew she loved the stuff. "You finish it," he murmured, since it might be a while before she got it again. "I've had my fill of tentacles and suction cups. So," he continued, his voice deceptively casual. "How does it feel to be back?"

He seemed as anxious as she was to change the subject. Grateful for that, she tried to shake off the thought that he wasn't looking for what she wanted. Not that she was looking now, either, she reminded herself and forced her focus to his question.

Oddly, thinking about how to answer him, she found that her response wasn't what she would have expected at all.

The restaurant was wonderful, she hurried to tell him, the food delicious, the wine incredible. But now, having spent hours surrounded by the noise and hustle beyond these relatively tranquil walls, she realized she didn't miss the city quite as much as she thought she had. She didn't miss standing on a train and being pressed like panini between someone who forgot to bathe and someone else who bathed in her perfume. Or the stress of last-minute deadline changes, the chaos at the deli trying to get a sandwich for lunch, or trying to get a cab in the rain when she was already late for a meeting.

Beneath the table, their legs brushed. Above the table, their fingers bumped as they each reached for the wine that kept disappearing from her glass.

As other diners came and went around them, she conceded that she'd pined for the wonderful variety of movie theaters, stage theaters and restaurants. But if she still lived there, if she'd never changed anything and not gone to Rosewood, she wouldn't have met him and learned that she didn't need to be afraid of cats.

That was what she told him, anyway. What she was thinking was that if she lived in the city, she never would have met the rugged, determined and undeniably intriguing man who cared enough to give her a taste of what she thought she'd missed.

"So why Rosewood?" he asked. "Why not Hudson or Stuyvesant Falls?"

It seemed that every time she saw him he asked what had taken her to that particular town.

Not about to ruin the evening by going anywhere near that mental minefield, she slowly shook her head—only to stop when the motion threatened to make her dizzy. Surprised to see her wineglass nearly empty again, she pushed it back.

"Not now," she murmured. "I'm having too nice a time. Do you want to walk down the street and do the art showings?"

Joe's glance slipped from the quick resistance that had come and gone from her face to the soft curve of one shoulder and over the gentle swells of her breasts. She hadn't been her totally animated self since he'd told her about leaving the woman it truly would have been a mistake to marry. But his mind was more occupied at the moment with her admission that something specific had, indeed, taken her Rosewood, something she clearly didn't want to talk or think about just then. Another part of his brain was busy with thoughts of how perfectly her small breasts would fit his palm. Lifting his eyes to her mouth, he imagined she would fit him perfectly everywhere.

Having her put on her coat sounded like an excellent idea.

"Only if you can explain the appeal of splashes of bloodred paint on white canvas."

To Rebecca, his tone sounded utterly nonchalant. But there'd been no mistaking the path of his glance, or the way his jaw hardened an instant before he turned his attention to the waiter to ask for the bill. As with every other time his glance had wandered over her, she felt warm wherever his eyes had touched.

His focus had strayed to her mouth while they'd talked. Occasionally, it had moved over her as it did now, lingering at the hollow of her throat, quickening the pulse beating there before sliding away. His visual caress unsettled her enough. Thoughts of how his hands would feel skimming over her body disturbed her even more.

She reached for her purse. He had deliberately touched her only in the most casual of ways, to help her from the cab, to usher her through the door, to help remove her coat.

She had no idea where he expected the evening to lead, if anywhere at all. She wasn't sure where she wanted it to go herself. She didn't trust what he made her feel on any number of levels, and she most definitely didn't trust what she was beginning to feel for him. As they left the table and he helped her with her coat, the only thing she knew for sure was how hard it was becoming to deny how drawn she was to him.

Without a word, he slipped his fingers through hers as

they left the warmth of the restaurant and stepped into the cold, damp air.

The evening crowd moved along the wet sidewalk, coming and going from the restaurants and galleries that drew foodies and art lovers from all over the city. She barely noticed the other people as they moved up the street. Her attention was on the odd distance she sensed in Joe. Considering the protective feel of his hand around hers, that distance had her thoroughly confused.

That confusion remained as they entered the first gallery where their feet and voices and those of dozens of others echoed off hardwood floors and the brick walls where the huge canvases were displayed. It was still there when they walked out five minutes later to see that the rain that had earlier dampened the streets had returned.

Instead of going into the next atelier, Joe tugged her back into the slightly recessed entry of the gallery. Ahead of them people bundled in coats and scarves hurried by, umbrellas popping up like mushrooms.

She thought he meant to protect her from the breeze as he turned his back to the sidewalk. But with his face inches from hers, it didn't seem to be anything so gallant that he had in mind. In the kaleidoscope lights from the window display, she watched the preoccupation she'd sensed in him since they'd left the restaurant intensify as a muscle in his jaw jerked.

"I'm not Jason, Rebecca. Just keep that in mind. Okay?"

She had moved on from their conversation at dinner. Most of it, anyway. The wine she'd apparently consumed a tad too much of had started catching up with her about the time she'd stood up from the table. Since then, the warm lethargy filling her body had taken over most of her concentration. Something about that conversation apparently still bothered him, though.

If she had to guess what that something was, she would venture that it had been her reaction to it—although she honestly thought she had masked her thoughts rather well.

Twin lines formed between her eyebrows. "I could never confuse you with him. Ever." Jason would never have thought to do what Joe had done for her tonight. He'd never paid much attention at all to little things she liked. With the exception of a pair of teeny tiny diamond earrings he'd given her one Christmas, the only gifts he'd ever presented her with had been flowers. Since he didn't like oriental cuisine, if she'd wanted Thai she'd had to order takeout or go out with a friend.

Her quiet insistence made the muscle in Joe's jaw relax.

"Just so you know I have no intention of leading you on."

She thought about giving him a nod. Afraid it might make her dizzy, she took a deep breath instead.

The ground seemed to tilt. "Understood," she assured him, flattening her hand against the soft leather covering his chest for balance. "I don't think you have intentions about me at all."

The lines between her eyes deepened as she blinked at the soft gray wool of his turtleneck. She hadn't intended to actually say that.

"I wouldn't go that far."

"You wouldn't?"

She hadn't meant to sound that hopeful, either.

His smile increased in direct proportion to her consternation.

Leaning forward, he brushed his lips over hers.

Her breath had barely caught before he did it again. The

touch was light, warm, teasing. Or maybe what she felt as warmth gathered deep inside her was more like...promise.

He edged back. "Just so we're clear on the other."

With the rain beating harder on the sidewalk, she felt him move closer as another couple squeezed past them. "We're clear," she assured him solemnly. "I know you're nothing like Jason."

"Good. Now, I'd better get you home. We've got a long drive."

She wasn't sure if she felt disappointed or relieved that he hadn't suggested they stay the night as he left her in the shelter of the entry to move to the curb. With one hand out, two fingers of his other hand to his mouth, he gave a sharp whistle that he'd undoubtedly learned herding things on the farm. It worked just as effectively in the city.

A yellow cab immediately pulled up beside the row of parked cars. Thinking she needed to ask him how to do that, she dashed through the rain herself, and would have slipped off the curb had Joe's arm not been there for her to grab.

She definitely should not have had that last glass of wine, she thought, and promptly suppressed a giggle as she climbed in ahead of him.

"Are you okay?" he asked, closing the door behind him.

"I'm fine," she insisted, doing her best to look serious. She never giggled. Ever.

Sure you're fine, Joe thought, and tried not to smile himself at the way her lips twitched as they settled back for the ride to the station to catch the train where they'd left his truck.

An hour later they were in the cab of the truck, waiting for it to warm up and the fog to clear from the windows. It was cold. So cold Rebecca was shivering. But being cold was good because it helped keep her from feeling as sleepy and relaxed as she'd started to feel leaning against Joe on the train. It also gave her something to think about other than those moments outside the gallery when she'd felt the lovely warmth of his kiss. Not that the thoughts were far from her mind even now.

"It'll be warm in here in a minute."

They were parked beneath a security lamp, the other cars little more than blurs beyond the windows. "No hurry," she murmured, watching his profile in the pale light as he flipped switches. "At least the rain stopped."

She would have felt awful if he'd gotten soaked. And he would have in the dash between the station and his truck had the rain still been coming down.

She still couldn't believe he'd given her a night in the city.

He leaned forward, shrugged out of his jacket. "Put this around you."

"Joe, no. Put that back on. You'll freeze."

"Cold doesn't bother me. Turn this way." Totally ignoring her protest, he reached toward her and slipped his leather jacket around her shoulders. Pulling the lapels together with one hand, he tucked her scarf closer to her neck.

He was doing it again, she thought.

He was taking care of her. The way he had that day by the stream.

She looked away, looked back. The warm citrusy scent of his aftershave lotion clung to the buttery soft leather. The scent seemed to surround her, much like the warmth she could feel slowly working its way from his jacket through the wool of her coat.

"There," he pronounced, apparently satisfied that she would be warmer now.

Watching him adjust her scarf, her alcohol-freed tongue

got the better of her sense of self-protection. "May I ask you something, Joe?"

She didn't know if it was the reluctance in her tone or the question itself that drew his eyes to hers. She just knew she needed an answer to what she'd been wondering about ever since he'd told her where he was taking her. She hadn't wanted it to matter. But it did. A little too much.

"Why did you do that for me?"

"Because you're cold."

She caught her hand over his, stilling it at her throat before he could pull back. "The evening, Joe. Why did you take me all the way into the city for dinner? And, please," she murmured, "don't tell me you just wanted to see where a city girl grew up."

He had spent far more time watching her reactions to where they were than to the places she'd shown him. From the deep breath he drew, it seemed he knew that, too.

He seemed as reluctant to answer as she'd been to ask. He seemed to know, too, just how important the answer was to her.

"I did it because I thought it would make you happy. And happy isn't something you truly seem to be."

It was clear to Joe that she hadn't expected that. He didn't know what she had expected, though. All he knew for certain was that she was about to protest his conclusion, simply because protecting herself was what she always did.

"You don't," he insisted, and leaned forward to silence that protest with his lips.

Rebecca felt her breath stall in her lungs. He didn't kiss her the casual way he had outside the gallery. As he curved his hand at the side of her face and coaxed her to open to him, he kissed her slowly, thoroughly, methodically melting her insides and completely vaporizing any thought of contradicting his dead-on insights.

Not that she could produce anything resembling a rational argument just then. Her head was already muddled from the wine, but something about closing her eyes—and Joe's kiss—made her head seem to spin.

Joe eased back. "We'll talk about it later," he promised, and settled into his seat to put the truck into Drive.

Rebecca said nothing. She didn't utter a single word as he headed them out of the parking lot and onto the freeway. As verbal as she usually was, he didn't know what to make of her silence, either, until he saw her lean her head back against the seat. An instant later, she jerked upright again.

She wasn't upset with him, or mulling over what he'd said. She was just having a hard time staying awake.

"Sorry," she murmured.

"Don't be." Reaching behind him, he pulled a folded blanket from behind the seat and laid it across the low console between them. "Slip your arm through the shoulder harness and put your head in my lap. You can sleep on the way back."

Her only response was a faint smile before she settled into the spot prepared for her. Laying her head on his thigh, she curved one hand above his knee. A moment later, he heard her sigh.

He'd just brushed her hair back from her temple when he heard her breathing grow deep and rhythmic.

He didn't think she'd passed out, but he would concede that it was a possibility. Knowing that he'd have to drive, he'd only had one glass of wine himself. Considering that there hadn't been much left in the bottle, she'd had considerably more.

She'd giggled.

He hadn't expected that. He had the feeling, she hadn't, either. The thought made him smile. He suspected that relaxing wasn't something that came easily to her. He also sincerely doubted that she often willingly let go of her control. The fact that she'd felt comfortable enough with him—safe enough—to drop her guard that much tugged at the sense of protection that was coming to feel far stronger than it should.

The more he learned about her, the more he wanted to know. Mostly, what he wanted to know now was how much longer he thought he could keep his hands off of her, and why he wasn't simply letting her go.

He wanted to think he wasn't walking away from her because she needed a friend. He didn't doubt for a minute that the guy she'd hoped to marry had left major scars. He just had no idea where those scars were in the mending stages. Wounds were funny things. They could look healed on the surface, but it took time for tougher tissue to form beneath that new and tender skin before it could withstand much pressure. Even then, tenderness could remain.

Then there was her reason for being in Rosewood. The fact that she didn't want to talk about it warned him that there might be other scars, too.

The rain beat against the windshield, the wipers worked to keep up.

In the glow of the dashboard lights, he punched on the radio for company and settled his hand on Rebecca's head.

That was how he drove back to Rosewood, with her head on his thigh while he absently stroked her hair, all the while wishing he knew her secrets.

* * *

"Rebecca? Hey, honey. You need to wake up."

The deep voice came from above her, quiet and coaxing, deliciously deep.

"You're home."

She wasn't home. She didn't have a real home.

Frowning at the thought, she tried to ignore the voice and snuggled her head against the warm pillow under her head. The crick in her neck ruined the attempt.

It also made her conscious enough to realize that what supported her head wasn't a pillow. It was a man's thigh. A very hard, muscular, masculine thigh.

"Come on."

Joe.

She felt his hands slip under her shoulder as the will to straighten up on her own fought the lethargy that pulled the strength from her bones—and the dizziness that made her want to lie right back down when she pushed herself up.

"Let's get you inside. Where's your key?"

She fumbled for her purse, then fumbled for the passenger door. By the time she had it open, he was there, sliding his arm around her in the cold and guiding her inside the house.

Leaning against him felt nice. All that solid muscle supporting her.

"Where's your bedroom? Upstairs or down?"

The bedroom she was using was upstairs. The thought of climbing all those steps, however, held no appeal at all.

"You don't have to take me," she insisted, thinking she'd just lean on him for another minute. "I'm just tired."

"And drunk."

"Am not."

"Are, too. Come on."

He moved her into the short hallway beside them, his arm still around her as he led her into the frilly, rosebud-covered guest room where he'd once examined Columbus.

Taking her by the shoulders, he turned her around when they reached the side of the bed.

She sat, looked up. Seeing him blur, she closed her eyes, tipped sideways and let her head land on the pillow. The last thing she remembered was her coat and boots being tugged off and the quilt at the bottom of the bed being tucked over her.

Chapter Seven

It was midafternoon before Rebecca worked up the courage to return Joe's call. The worst of her headache was gone, thanks to a couple pots of coffee, headache tablets and the hamburger she'd made herself go get a little after noon. The weather had cleared, leaving the sun shining on another glorious fall day, but all that bright light had made her leave the house wearing a baseball cap and sunglasses for reasons other than fashion and the prevention of future squint lines. It was while she'd been out that Joe had left a message that said little more than he wanted to make sure she was all right.

She hadn't had a hangover since her friends Cindy and Rachelle had taken her out the night after Jason had broken up with her. The good news was that, physically, she didn't feel anywhere near as bad as she had mixing Cosmopolitans with Chardonnay. She didn't even like Cosmos. She just liked the glass they were served in.

The bad news was that, in other ways, she felt so much worse.

If she wasn't mistaken, she'd practically passed out on Joe. Literally.

From across the room came the low sounds of the television. She almost always had it on, just as she had when she'd lived in the city. There, it had drowned out the noise that filtered up from the streets when she'd had her windows open in the summer, or the noise from the plumbing pipes in the walls, closing doors and the occasional argument from other tenants when the windows were closed.

Here, the disembodied voices filled the silence and provided the illusion of not being the only human in the large and rambling house.

Walking away from where she'd just nudged the volume down with the remote, she punched Joe's number into the phone, took a deep breath and pressed the phone to her ear.

He answered on the third ring.

"Hi," she murmured.

"Hi, yourself. How's your head?"

She closed her eyes. She couldn't tell if he was serious or smiling.

"Better. Thanks. Look, Joe. I'm sorry," she hurried on. "I really am. I honestly hadn't realized how much I was drinking. We were just talking and the wine was there and I wasn't paying attention to anything except all the things we were talking about. What you did was so nice. The nicest thing anyone has done for me in longer than I can remember. I'd just been enjoying myself so much—"

"Rebecca—"

"—that I wasn't keeping track—"

"Rebecca."

She took a deep breath.

"What?"

"Slow down. And stop worrying. I had a good time, too."

The admonishment, or maybe it was the admission, had her sinking onto the sofa by the bunched-up quilt she'd spent much of the morning curled beneath.

"Even though I totally blew the end of the evening? I should have kept you company on the drive home. I should have asked you in for coffee."

"Caffeine would have just kept me awake all night. It was better that I just covered you up and left."

She winced. "About that—"

"Rebecca. Let it go," he said, not unkindly. "There was a lot about the evening that really was good. Like seeing where you grew up. You couldn't get me to live in Manhattan," he admitted, a smile now audible in his voice, "but I can see where parts of it would always be in your blood."

"Like parts of the country will always be in yours?"

"We can't escape who we are," he concluded.

Those of you who know, she thought, only to sigh at the way her mind inevitably wandered back to the part of her life still missing.

With the phone pressed to her ear, she reached for the quilt, folding it to make herself think of something—anything—else. "Well, I know who I am," she insisted, because she couldn't escape what she'd done. "I'm the person who needs to make up for last night."

"That's not necessary."

"It is." She knew he liked football. Any kind of ball for that matter. "Rosewood High has a home game Friday night. If you want, we can go to the game and afterward, I'll take you anywhere you want to go for dinner."

She hoped he'd choose Entrée. The restaurant her next-door neighbors, the Vincents, owned was the nicest in town—intimate, quietly elegant, excellent food, nice little bar. Promising herself she'd stay away from wine, suspecting he'd prefer pizza to picatta, she added, "You name the place."

"How do you know about the home game?"

Clearly he hadn't thought she'd know a thing about local sports.

"I drive by the high school when I go to the printers. There's a billboard out front that posts what's going on for the week." Quilt folded, she draped it where she kept it over the sofa's arm. "So?"

"It sounds good," he said, though something in his tone killed her hope. "But I'm not going to be here this weekend. I told my dad and brother I'd help them with the barn. I'm leaving for Peterboro Friday after work." He hesitated. "How about I call you when I get back and we'll work something else out?"

He was going home. Back to the place where his mom lay in wait with women lined up for him to marry.

"That would be good. Just don't come back engaged. I don't take engaged men to dinner."

He chuckled, told her that wasn't going to happen, then said he had to go because he was working on his loan application and he was going to finish the thing if it took him until morning.

She hung up a few minutes later, more relieved than she would have thought possible that he still wanted to see her, and thinking she would very much like to see where Joe had grown up himself. The main problem there was that his parents still lived on their farm, and meeting parents implied a direction in a relationship that neither one of them was prepared to go.

She wondered, though, if he had any idea how lucky he was to have such great relationships with his parents. More important to her just then, she couldn't help thinking how lucky he was to know who both of his parents were.

She was still thinking much the same thing six nights later when she turned from peeking out the drapes in the family room and frowned at the fire dancing in the fireplace.

The beautiful fall weather had officially turned ugly. It was raining so hard the gutters were overflowing. The noise she'd heard outside was water cascading from the gutter above the window and beating into the flower bed below it.

She wasn't supposed to be missing Joe so much. She wasn't supposed to care about him enough to be missing him in the first place. She wasn't supposed to want to be in his arms as badly as she did, either.

What she should have wanted was to celebrate. Her editor had called Thursday to tell her she loved her piece on "sexy summer feet" and overnighted the press kits of three major designers' new summer swim lines for her to caption. She'd also given her the dates for next fall's fashion previews in February and asked her to block three days to go with her. New York Fashion Week in Bryant Park was the place to be for editors, buyers and stylists. Over a hundred major designers previewed their collections.

With the invitation from her editor, she was all but guaranteed major article assignments.

Her make-over-your-mate article was also shaping up nicely. She'd had a positive response on another proposal she'd sent out a couple of weeks ago and she'd picked up a job writing fashion copy for Felice's Nieces for their Web site and print advertising. Angela had told the trendy boutique's owner about her. Impressed with her big-league credentials and with the store needing a major Christmas push, the owner had all but begged for her help.

Begging hadn't been necessary. Rebecca had been delighted to do it. Joe had even sounded happy for her when he'd called Wednesday evening just to see how her week was going and to remind her that he'd call her when he got back on Sunday.

Feeling pleased was just hard to come by tonight.

She'd had no desire to go out in the pouring rain to pick up dinner, so she'd nuked a bowl of canned soup and opened a can of tuna for her roommates so they could help her celebrate her successes. But as celebrations went, hers was pretty pathetic. Judging from the way the cats now contentedly groomed their paws in front of the fire, they were definitely having the better time.

She paced into the kitchen, made herself a mug of Chai tea. Then, restless, she decided she didn't want it and left it cooling on the counter. Hugging her arms over the empty sensation in her stomach, she paced around her kitchen table desk instead.

Nothing in the neat stacks of files, drafts of articles and magazines feathered with sticky notes caught her interest. Neither did the novel turned upside down on the coffee table or the program on Home and Garden Television showing how to decorate small spaces. Accessorizing anything usually appealed to her, but tonight nothing seemed to hold her attention.

Missing Joe was running neck and neck with her need for Russell Lever to acknowledge her as his daughter.

Beneath that desire was the need for him to be a decent person, and not the unfeeling, self-centered egoist Jack had described.

Thinking there had to be something positive she could learn about the man, she turned to where she'd left her laptop on the table, plugged in the phone line and sat down to see if she could find anything she hadn't already found all the other times she'd searched his name. A newspaper article about donations to charity. His name on the board of directors for a homeless shelter, an animal shelter, a shelter for abused women. Anything that might prove him redeemable and offer a possible way to meet him since the man had proven to be so elusive.

After twenty minutes of nothing and feeling more dejected by the second, she was about to shut the computer down when the icon popped up that told her she had an incoming call. Unable to imagine who would be calling at eight o'clock on a miserable Saturday night, she clicked the icon to check caller ID.

Her heart bumped her breastbone.

Quitting the Internet, she rose with the scrape of maple chair legs on pine flooring and snatched up the phone. "Joe. Is everything okay? Are you all right?"

She wasn't sure why her first thought had been to make sure nothing had happened to him. Maybe it was because he'd gone to work on the farm with his dad and accidents seemed like something that could easily happen in such a place. Maybe it was because she couldn't imagine him calling from his parents' house simply because he missed her as much as she did him. Whatever it was, it seemed he'd heard that unguarded concern.

"Hey," he murmured, his deep voice instantly reassuring.

"I'm fine." Having heard her worry, something like that same concern slipped into his tone. "Are you okay?"

"I'm…sure. Of course," she insisted. Even as her protective bravado automatically slipped into place, she gripped the phone more tightly. "I'm just surprised to hear from you is all."

"Am I interrupting anything?"

Yes, thank heaven. "Not really."

"I said I'd call when I got back," he reminded her, sounding as if he needed to explain why he was calling so late. "We finished the weather stripping on the barn this afternoon, so I thought I'd head back. I just took the dogs home and went by the clinic to make sure the roof wasn't leaking. We have a bad spot in the file room."

"Was it leaking?"

"Not yet." The distant sound of a honking horn filtered through the line. "Look. I know it's late, but if you're not doing anything, I thought I might come over for a while."

There was nothing she wanted more at that moment. Desperate to shake the awful sense that she didn't really belong anywhere, and wanting to see him no matter how much smarter it would be to protect her heart, she headed for the sofa to stuff the load of clothes she hadn't folded back into the dryer.

"Where are you now?"

"About a block from your street."

Her hand shot to her hair, specifically the scrunchie she'd whipped it into that morning. An instant later, her glance darted to the slim black sweatpants and hoodie she'd spent the day in. She hadn't left the house. She wasn't even wearing shoes. Keeping her feet warm were a pair of thick black fleece socks she'd bought last week at the mall.

"Rebecca? You there?"

She told him she was. She also told him she'd see him in a minute as she scooped up the clothes and headed for the laundry room off the kitchen.

She didn't have time to change. She had no time for makeup, either. Thinking that she'd picked a fine day to let her skin breathe, she headed for the entry to turn on the porch light and heard the slam of a truck door over the beat of the rain. Looking out the little window on the door, she saw Joe in the outside lights jogging toward the porch.

She had the door open before he could knock.

He'd just reached the shelter of the overhang. Pulling off the baseball cap keeping his head dry, he started to smile, only to have that smile stall when his glance moved over face. With his eyes narrowed questioningly at her attire and lack of makeup, she stepped back for him to enter.

The scents of fresh air and rain came in with him as he moved into the dimly lit entry. They clung to his leather bomber jacket as, dripping on the inside mat, he shrugged it off so he wouldn't drip anywhere else.

"It's warmer in the family room," she said, uncomfortably aware of his scrutiny as she took his cap and jacket and hung them on the coat tree beside the door. "There's a fire in the fireplace. It's been nasty outside all day."

"Same up north. It started there about one."

"It hit here about noon."

She turned back to face him. Usually standing near him, she barely had to look up to meet his eyes. Without the benefit of heels, her eyes were even with the crew neck of a blue thermal sweater that made his shoulders look impossibly wide. Worn jeans clung to his narrow hips.

Lifting her head, she saw his smile finally form.

"Do you really want to talk about the weather?"

She shook her head as she drank in the rugged lines of his handsome face. She didn't want to talk at all just then. What she wanted was for him to reach for her, to pull her against his very solid-looking chest, wrap her in his arms and tell her he was here because he'd missed her.

"Not really," she murmured, and looked away so he wouldn't see her disappointment when he pushed his hand through his hair instead.

Her feet soundless on the pine flooring, she headed for the lights and warmth in the back of the house. As she did, she could practically feel his curious glance moving over her as he followed. He remained oddly silent as she swiped up a magazine from the floor by the sofa and dropped it on the coffee table.

The cats had uncurled themselves from their spots by the gas-fed fire and moved in to sniff at his boots. Giving them both a scratch behind their ears, noting that Columbus's injury had healed nicely, Joe glanced up to see Rebecca continue through the open room to the kitchen table.

Seeing the computer on, his brow pleated. "Were you working?"

"No. No," she repeated, because she really hadn't done a productive thing all day. Cleaning the house didn't count. That had been therapy. With a few deft strokes on the keys, she shut the computer off. "I was just looking up...someone."

There was strain behind her smile. It was as obvious to Joe as the delicacy of features that looked even more fragile without the expertly applied makeup she usually wore. With the model-perfect eye shadow, lip gloss and whatever else she used, she was undeniably beautiful.

Without it, the physical beauty remained, but she looked younger, definitely less sophisticated and infinitely more vulnerable.

He'd noticed that vulnerability the moment she'd opened the door. As for the fragility, that was compounded by her unexpected lack of height. He hadn't realized how much shorter she really was compared to him.

His glance skimmed the casual black jogging suit molding her slender body. There really wasn't much to her at all.

"Are you sure I'm not interrupting something?"

She shrugged, tried again to smile. "Okay," she conceded. "You were. But I'm grateful that you did. Can I get you something. Coffee? Tea? Hot chocolate? That's about all I have."

"I'm good. Thanks." With the low voices on the television extolling the virtues of proper lighting, he walked over to where she remained by the table. Beyond the closed curtains of the bay windows, rain pounded the roof, the ground. Wind tossed sheets of it against the glass.

He stopped in front of her. Despite her obvious efforts to hide it, the sadness he'd sensed in her on occasion seemed so much more pronounced tonight.

"What is it you're grateful I interrupted?"

The overhead lights caught the shimmer of gold and sable in her loosely restrained hair as she tipped her head. "It's a long, boring story," she assured him, hints of her intrepid spirit shining through. "It's even boring me."

"You said you were looking for information on someone."

He lifted his hand to her face. He'd come home early for this. Just to see her. To touch her. He didn't care that there wasn't anything logical about that need. He didn't even care that he was probably being driven by hormones and some crazy need he felt to be there for her because no one else seemed to be. It didn't even matter that that particular combination felt inherently dangerous. The need to touch her was strong. The need to know why that underlying sadness existed felt stronger still.

"I'm pretty good at listening if you want to talk."

His fingers felt cool against her cheek, their tips slightly rough. He was a man who worked with his hands in ways she once would have never considered. He used them to build things, to repair and restore, to heal and to care for.

His touch now offered reassurance. Yet, instead of calming her, instead of easing the sense of being alone and adrift she'd been fighting all night, having him so close somehow made that loneliness even more pronounced.

Maybe it was better to have nothing at all, than to be teased with a taste of something she couldn't ever truly have.

With the awful feeling that might well be true for her with both her father and Joe, she crossed her arms beneath her breasts and stepped back.

"It's…complicated," she said, hating how torn she felt just then. Moments ago she couldn't have imagined anywhere she'd rather be than in Joe's arms. Now, the possibility only promised to make her feel worse when he let go. "And…awkward."

The situation truly was complicated and awkward. But more than anything, she didn't want him to think of her as lost, ungrateful and confused as she was afraid she'd sound if she tried to explain how incomplete her life had always felt with a major part of it missing.

"Does this have anything to do with what you didn't want to talk about last week at dinner? The reason you came here?" he reminded her.

Rebecca's glance shot to his, only to fall away in

what almost felt like defeat. Or maybe it was simply acceptance. Joe had developed a way of reading her all too easily it seemed. She just didn't know if it was pride or her need for self-preservation that hadn't allowed her to confide in him or anyone else about how incomplete her life had always felt. She had the feeling Joe already knew that, though. He knew how she'd grown up. He knew her parents had never married, that she didn't know her father, that it had always pretty much just been her and her mom.

He was also the most realistic and practical person she'd ever met. Since she was afraid she wasn't being either, she could desperately use his advice.

She turned from straightening an already straight stack of files. "May I ask you something?"

"Of course you can."

She could do this logically, methodically. He'd never have to know what a train wreck she felt like inside.

"Would you want to know who your father is if you didn't know already?"

His eyes narrowed on hers. "I can't say I've thought about that before." Leaning against the end of the breakfast counter, he crossed his feet at his ankles and his arms over his broad chest. "But yeah," he concluded, apparently thinking about it now. "I'm sure I would."

"Would you think I was being ungrateful to my mom if I needed to know who my dad is?"

As if realizing where she was headed, caution entered his tone. "I wouldn't," he told her. "But the question should be, would she?"

Rebecca's shoulders rose with the deep breath she drew. "Probably. Most likely," she had to amend, because her mother had been so adamant about leaving the entire matter alone. "But I'm not ungrateful," she defended. "She could have given me up. I think her relationship with her parents wouldn't have suffered so badly if she had, but she kept me with her and did the best she could to take care of us both. I love my mom. I just need—"

"—to find your father," he concluded for her.. His glance slid toward the dark computer. "You think he's somewhere around here?"

"I know he is. That's why I came here," she finally told him. "I ran across an old diary of Mom's last spring." Her mom hadn't made entries every day and the last entry had been before some big dance, but Rebecca hadn't had any problem with the missing details. There had been more than enough to go on without them. "She was crazy in love with him. The dates coincide with the time I would have been conceived, so I'm almost positive it's him."

She hesitated, something like hope entering her voice. "Russell Lever," she said, wondering if it wasn't trepidation she felt instead. "Have you ever heard of him?"

Contemplating the question, Joe gave a slow shake of his head. "The name Lever sounds familiar," he murmured. "I'm not sure why. But Russell Lever doesn't sound familiar at all." The dark slashes of his eyebrows merged. "How did you track him here?"

She needed to move. Plagued by the same restlessness she'd felt all evening, she started to pace

"I hired an attorney," she told him, moving past the breakfast bar. "The Russell Lever in Mom's diary went to Columbia University. According to what she'd written, she met him at a frat party there. Columbia is on the Upper West Side and the Fashion Institute where Mom went is Midtown," she explained, so he could understand how close the schools were, relatively speaking. "The lawyer found a Russell Lever who'd graduated from Columbia a couple of years before Mom graduated from FIT. That put him in the right location at the right time and in the right age group. The alumni records showed that he'd moved to Rosewood," she went on to explain. "Through those records, he learned that he had a wife and a stepson."

She turned, paced back. "That would be Jack. Jack is the attorney I went out with a few times here. The one who dumped me for his nanny," she reminded him, in case he'd forgotten her less-than-illustrious history with men. "I wanted to get to know Jack because I was having a hard time figuring out how to meet Russell. I also wanted to find out everything I could about him, but all I learned is that the man was a terrible father to Jack."

"So this Jack knows you're Russell's daughter?"

She quickly shook her head, fidgeting with the strings on her hoodie as she paced past him again. "I never told him. I haven't told anyone except you. I didn't want anyone to know why I was here until I felt ready to face my father myself. I wanted to know everything about him that I could," she hurried to explain. "I wanted him to know that I'd learned about him so I'd fit in with his family. But I haven't found anything at all encouraging and now I'm torn between wanting to finish what I came here to do and wondering what's wrong with me that I can't just leave everything be the way Mom always wanted me to.

"I always imagined my reunion with him to be so perfect," she went on, turning to pace back again, "but even the work he does sounds selfish. I don't know if I'll get a father or if I'll be opening Pandora's Box and some monster will come out," she went on, only to find herself cut off when Joe reached out and snagged her arm on her way by.

Unfolding his nicely muscled frame, he straightened in front of her.

"Take it easy," he coaxed, pretty much proving to her that she'd moved a tad beyond methodical with her recitation. "First, what you said about learning about him so you'll fit in? Meeting him isn't a job interview. You're not applying for the position of daughter."

Beneath his hands he could feel the tension in her slender muscles increase. "And there's nothing wrong with you."

He had told her that before, the day at the park when she'd confided that she'd been dumped twice in a row. He really didn't feel that she was the problem. From what he knew of her, he suspected the problems were with everyone else who'd come and gone from her life. Starting with the father who'd disappeared before she was born.

"It's natural for a person to want to know her roots," he told her. Slipping his hand up her arm, he curved his palm at the back of her neck.

"You just need to prepare yourself for a less-than-perfect reunion."

"What about my mom?"

"Personally?" he said, wondering if she had any idea how unguarded she looked just then. "I'd see how it went with your father, then take my cue from there. If he's good with it and not too upset about discovering he has a daughter, then I'd tell her you found him. If he's ugly about it, or her, then I'd keep it to myself. There's no reason to tell someone something that will only hurt them, especially if there's nothing she can do to change it."

Her eyes remained on his, her shoulders lifting slightly

beneath his hand as she drew a deep breath. Quietly absorbing all he said, she gave a small nod.

The motion only made him more aware of how soft her hair felt as it shifted against the back of his hand.

"One last thing," she asked. Her brow furrowed as her glance fell. "How do I meet him?" Lifting her hand, she touched her fingers to the middle of his chest. "I have no way of contacting him other than to leave a message asking him to return my call. I can't explain who I am in a message, and why would he return the call of someone who doesn't say who they are or what they want?"

She kept her focus on his sweater as she smoothed that small patch of fabric. "If I say who I am, there's always the chance he won't call back."

There was no denying the amount of thought she'd given the situation. There was no denying how afraid she was of being rejected, either.

Between that and the certainty that her mom would be upset, it was no wonder it had taken her so long to do what he would have done pretty much the moment he'd met the man's stepson. He just wasn't crazy at all about the most obvious solution to this particular aspect of the problem.

She had made it clear from the beginning that there hadn't been anything of any consequence between her and Jack. When she'd first spoken of him, he had detected more embarrassment than hurt over the way the relationship had ended. When she'd spoken of him now, he'd sensed no particular feeling at all.

Still, he found it rather telling that he envied the guy the time he'd spent with her.

"Maybe you should go to Jack and tell him who you are. He lived with the man. He's probably in the best position to help you arrange a meeting."

At the suggestion the furrows in her brow deepened.

"Unless you'd rather not see him," he continued. "You said you weren't that involved with him, but if it would be difficult for you—"

"I wasn't involved with him. Not *involved* involved," Rebecca insisted.

"That's not what I meant. I wasn't questioning you," he insisted right back. "I was going to say that if it would be difficult for you, I'd go with you."

She blinked in disbelief. "You'd do that for me?"

The look on her face nearly broke his heart.

"Of course, I would."

Disbelief turned to doubt. "Why?"

He wasn't about to tell her it was because he felt sorry for her, though that sympathy was definitely there. It didn't seem wise to mention the increasing need he felt to protect her, either.

Taking her face between his hands, he looked straight into all that sad confusion and answered the simplest way he could.

"Because it's what a friend does," he said, and lowered his mouth to hers.

Rebecca felt her entire body go still. There was such tenderness in his strong, capable hands as he cradled her face. She felt that same disarming gentleness in his kiss as she opened to him, and in the touch of his tongue to hers in the moments before she drew in a long, shuddery breath.

Warmth seemed to flow through her, moving from his mouth to hers and quietly soothing all the restless nerves in her body. She could practically feel the knot of anxiety in her stomach slowly unravel. The tautness in her shoulders seemed to drain toward the floor.

She had felt calmed by his touch on occasion. Yet, what she felt as his mouth caressed hers moved light-years beyond anything he had made her feel before.

No man had ever touched her the way Joe touched her now. No man had ever kissed her as if she were something fragile, something…precious. But that was how he made her feel as he held her there, as if she truly mattered to him. She just didn't know which disconcerted her more. The way the heat he caused to flow through her turned liquid low in her belly, or the realization that, along with everything else, that feeling of truly mattering to someone had been missing from her life, too.

Joe lifted his head, watched her eyes slowly open. The heartrending disbelief was gone. But the naked need he saw in its place did nothing for the heat burning low in his gut. He'd realized before that all he had to do was think about this woman to want her. The taste of her turned want into smoldering need.

The strength had left her voice. "I've never had a friend do that before."

With the pad of his thumb he traced the fullness of her bottom lip. "Kiss you?"

"Not…like that."

He felt the slight movement of her cheek toward his hand as she unconsciously sought more of his touch. Drawn by that, drawn by her vulnerability to him, he figured now was as good a time as any for honesty. He'd told her when they'd gone to dinner that he wouldn't lead her on. And he wouldn't. But he couldn't deny the need to follow wherever she would willingly go.

"Maybe I don't want just friendship. Maybe," he said, warning her, "I want a little more."

Need remained achingly visible in her eyes.

"How much more?"

His glance drifted to her mouth. "Show, or tell?"

Rebecca's breath thinned. Craving what he'd made her feel, wanting him in ways that felt all too essential, she whispered, "Show."

The pounding of the rain seemed to echo around them as he eased his hand around her back. Drawing her to him, he held her against his body with his fingers splayed low on her spine and covered her mouth with his.

He kissed her deeply, his tongue mating with hers as he aligned her more intimately to the solid wall of his thighs, his stomach, his chest. She could feel him hard against her, his need as obvious as his restraint in the long moments before she felt his hand slip under her top and curve beneath her breast.

An aching little moan escaped from her throat at the feel of his fingers cupping her fullness. The flick of his thumb over her nipple nearly buckled her knees.

She curved her arms around his neck, as much to stay upright as to get as close to him as possible. The sensations he created in her body were as compelling as the sense of being cared for that he'd exposed in her heart. She wanted to know more, to feel more, because what she experienced in his arms seemed to erase all the empty feelings she'd been struggling with while she'd been missing him so desperately.

His breath felt warm and a little ragged when he carried his kiss to her temple. Easing the hand under her hoodie to her waist, his palm hot against her bare skin, he nipped at the lobe of her ear.

"I think you get the general idea."

With his lips creating little shimmers of heat down the side of her neck, she tipped her head to give him better access. "Maybe."

He chuckled against her ear, the sound deep, rich, seductive. "Do I need to be more specific?"

"Please," she murmured, only to have what little was left of her common sense struggle past sensation. Though the thought of him letting her go was almost more than she could bear, she added, "If you're prepared to be."

She thought she felt him go still. Or maybe it was her own stillness she felt as he drew back to skim a stray lock of hair from her cheek.

There was no mistaking the tautness carved in his features, or the way his blue eyes darkened as they held hers. He knew she was asking if he had protection with him.

"In that case," he said, his voice going husky, "I can get very specific." His hands settled at her waist. "By the way," he told her, his mouth hovering over hers, "I like you short. You fit better."

She would have argued his opinion of her height but he was kissing her again. Under that tender assault, the thought fled right along with any consideration she might have given to how completely he had annihilated her defenses. As he backed her across the room, unzipping her hoodie and pushing it over her shoulders, all that mattered was that he was touching her. As he angled her toward the sofa while he drew the scrunchie from her hair and unfastened her bra, all she cared about was that he was with her now.

She felt the backs of her calves bump the sofa. His hands left her only long enough to turn out the lamp beside it, to grab the quilt from the arm, and to pull his sweater over his head. Even before it hit the floor, she was working at the buttons of his shirt. His flannel had barely landed on her fleece and lace when his hand skimmed down her bare back and he lowered her to the cushions.

In the flickering firelight, his muscles backlit by the light from the kitchen, he eased down on top of her.

With his hands in her hair, he kissed her slowly, thoroughly, as if he intended to learn all her surfaces and textures before the night was through. He told her by the easy way he skimmed his hands over her breasts, her belly and followed those debilitating caresses with his lips, that he was in no hurry. Even when he moved long minutes later to rid them of the rest of their clothes and he drew her soft curves against his harder, rougher body beneath the quilt they were covered with, he seemed intent on doing nothing but driving her slowly out of her mind.

She had been told before that she was beautiful, but no man had ever made her feel that way. Yet, that was what Joe did with every kiss, every caress.

He also had her entire body aching with need. She'd had no idea such incredible yearning existed.

Wanting him to ache just as badly for her, she mimicked his every caress, turning each touch into an erotic game of following the leader that finally had him grabbing her wrist and pinning it above her head.

"Easy."

The word was a harsh rasp as Joe gritted his teeth against the raw hunger burning through his body.

He hadn't shown up on Rebecca's doorstep intending to take her to bed. He had just wanted to see her. Or so he'd told himself before he'd been hit with the need in her eyes, and felt her curvy little body melt into his. It seemed there were reasons he'd intended to go slow with her, to take the relationship at a leisurely pace. But whatever those reasons were, they were lost to him as he rolled their protection into place and eased back over her.

With his control hanging by a thread, he tucked her

more intimately beneath him and drew one long slender leg over his. He'd wanted to savor her longer, to linger over the sensual curves and textures of her body. The desire sinking its claws deep inside him made lingering impossible. He knew what it was to give a woman pleasure, to take pleasure himself. Yet, what he felt as her soft hands urged him closer went light-years beyond anything so simple as the need for sexual release. What he felt for this woman seemed to be getting all mixed up with a need to be there for her, to be part of what she was going through, to erase the thought of any other man she'd ever known from her mind.

He whispered her name. Watching her open her eyes to meet his, he slowly sank into her warmth. He heard her breath catch, saw her eyes close once more as she arched toward him.

The white hot heat rippling through his body threatened to melt what little remained of his restraint as he lowered his head to her shoulder and she began moving with him. He'd never felt anything so powerful as he did the need to claim her as his own. There were consequences to that need. Complications. Somewhere in the back of his brain he knew that. But he didn't care. With her clinging to him, whimpering his name, he felt her shatter. In that mindless instant, the red haze of pure sensation took over—and he wasn't aware of conscious thought at all.

Chapter Eight

Rebecca didn't want to move. She didn't want to think. All she wanted, for however long she could make it last, was to be right where she was—curled up under the heavy quilt, protected by Joe's embrace.

Protected.

That was how she'd felt when she'd awakened moments ago. The sensation was new to her, something she couldn't honestly say she had ever felt with any other man before. But then, Joe had introduced her to so many feelings she'd never experienced. So many feelings she wondered now if she was better off not having experienced at all.

She closed her eyes, tried not to breathe in too deeply for fear she might wake him and the feeling of being protected, cared for, would come to an end. She couldn't deny how badly she'd wanted to be in his arms. She'd just never intended to make love with him until the thought of him letting her go had become more than she could bear. She didn't doubt for a moment that she was in serious lust with him. She was afraid to call it anything more. He was a wonderful man, almost too good to be true, but with her abysmal track record with men, it wasn't a matter of if they would end, it was simply a question of when.

Joe knew the moment Rebecca woke. Curled up to her back, her soft curves fitted perfectly to him, he could feel the subtle tension move through her slender body. That tension tightened her breathing, tensed her supple muscles and slowly curled her fist where it lay beneath his hand on one of the sofa's throw pillows.

He didn't doubt for a moment that she was questioning the turn their relationship had taken.

He was doing a little mental struggling of his own. He wasn't totally sure what it was he felt for this woman. All he knew for certain was that he didn't want her to withdraw from him. And she would if she was regretting what they'd just shared.

Wanting to distract her from her thoughts, he raised himself on one elbow, smoothed her hair from her neck and kissed the soft skin behind her ear. "I'm going to get dressed and go," he murmured. "The neighbors don't need to get their newspapers in the morning and see my truck out there."

In the light slanting in from the kitchen and the glow of the fire, he watched her roll to her back and cautiously lift her eyes to his.

"What time is it?"

"Four-thirty."

Her dark hair was thoroughly tousled from his hands. Pushing the long locks back from her forehead, she listened to the steady drumming on the roof. With a faint frown, she touched her fingers to his jaw. "You're going out in the rain."

"I got here in the rain." Drawn by her concern, he took her hand in his, pressed a kiss to her palm. "I can either call you in a few hours, or you can come with me now."

"Come with you?"

"Sure," he murmured, smiling. Lowering his head, he brushed his mouth over the sweetness of hers. "You can fix me breakfast."

Drawing back, he found her looking as apologetic as she sounded.

"I'm not much of cook." Having warned him, caution entered her tone. "What did you have in mind?"

"Eggs, bacon, hash browns, toast."

"I can do toast and eggs," she said, brightening. "But I don't think you want to risk bacon or hash browns. I don't have them, anyway."

"I do. Come on. We'll shower and go to my place." Seeing a smile curve her lovely mouth, he lowered his head toward hers once more. "I could use some help at the house. I'll bring you back tonight."

He'd feared she was regretting the turn their relationship had taken. He still suspected she harbored second thoughts. Yet it wasn't regret he heard in her whispered, "Okay." It wasn't regret he tasted on her lips when she met his kiss, either. Nor was it what he felt when her arms curved around his neck and her body flowed toward his.

With her responding so completely to his touch, any doubts he might have felt himself were put on hold. Gathering her to him, he slipped his hand down her back, felt himself craving her all over again—and decided leaving could wait for a while.

* * *

Daybreak hadn't provided much difference between the dark rain of night and the dreary gray rain of late morning. To Rebecca, it seemed the day had simply lightened enough to reveal the charcoal-colored sky and the rain-blurred fields and trees being beaten bare beyond the windows of the partially remodeled house Joe called home.

Thunder rumbled in the distance. The weather was still miserable. Yet, it felt different to her here. Instead of feeling isolated as she had yesterday, she felt sheltered. Rather than being conscious of the wind, the rain and the cold, she was more aware of the coziness of being inside in the warmth. Instead of feeling restless, she felt almost…calm.

Or would have, had it not been for the pathetic and insistent whine coming from beside her feet. Rex had run out of water. With Joe somewhere at the other end of the house, the little gray dog who seemed to bounce rather than walk had brought her his dish.

She turned from the deep stainless steel sink Joe had installed in the kitchen himself last year. There were no curtains or blinds over the large window above it. Other than a coffeepot and toaster, the open space had no accessories of any sort. The other rooms were equally spare. But in here he'd put in new cherrywood cabinets, counters that almost looked like granite and was working on the molding he was apparently staining by hand.

"There you go, boy." Setting the water dish by the dogs' food bowls under the built-in kitchen desk, she scratched Rex's soft head, received the wiggle of his back end in return and went off in search of the only man she'd ever known who actually owned power tools.

While Joe had fried bacon and she'd scrambled eggs,

he'd told her he'd bought the house three years ago, then gutted the whole thing. He'd finished his bedroom and bath the first year. The next, he'd finished the living and family rooms. Last year, he'd tackled the kitchen. His latest project was stripping and staining the hardwood flooring. He hadn't done anything yet with the other two bedrooms and the main bathroom.

Over breakfast, he'd gone on to tell her he figured the house would be done right about the time he needed to turn his attention to the new building for the animal hospital. He could do much of the finishing work himself.

The man had major portions of his life all mapped out for the next couple of years. As much as she admired his tenacity with his goals, she found his drive disheartening, too. From what he'd told her before, she knew he didn't intend to add anyone else to those plans.

Not wanting to think about that now, wanting only to enjoy being with him, she headed into the family room where he'd returned with his camera and tripod to set them up in the middle of the sparsely furnished space.

This room had more in it than the rest. One side of the stark off-white room was occupied by a long, sage-green sofa, a matching barrel chair and a low, black coffee table. Opposite the sofa rose a bookcase and entertainment center dominated by electronics and a big-screen TV. His only nod to any sort of decoration was the temperature gauge he'd hung above a six-foot-long terrarium down by the doorway that opened to the bare living room. The rectangular glass box contained what looked like a miniature version of the Pleistocene era to Rebecca. Ferns, a little rock waterfall, a pool surrounded by moss. It also contained a foot-long striped iguana that Joe had tried to introduce to her, but she wasn't going anywhere near.

She was okay with cats now. Those she lived with anyway. And Joe's dogs seemed to be becoming her buddies. She was drawing the line, however, at things with scales.

Her thoughts slid back to his blank walls.

The man could seriously use a decorator.

"Why don't you hang your photography in here?" she asked, moving to where Bailey lay curled up on the small braided rug in front of the welcoming fire. Sitting down on the stone hearth by the German shepherd and the heat, she let her glance skim the blue fleece shirt covering Joe's strong shoulders. "You could put a row of them similar to those in your office all along that wall," she pointed out, indicating the empty space above the deeply cushioned couch. "If you picked scenes of trees or something in all four seasons, the colors would go great with your sofa. They'd need to be larger than what you have in your office. For scale," she explained, reaching toward the end of the hearth where he'd put the Santa hats and collar she'd dropped off at his office a couple of weeks ago. "Unless you wanted to use small photos with big mats and black frames," she suggested. "That would look nice, too."

Joe looked up from where he'd just aimed the camera at the hearth and fixed it into position. Rebecca had put makeup on after they'd showered. Not as much as she usually wore, but enough to take the edge off the vulnerability he'd seen last night. Wearing a snug burgundy sweater, designer jeans and her usual, high-heeled boots, much of her sophistication was back, too, along with a fair amount of her appealing animation.

He never would have thought it when he'd first met her, but sitting there absently patting his dog, she looked very much as if she belonged right where she was.

He glanced at the wall that had her attention. He'd had no clue what to put on his walls, although the bank teller he'd casually dated for a while last year had seemed to think he needed art prints and to lose all the green.

He liked green. He didn't like art prints. He did, however, find a certain appeal in the way Rebecca automatically seemed to know what would make the space personal.

"I have a whole darkroom full of photos back there. If you want to go through them, maybe you can find some there I could use."

She popped to her feet. "Where are they?"

"Can we do this first?"

She looked at the Santa hats and collar she'd just picked up. As if she'd intended to do both at the same time, which wouldn't have surprised him at all given her usual energy level, she gave him a shrug.

"Sure," she said, and handed him the stretchy circle of white fur.

It was as clear as the blue of her eyes that she had no intention of putting the thing on his iguana. If the way she'd skirted the terrarium every time she passed it was any indication, she had no intention of getting anywhere near his pet lizard.

His nieces were like that. "Where's Rex?" he asked.

"Getting a drink."

"If you'll get him, I'll get Iggy."

"What about your backdrop?"

"I thought I'd use the fireplace."

"Just plain like that?"

That had been his plan. Stopping short of Iggy's confines, he turned to where she frowned at the leaping flames.

"What's wrong with it?"

"Inherently, nothing. It's a lovely fireplace," she insisted. "And the fire and andirons will look great in a Christmas photo. It just needs something else."

"Else?"

"Something…Christmassy."

"Bailey and Rex have their hats." He dangled the circle of fur from his finger. "Ig has this."

"That's not backdrop."

He knew she had a good eye. He did, too, when it came to framing pictures outdoors. But in the outdoors, the background was already there.

"So what do you suggest?"

"What was in your picture last year?"

"Bailey in the snow."

"That was it?"

"One of my assistants gave me a red bow to put on his collar."

They didn't have an early snow to work with this year. Nothing in the room offered inspiration, either. But it seemed to Rebecca that he definitely needed something more festive than a plain fireplace on his office holiday card.

"Do you have any Christmas decorations?"

"A few tree ornaments. They're in the garage."

"Do you have stockings?"

The slow arch of his eyebrow clearly said he did not.

She turned to the long, bare mantel. "You need stockings," she decided, trying to remember what she'd seen on greeting cards and in department store windows last Christmas. She never decorated for the holiday much herself. As a child, she and her mom had always put a little tree up on a table in a corner. She and her roommates over the years had done the same thing. Some of the decorations the commercial establishments put up were incredible, though. Store windows and the lobbies of the big hotels were practically transformed into winter wonderlands.

She adored the holidays in New York.

"And a big basket filled with pinecones. And a wreath up there," she continued, pointing to the middle of the un-adorned white wall above the fireplace. "And fir boughs and candlesticks." She whirled around. "Do you have any brass candleholders and candles?"

The animation in her eyes met what looked like indulgence in his.

"I'm not cutting down fir boughs. They'd be soaking wet."

So would he, he could have said.

"What about the rest of it?" she asked, undaunted.

"I don't have any of that stuff. I have no idea where to get it, either."

Rebecca's smile came easily as she walked over to where he stood smiling back. "I do," she said.

Settling his hands on her hips, his glance dropped to her mouth. "Where?"

"The craft store."

His eyes jerked back to hers.

"I'd never been in one until a couple of weeks ago," she admitted, removing one of his hands to slip into hers, "but it'll have exactly what you need."

What he needed was her, in his arms, down the hall and in his bed. She gave him little time to indulge the taunting little fantasy, however. Clearly on a mission, she hauled him to the closet for their coats, planning aloud the tableau she had in mind while he marveled at the fact that she was actually getting him to go to what he'd always thought of as the female version of a home improvement store. Of all the things he'd found unexpected about her, so far, that was the most unexpected of all.

Daylight had disappeared. What shouldn't have taken more than half an hour at the craft store took over two. Partly because the store had a custom frame section and Joe wanted to know what style of frame she thought might work in his family room, and partly because the place was packed and the lines forever long.

They never did go through his photographs, either. By the time they returned to the house, decorated the fireplace, decorated the dogs and the iguana, got the shot they were both satisfied with and took the decorations back down, it was after five o'clock and the ease she'd been feeling with Joe had turned to a self-protective sort of disquiet.

Smoothing the three stockings she'd just taken down, one for each pet, she laid them atop the bag on the coffee table holding the faux pine bough she'd just removed from the mantel.

The setting they had created for the photo had been nothing but a prop. Already, the charming little scene was gone, relegated back to the bags from which it had come. Nothing remained but the large brown basket of pinecones Joe had decided to leave on the end of the hearth, sans the red plaid ribbon, because he liked it there. But laughing with him while they'd hung the wreath and having him turn her in his arms to kiss her breathless as he'd lifted her from the hearth had made her long for special moments like that during the real holidays.

Jason had never kissed her like that. But then as she'd realized in Joe's arms last night, no man ever had. No man had ever seemed to simply care the way Joe did. Not just about her. About so many things.

Turning her back on the bags, she snagged the hearth broom from its brass stand and started sweeping up plastic pine needles and sparkles from the stones.

She didn't want him messing with the little dreams that had always been in her heart. But there was no question that he was. He was putting a face on them, showing her what those dreams could be like for real and she definitely didn't need to tease herself that way.

"There." She pronounced the word with a self-protective smile as she swept the bits of silver and green into the dustpan Joe had brought in. "All done."

Taking the pan and broom from her, Joe set them on the hearth. Instead of taking her by the shoulders as she thought he might, he jammed his hands on his hips. "I told you, you didn't have to clean this up."

"And I told you that I helped make the mess, so I'd help clean it."

"It wasn't a mess. It looked great."

"It was a figure of speech."

"You're too stubborn for your own good sometimes. If you'd left this, I could have had you home an hour ago."

He hadn't intended to keep her all day. He had book work for the clinic to do and hadn't done a single load of the laundry he'd put off all week. It was either wash a load of whites or hit the mall tomorrow and buy a couple packages of briefs and undershirts.

Doing the laundry while he paid the clinic's bills made more sense.

So did getting her home.

He had the feeling from the distance that had crept into her expression while they'd put away the instant

Christmas she'd created that she was retreating from him somehow. The last thing he wanted was for either of them to feel crowded—or to get burned.

He didn't want to be a rebound relationship from her boyfriend of six months ago. As he'd told himself before he'd ignored his intentions to take it slow, she needed time to deal with her past before she could think of a future. Then, there were her unresolved issues regarding her father.

If he were in her position, he'd want breathing room. So that was what he would give her—and himself—just as soon as he made sure she would be all right.

Not wanting her to overthink whatever was on her mind, he ventured into territory guaranteed to keep her side-tracked.

"Are you going to see Jack about your father?"

As incredible as it seemed to Rebecca just then, being with Joe, she had actually forgotten about Russell.

Joe had said last night that Jack was probably in the best position to help her arrange a meeting. Any thought of Russell or his stepson, however, had evaporated shortly after that.

Thinking it best not to consider how effectively Joe's touch had overshadowed the doubts and disquiet she'd been grappling with then, she focused only on the practicality of his suggestion.

"He's the only person I know with access to him. I don't know if I should just show up at his office or call first."

"Call and make an appointment. You don't want him rushed." He finally lifted his hand, skimmed his knuckles over her cheek. "Are you okay seeing him alone?"

He would go with her if she wanted him to. Rebecca knew that because he'd told her he would last night.

Her need for distance fought the need for his friendship. The thought that he would stand beside her felt almost like a balm to the tender parts of her heart.

She touched her hand to his chest. "Thank you," she murmured. "But I can do this myself." Seeing Jack might be a bit awkward at first. But she needed to go to him on her own simply because she wasn't prepared to let herself lean that much on anyone else. There would be a side benefit to seeing Jack, though. Explaining why she'd been so interested in getting to know him would take some of the sting out of what he'd done.

Joe didn't seem particularly surprised by her refusal. He simply gave her a nod that seemed to say he'd expected it. "When will you call?"

She took a deep breath. "First thing in the morning."

The offices of Wasserman, Kendall, Lake and Lever were on the tenth floor of the bank building across the street from a Starbucks. Having fortified herself with a double skinny, sugar-free vanilla latte, Rebecca stood in the elevator watching the numbers ascend and did what she always did before going into a life-altering meeting. Not that she'd walked into that many. Only one came to mind. The meeting where she'd told her editor she was quitting to move to the suburbs and freelance.

Still, as then, she took a deep breath, prayed she was doing the right thing and made herself put aside her doubts the moment the elevator doors opened.

The brass letters identifying the law firm were on the wall directly across from where she stepped out. Not allowing herself to consider, again, that she was closer than she'd ever been to meeting her father, she walked through the double doors, up to the receptionist at the large and curving teak desk and, with a polite smile, asked for Jack.

"I'm Rebecca Peters. I have a three o'clock appointment."

The receptionist, a very attractive brunette in her own right, had already noted her stylish black coat, high-heeled boots and the black-and-tan scarf slung around her neck. With an approving glance at her large gold earrings, she punched a button on her console and smiled back.

"Miss Peters to see Mr. Lever," she said into the tiny mouthpiece curving from her earphone. "Of course. I'll send her right back."

The woman motioned to her right.

Rebecca knew Jack was from money. She'd also heard how successful he was in his own right. Aside from what she'd discovered on her own in the past several months, her neighbors had mentioned both. Yet, only now did she get the sense that success was something that simply surrounded him. Rather like the sense of quiet command surrounded Joe.

A sharply attired middle-aged woman with a short, graying bob appeared ahead of her to provide escort through the labyrinth of mahogany-paneled halls and walls hung with what looked suspiciously like original artwork. Secretaries occupied rows of cubicles, looking up when she passed. Men and women in dark suits glanced her way when her guide, who'd introduced herself as Jack's secretary, led her past a huge conference room.

Had she not already been running on pure need and nerve, she might have paid more attention to her surroundings, checked out more details. As it was, her only thought was to get her meeting over with.

Jack's secretary stopped by a closed door, knocked once, then pushed the door open for her to pass.

She found herself facing a wall of law books. Jack rose from behind the large mahogany desk in front of it.

Six feet tall, all blond hair and muscle in a tailored navy suit, he met her halfway across his impressive office.

"Rebecca." His smile was questioning and more than a little hesitant as the door was closed behind her. In front of his desk were two red leather wingback chairs. He motioned her toward them. "I'm kind of at a loss here. What's so important you couldn't talk about it on the phone?"

"It's just something better handled in person. How's Zooey?" she asked, because she really did like his nanny and wished them both well.

"Zooey's fine." Looking guarded, or simply wary, his brown eyes narrowed. "What's this all about?"

"Nothing personal," she assured him, pretty sure he was thinking she wanted him back. Guys, even nice ones, were so predictable. "At least not personal between us." That didn't sound right, either. "I mean, I'm not here about what happened with you and me," she concluded, thinking that was as clear as she could get.

His wide forehead pleated. "Nothing happened."

"Sure it did. You dumped me."

"Rebecca…"

She offered a forgiving smile. "But my being here has nothing to do with our nonrelationship."

Patience joined confusion. "Then you're here because…?"

Covering her nerves, she moved to one of the chairs in front of his desk. He remained by the other.

"Because I need to talk to you about your father."

His confusion turned total. "My father? Russell? What for?"

She took a deep breath. "Because I think he's mine, too."

Jack opened his mouth, closed it again.

"May I sit down?" she asked.

"*Your* father."

"Can I sit?"

"Yeah. Sure." His eyes never leaving her face, he swung the chair beside him around and sat down, too. "Your father," he repeated. "As in biological?"

"I believe so."

Doubt was probably second nature to an attorney, she thought. Surely skepticism was. A heavy dose of both crept into his already disbelieving expression. "You have proof?"

"I don't have DNA if that's what you mean, but I tracked him through an attorney I hired before I came here. I'd found my mom's diary," she explained, and went on to tell him about how she knew Russell had gone to Columbia. She told him about how she'd tried to find Russell since she'd arrived here, how difficult it had been and how she'd had no luck even catching a glimpse of him.

She even admitted how hugely jealous she'd been when she'd first realized that Russell had a stepson.

"When I first heard about you, all I could think about was that you grew up with everything I didn't have as a child. I was so envious of you," she admitted. "You grew up with my dad. You had a mother and a father. Money. Security. But this isn't about money," she insisted, needing him to know that. "And I stopped envying you your childhood when you told me how he was never there for you and your mom."

That was probably when she'd first thought herself attracted to him, she realized. But that attraction had never had any chemistry to it, as she'd once confided to Molly. If anything, her feelings toward him had been mostly...empathy.

As if recalling what little he'd told her about his step-father, Jack's glance fell to the toes of his wingtips.

"All I want is to meet him, Jack." Joe had said this man would be her best shot at that. She desperately needed for him to be right. "I'm not expecting a big welcome into the family." Not anymore, anyway. "I just want to see what he's like for myself." She hesitated. "I just don't know how to do that without your help."

The thought that he might not be willing to offer that help moved to the center of the sudden silence.

For long moments, the fair-haired, widowed father of two said nothing. He simply took a deep breath, gave her a look she couldn't read at all and rose to jam his hands onto his hips.

She rose, too. Mostly because she couldn't sit still any longer herself. What she was asking him to do was huge. And without his help, she was back to square one.

He quietly studied her in the growing silence. She just couldn't tell from that hard scrutiny if he was looking for signs of honesty or traces of guile.

He was looking for familial resemblance.

"You've got the Lever coloring. They're all dark-haired and blue-eyed."

Unlike him, his quick silence said.

His own eyes narrowed. "What color are your mom's eyes?"

"Brown."

Hers were unquestionably blue. She had the dark hair, too. But then, her mom had also been a brunette—until she'd started covering up the gray with shades of caramel and blond.

The only picture Rebecca had seen of Russell was the tiny black-and-white photocopy of a photocopy the attorney had obtained from a Columbia yearbook. She'd seen no similarity to herself in the grainy image at all.

"And you have the dimple in your chin. It's not as deep as the men's, but it's there."

Her heart gave a funny jerk. She actually bore a physical resemblance to her father.

Jack blew out a breath.

"What's your mother's name?"

"Lillian Peters."

"Is Peters what it was back then?"

Her hands were shaking. Clasping them in front of her, she gave him a nod. "She never married."

"And this would all have been…twenty-six or seven years ago?"

"Twenty-nine. I'm twenty-eight now."

He lifted his chin. "In Manhattan," he said, obviously wanting to make sure his facts were straight.

"Yes."

"Does he know he might have a daughter?"

"I don't know if Mom told him she was pregnant with me or not. I have no idea what happened between them. She would never talk to me about him."

His response was the hardening of his jaw while she all but held her breath.

As if looking at her from an entirely different perspective, he finally gave a nod, muttered, "Okay. I'll see what I can do. I can't promise you a thing," he was quick to inform her. "The man runs hot and cold.

"Today is his birthday," he continued. "Mom's having a family dinner for him tonight. I'll ask him then if he'll call to arrange a meeting with you." He shook his head again. "You're going to be one heck of a birthday surprise."

Chapter Nine

Rebecca pulled into her driveway as Molly and Adam pulled out of theirs. Thinking they must be on their way to Lamaze class, she waved to them through the drizzle while she waited for the garage door to lift, then pulled in and hurried inside to get the envelope she'd forgotten.

Her concentration was shot. She had spent the day captioning swimwear, finalizing and printing her make-over-your-mate article—and waiting for the phone to ring. Jack had said he'd call to let her know how Russell had reacted to his little bombshell and whether Russell wanted to call her or for her to call him. But the only call she'd received all day had been a local charity wanting usable discards.

With that distraction lurking in the back of her mind, she obviously hadn't been as focused as she had thought she'd been on her work. She'd left five minutes ago for the FedEx office to courier her article to her editor only to leave the set of photos she'd intended to send with it on the table.

Snagging the envelope, she checked to make sure the cats weren't following her and heard the phone ring just as she started back through the utility room.

With a glance at the envelope in her hand, she dismissed any possible thought of not seeing who was calling and darted to the kitchen counter where she'd left the portable phone.

The caller ID read Wasserman, Kendall.

Recognizing the name of Jack's law firm, she snatched the phone up with a suddenly cautious, "Hello?"

"Rebecca. It's Jack. Do you have a minute?"

"Sure," she replied, thinking her heart had never beat so hard. "Did you talk to him?"

"I did." He paused. "I talked to him alone in his study," he began, his even tone betraying nothing. "I figured it was up to him to break the news of you to Mom or whoever else he chose to talk to. But he said he barely knew your mother, Rebecca." His voice dropped. "He also said there's no way he could be your father."

For a moment, the only sound on the line was the steady hum of silence. Rebecca blinked, unseeing as she sank onto a stool at the counter.

In the interest of self-preservation, she had already given up the idea of a warm and welcoming family reunion. She hadn't been prepared, however, for Russell to totally deny being her dad.

"But you said I look like him. Did you tell him that?"

"I was just the messenger," he reminded her. "It wasn't my place to convince him."

"Of course it wasn't," she murmured. "Maybe if he saw me…"

"I don't think that will help. He doesn't want to see you." His bluntness made him pause. "I'm sorry, Rebecca. I don't know what else to say, except that these things happen. He's denied that he's your father. Short of coming up with DNA, there's nothing you can do to convince him otherwise. Even then…" *Even then, you can't make him care about you,* he could have said.

"Let's just say that not having him in your life isn't exactly the worst thing that could happen to you," he said instead.

She could hear the empathy in his voice. What she needed just then was his insight.

"Do you believe him? That he's not my father?"

"I don't know if I do or not. He didn't seem to recognize your mom's name until I mentioned where she'd gone to school. But it has been nearly thirty years," he reminded her. "There's definitely a resemblance between the two of you, though."

"Did he ask any questions about her? Or me?" she added, praying she didn't sound as desperate as she felt.

"Not about your mom. All he was interested in was finding out what you wanted from him. He figured it was money. I told him I really didn't think you were after anything like that from him."

"What did he say?"

"That if I believe that, I was a bigger fool than he'd thought. All women are after money."

At his admission, Rebecca closed her eyes, slowly shook her head. "I'm so sorry, Jack. I didn't mean to cause you more problems with him."

"Don't worry about it. I stopped letting what he said to me matter years ago. As for you," he offered, sounding almost brotherly, "if he isn't your father, count your blessings. If he is, then I'd forget about him and go on knowing that you're better off just as you are."

Just as you are.

The words did nothing to ease the sense of desolation slowly overtaking her. "Thank you," she said, anyway.

"Sure," he replied. Then, because there was nothing else to say, he offered a quiet "Take care," and "Goodbye."

After murmuring "Goodbye" herself, she punched the End Call button on the phone and carefully laid it on the counter.

The huge knot behind her breastbone made it difficult to breathe. Taking another deep, deliberate breath, she slowly rose and pushed her fingers through her hair.

Russell Lever had denied being her father. He'd said he'd barely even known her mom. Given everything her mom had written about him, about the times they'd had coffee together, their conversations, their first kiss, she didn't see how he could even begin to claim that. Her mother had so clearly been in love with him.

Then, there was the family resemblance Jack had noted.

It seemed a true measure of her hope or her naiveté that it hadn't occurred to her that Russell wouldn't be honest. But it seemed to her that he couldn't possibly be telling the truth. There just wasn't a thing she could do about it. He didn't want to claim her, much less have anything to do with her. End of story.

End of search.

End of a lifetime of being so certain she wouldn't feel so incomplete if she could just connect with the man who'd always been missing from her life.

End of months of trying to fit into a place she didn't belong.

The thoughts crowded in on her, all the more chaotic for the silence that filled the big, rambling house.

She looked from the dark television to the cats contentedly grooming themselves by the heater vent.

This house wasn't her home. Except for her clothes and a few odds and ends, the bulk of her possessions resided in boxes in the corner of the Turners' garage. The pictures on the walls were of someone else's family. The pets weren't hers. She had no truly close female friends in this town. Molly was as close to a real girlfriend as she had, but even she didn't know that she'd come there desperately hoping to find the sense of family that had always escaped her. But now she'd discovered she didn't have family there after all. At least, none that wanted her.

With those distressing thoughts echoing in her head, she reached for the phone. The only person who could possibly begin to understand what Jack's call meant to her was Joe, but before she could even try to recall the clinic's number she put the phone back down. She didn't want to disturb him at work, not when he would be finishing the last appointments of the day. She didn't know what she wanted him to do, anyway. It wasn't as if he could change what had happened.

Still wearing her coat, she turned a slow circle and shoved her fingers through her hair once more. When she'd left the city, she'd felt like a total failure in her personal life, but she'd had a purpose in coming to Rosewood. With that purpose gone, feeling like an even bigger failure, she realized now that she had no direction at all.

At least in the city, she'd been in a familiar place. Thinking only that she never should have left it to begin with, she snatched the phone back up and reached her friend Cindy. With the connection cutting in and out, it was hard for her old college roommate to hear on her cell phone, but Cindy seemed to catch enough to understand that Rebecca needed a place to stay for a few days and told her to she was welcome to her couch. She had taken the week off and was on her way to her parents in Connecticut with her fiancé for Thanksgiving. Her current roommate, a flight attendant, wouldn't be back until next week, so the place would be all hers for the long weekend. She'd leave her extra key with the building super.

Rebecca had forgotten about Thanksgiving. Not wanting to think about it now, she hurried upstairs, packed her things and loaded them into her leased car. Eyes stinging, throat constricted, she picked up her work from the table, dumped it into a box and added that to her trunk. She would come back later for the boxes in the garage and to clean the house. Right now, she just needed to be where she didn't feel she had no business being.

With her things in the car, she left a message on Molly and Adam's answering machine asking if they would please feed and check on the cats for her for a few days. After adding that she'd leave a key for them under the back doormat and extra food and litter on the washing machine, she punched in Joe's number at home.

She didn't realize how close her tears were to falling until she heard his deep voice on his answering machine. Swallowing them back, telling herself that she was just saving him the trouble of breaking up with her later, she told his machine what Jack told her about his meeting with Russell, that there was no point in her staying in Rosewood and that she hoped everything worked out for him with his new clinic.

Once that was done, it was simply a matter of locking up the house—and leaving.

The only problem was that once she found herself back

in the city, back on streets that were so familiar she could have walked them blindfolded and back in an apartment two floors up from where she'd once lived herself, she had the feeling she no longer belonged there, either.

That disheartening feeling greeted Rebecca within seconds of waking up the next morning. But rather than pull the blanket over her head and escape in sleep all day, which she was sorely tempted to do, she made herself get up, shower, dress and head out onto the bustling sidewalks. Since she hadn't couriered her article yesterday, she would take it to Cleo, her editor, herself. Depending on how busy Cleo was she would also ask if there was any possibility she could have her old job back.

Cleo wasn't there, though. It was only Wednesday morning, but nearly everyone she'd once worked or played with was either out or getting a jump on the holiday. After leaving the envelope on her editor's desk, she left the building and spent the next hour doing what she'd always loved to do this time of year. Yet, looking at the elaborate department store holiday window displays and trying to find a crack in the window coverings of those yet to be unveiled to see what was behind them provided none of the pleasure it once had. Neither did watching the workers finish stringing the lights on the huge tree in Rockefeller Center that had been trucked in from the woods. Or watching kids skate while she warmed her hands around a latte.

The last time she'd been in Manhattan, Joe had been with her. The last time she'd seen a fir tree, she had been with him, too. As odd as it seemed, not having him there sharing with her now made her feel even more miserable than she already did. By one o'clock, she was back in her friend's apartment. By two, she had climbed back into the pink thermal leggings, shirt and socks she'd slept in to watch one of the six movies she'd picked up at the video store.

She should call her mom, she thought. They'd made no arrangements for tomorrow. Being the only family they each had, they should spend the day together. But her mom didn't answer her phone.

Lillian Peters had been in the shower.

She had her head wrapped in a white towel, a white spa robe wrapped around her body and a look of what Joe could only call skeptical curiosity on what he could see of her unlined face as she looked at him through the crack in the door. No less than three chains spanned that negligible space.

She'd buzzed him into the building only after he'd told her he was a friend of Rebecca's, that Rebecca had left Rosewood and that her friends were worried about her. What he hadn't told her was that he'd been concerned about her ever since he'd received her message last night. She'd sounded close to tears. It was because of that that he'd left straight from the clinic when they closed up a little before noon for the holiday.

"You said Rebecca left Rosewood?" she asked.

"Sometime yesterday afternoon or last night. She left a message for one of her neighbors asking her to feed the cats she was taking care of and left a message for me saying she was coming back to Manhattan. Is she here?"

Mention of the cats seemed to finally convince her that he really did know her daughter. The door closed, metal clanked and rattled and the door finally opened to reveal a beautiful, forty-something woman about Rebecca's height without heels, with a slender frame and doe-brown eyes.

"Your name again?" she asked, stepping back for him to enter.

"Joe Hudson." He held out his hand. "It's nice to meet you, Ms. Peters."

"Please," she replied, her hand delicate in his, her handshake firm. "It's Lillian. Come in. You'll have to excuse me," she said, leading him into the apartment that almost would have fit into his family room. A mauve sofa and chair and a television occupied one side. A dining table and hutch, the other. Through a doorway to his right, he could see a neatly made double bed with a suitcase open atop it. Two other doors were closed.

"This is just an insane time of year," she continued, motioning to boxes marked Sample piled on the table. "My flight didn't get in until four this morning. I haven't even unpacked. I haven't even made it into my office yet," she stressed. "We're buying for summer and trying to iron out vendor glitches with holiday orders that should have been on the floors weeks go. May I get you some coffee?" she asked, sounding very much like her daughter as she jumped from one subject to another. "I'm out of milk, so it'll have to be black. I haven't been to the market yet, either."

"Not for me. But thanks," he said from where he remained standing between the overstuffed chair and the small magazine and sample-box-covered coffee table. "I'd just like to know if Rebecca is okay."

Lillian gave the khakis and the flannel shirt he wore with his casual brown leather jacket a surreptitious glance before she turned to the little kitchenette and lifted a mug from the drying rack. Over the sounds of coffee being poured, she said, "Rebecca knows how to take care of herself. I'm sure she's fine. She's not here, by the way," she added, turning with her cup in hand. Enrobed from neck to ankle in thick white terry cloth, she remained in the doorway between the small rooms. "If she's come back, I imagine she's at her friend Cindy's. Have you tried calling her?"

Of course he had. He just didn't know if she wasn't answering his or Molly's calls on purpose, if she had her cell phone off, or if her battery was dead.

Because he'd known she was friends with Molly, he had called her after he'd listened to the message Rebecca had left him about her call from Jack. He wanted to see if she had seen her before Rebecca had left. She hadn't, though. It had also quickly become apparent that his basketball buddy's wife knew nothing about Russell or what happened with him, which meant Molly had been totally in the dark as to why her neighbor had departed so abruptly.

Since Molly hadn't seen or talked with her, he'd been left knowing only that the bottom had dropped out of Rebecca's world—and that he wasn't anywhere near ready to let her go.

"All calls are going straight to her voice mail." Wanting to leave now that he knew she wasn't there, it was all he could do not to back toward the door. "May I have Cindy's address?"

Lillian seemed to ignore his request. Watching him carefully, she squinted through the steam rising from her cup and took a sip. She didn't look at all disturbed to him. She didn't seem particularly troubled by the fact that her offspring apparently hadn't called her, either. If anything, she appeared to him to be totally lacking in concern of any sort for her daughter.

Or so he was thinking when, still watching him, she lowered her cup.

"Not until I'm sure she didn't come back to get away from you."

For a woman who looked as delicate and fragile as his grandmother's crystal, she clearly didn't pull punches. "What is your relationship with her?"

Pinned by her dark, discerning eyes, he found himself hesitating. He couldn't believe how it relieved him to discover that she actually felt as protective of Rebecca as he did himself. He just wasn't sure how to explain his relationship with her daughter.

Needing this woman's cooperation, he thought about saying they were friends, but they were much more than that. And admitting they were lovers wasn't something he could bring himself to say to her mother.

"I'm just someone…who cares about her," he admitted. "Lots of people in Rosewood do."

"Then why did she leave in such a hurry?"

"It's…complicated."

"Life is." She arched one perfectly shaped eyebrow, curiosity about him competing with maternal concern for her daughter. "I'm not telling you where she is until you tell me what's going on. Were you two dating?"

It was apparent that she believed they'd had some sort of quarrel. It was equally apparent that he was going to have to break Rebecca's confidence if he was going to find her. Not that she had asked him to keep what she'd told him to himself. As it was, he'd said nothing to Molly. But, he knew how much she had worried about her mom's response to having found her dad.

"Do you know why Rebecca went to Rosewood?" he countered, figuring that was the best way to start.

"She said she wanted to try freelancing for a while. I don't know why she couldn't have done that here, but I thought maybe she needed a change of scenery. She'd had a rather...difficult few months," she murmured, apparently referring to the time after Jason broke up with her. "As to why she picked Rosewood, I really have no idea."

The only way to find her was to level with her mom. He saw no way around that. Unfortunately, he saw no way to soften the blow he was about to land, either.

"She went there to find Russell Lever," he finally said—and watched the color leave Lillian's face a moment before she grabbed the cup with her other hand.

Afraid she was about to drop it, he covered the space between them in three long strides and took it from her himself.

"She what?" she asked, her voice little more than a whisper.

Touching her elbow, he nodded toward the couch. Rather than sit on one of its cushions, she sank to its nearest arm.

Joe handed back her cup. "She found an old diary of yours," he explained, half of his focus on her pale features, the other half on the cup for fear she might drop it after all. "Long story short, she traced him to Rosewood. He has a stepson she got to know, but when he...Jack...asked Russell about the two of you..." he explained, only to cut himself off right there.

He had just realized what he was about to say to this woman—and how hurtful it could be to hear that the man whose child she'd borne had denied responsibility for her pregnancy and claimed to barely know her.

Stepping back, he regrouped and put the focus on Rebecca.

"She didn't say much in her message to me," he continued, "other than that he denied being her father. I called Jack myself this morning to find out what all had been said and how Rebecca had seemed to take it. Jack said he thought she was okay. But I know your daughter," he told the woman with the death grip on her cup. "I know how strong she can appear to be. I also know how badly she wanted this and I'm not convinced that she really is all right."

For long moments, the only sounds in the room were the drip of the faucet in the kitchen sink and the muffled clank of radiator pipes. Lillian looked as stunned as she did distressed by what her daughter had done. That was how she sounded, too, when she slowly reached over to set her cup on the coffee table and rose to clasp her arms with her shaking hands.

"I had no idea she'd been looking for her father." Anxiety kept the strength from her voice. "I thought she'd given up that idea years ago." With her consternation, tiny lines appeared in the corners of her eyes. "Russell is in Rosewood?"

"He is. She never did get to see him, though."

"Does the rest of his family live there?"

"I have no idea."

Clearly agitated, she lifted one hand as if to run her fingers through her hair, only to have her fingertips bump the towel wrapped around her head. Clasping her arms again, she turned to face him.

For a moment, she said nothing. She simply studied the rugged lines of his face while seeming to come to grips with whatever it was she now needed to do.

"Will you do something for me?" she asked, seeming to compose herself right before his eyes. "A couple of things, actually."

"If I can."

"Will you give me this Jack's phone number? And,

please, don't tell Rebecca that you've told me why she went to Rosewood. I need to set things straight with her. I just need some time to do it.

"And one other thing," she asked, searching a cluttered desk for a notepad. "Since she's not answering her cell phone, please give me your number. I really do want to talk to her as soon as possible, and I'll need to know where she'll be."

Joe didn't like the idea of keeping things from Rebecca. It seemed to him that she would be relieved to know that her mom was willing to talk to her about her father. But this was between her and her mom. He was an outsider here.

Though not crazy about the feeling, he promised her he would say nothing, then wrote his cell and home numbers and the name of Jack's law firm on the paper she handed him so she could get the number from directory assistance. In turn, she wrote down Cindy's address for him, along with the building access code she'd written in her address book because until five months ago Rebecca had lived in the same building herself. She also wrote out directions to the apartment which took him twenty minutes to reach by car with all the traffic, but would have only taken him five to jog had he realized how relatively close it was. But, then, to him, everything was close in Manhattan.

The only thing that wasn't was a parking space. Finding one three blocks over, he stuffed the meter and hurried through the sea of tourists, businesspeople and shoppers. He felt like a salmon swimming upstream until he turned onto the block the apartment building was on and the pedestrian traffic thinned.

Since all he wanted was to get Rebecca back to Rosewood, he was thinking only of how he might convince her to do that as he entered the gray stone building using the code Lillian had given him and took the elevator to the twelfth floor.

He still wasn't totally sure what he was going to say when he knocked on the door of 12C.

He could hear a television through the heavy wood. Hearing no other sound or movement after a moment, he knocked again, then jammed his hands onto his hips and stood there wondering what he'd do if no one answered.

He had no Plan B. He had contingencies in his practice, his finances and when climbing the occasional mountain because it would have been irresponsible not to, and responsible was something he'd always been. With everything else in his life, he tended to go full steam ahead with whatever it was he wanted or intended to do and simply didn't allow for interference or failures. He always knew exactly what he wanted, and how and when he would obtain or accomplish it.

At least he had before he'd met Rebecca. Since he'd known her, he'd found little things like schedules, timetables and plans constantly changing on him. Since he liked his life orderly, since he liked knowing what to expect next, he would have found that disturbing, too, had he not realized that a guy couldn't plan for someone like her.

Rebecca Peters was nothing like the woman he'd thought he would look for in another year or two. She could barely cook, she had no interest in the outdoors, she knew next to nothing about animals. Yet, for seeming to have so little in common, they could talk about anything. She was strong in many ways, so very vulnerable in others. He liked her sass and her spirit and the way she responded to his touch. He had never wanted a woman the way he wanted her. Never craved the taste or feel of a woman the way he craved her. More than anything else, he had never cared about a woman the way he cared for the one who wasn't answering the door.

He knocked again.

Down the narrow hallway another door opened and a graying head of tightly permed curls popped out. The woman in the flower print housedress was eighty if she was a minute.

"Can I help you, young man?"

"I'm looking for a friend of Cindy's."

"Cindy's not here." Behind her silver-rimmed glasses, her rheumy eyes narrowed in suspicion. In her hand, she held a cast-iron frying pan like the kind his mom used to bake corn bread. "How'd you get inside?"

Thinking the woman must be hard of hearing, he raised his voice a notch. He hadn't said he was looking for Cindy. "Rebecca's mom gave me the code."

"Who's Rebecca?"

"The friend of Cindy's I'm looking for."

"I told you Cindy isn't home. She's gone to her folks."

The thought that the woman might actually intend to use that frying pan on him had just occurred to him when he heard the clatter of dead bolts being thrown. He'd barely turned when the door beside him jerked open.

He didn't have to look down to know Rebecca wasn't wearing heels. But her lack of height and the distress in her pale features were all that registered in the instant before she threw her arms around his neck and clung as if she was hanging on for dear life.

"Hey. Hey," he repeated, moving her back from the door and the prying eyes of the one-woman security force down the hall. With one arm around her shoulders, he closed the door with his free hand. "What is it?"

"I heard your voice." Her hurried words were muffled

against his jacket as her arms tightened even more. "I wasn't going to answer the door, but then I heard your voice and looked through the peephole and it really was you standing there...."

With her still clinging, he smoothed the silky hair at the back of her head. The familiar scent of her shampoo filled his lungs.

"It's okay," he murmured, more relieved than he'd thought possible to finally be holding her.

Beneath his hand, he felt her shake her head.

"No, it's not. It's not," she insisted. She looked up then, only to glance away the moment her troubled blue eyes met his. As if she couldn't believe she'd thrown herself into his arms as she had, she stepped back, hugging herself instead. "Nothing is okay."

She turned away, turned right back. "I'm so confused, Joe." The confession came in a rush. "I thought coming here was the right thing to do. I thought I'd try to get my old job back and find an apartment or a roommate and get at least the good parts of my old life back. But the good parts don't seem to exist anymore.

"I don't care about going out to shop the sales or finding someone to go out with for a drink or dinner or a movie or whatever it was I did before I left here. All I can think about is what a coward I was for leaving without saying goodbye to you, or letting you know how much I'd miss you and Bailey and Rex. I even miss the cats," she confessed, clearly upset by that, too. "I just didn't know what else to do. I don't belong there, but I don't feel like I belong here anymore, either. The worst part is that I have no idea what it is I'm supposed to do now."

Rebecca reached the sofa across from the stand that held the television and a CD player. Picking up the remote, she hit Mute, killing the voices on the movie she hadn't been interested in anyway, and plopped down on the comforter she'd slept under last night.

"Please, ignore me," she begged, shaking her head at herself. "I'm sort of a mess right now."

She hadn't even asked him why he was there. She'd just started dumping on him the moment she'd stepped out of his arms.

It seemed to her that any sane man would have turned and walked out the door. Since Joe remained within three feet of it, for a moment, that was what she was afraid he might do. Instead, he unzipped his jacket and walked over to crouch in front of her.

Picking up her hand, he turned it over in his.

"He didn't reject you as a person, Rebecca. He'd have to know you to do that. What he rejected was the idea of you."

She blinked at his bent head as he traced the heart line in her palm. Anyone else would have addressed the points in her little diatribe. They might have asked why she hadn't thought her plans through before she'd left, or why she was so quick to conclude that she didn't seem to belong much of anywhere. They might have even pointed out that being back in the city less than twenty-four hours was hardly enough time to come to the conclusions she'd drawn.

Joe, though, had gone right to the core of what had caused her to run so far so fast.

There wasn't another person on the planet who would have known what had left her feeling so lost, or whose touch could drain the fight right out of her.

Her voice fell. "It didn't feel like he was rejecting an idea."

CHRISTINE FLYNN   189

"Of course it didn't. It had to feel very personal. But the loss is more his than yours."

Her glance faltered as something seemed to squeeze around all the bruises on her heart.

"Come back with me," he quietly said. "It's almost Thanksgiving. You don't need to be here all by yourself."

With her focus on his strong hands, feeling as if he somehow held her heart in those broad palms, she almost gave him a little nod.

Instead, she murmured, "I need to find out what Mom is doing. She shouldn't be alone, either."

"She already has plans."

Two little lines formed between her eyebrows. "How do you know that?"

"How do you think I found you and got into the building?"

."You called her?"

"I went to her apartment."

"You remembered where it is?"

"Country boys can usually get back to a place once they've been there." He smiled then, relieved to see something other than the sadness that had drained the spirit from her lovely features.

"Come on." Joe rose, pulling her up with him. She had said she'd known even before she'd left that she would miss him. Missing her couldn't begin to describe what he'd felt when he realized she'd gone. But he hadn't questioned the odd mix of panic or possessiveness. Then, as now, nothing seemed more important than making sure she was all right—and getting her back home.

"Let's get out of here. Get dressed and get your things," he coaxed. "You can figure out what to do in Rosewood as easily as you can here.

"You don't have to make any decisions today," he assured her when she hesitated. She had enough to deal with without feeling any pressure from him. "You have friends there waiting to hear from you, anyway."

Chapter Ten

It was late when Rebecca and Joe entered the Turners' house through the garage. Since she had her car, he had followed her back through rush-hour traffic made worse by those trying to get out of town for the long weekend and an accident on the thruway that had backed up traffic for miles. The weather hadn't helped. The rain that had started as they'd left Manhattan had become mixed with sleet an hour south of Rosewood.

Rebecca had regarded the worsening weather as a good news, bad news sort of situation. The bad news was that the slick roads had required all of her concentration. That had been the good news, too. Since she'd had to concentrate so hard on her driving and the traffic around her, she hadn't been able to think about anything else—which meant she still wasn't sure what she was going to do about the sorry state of her life. All she knew for certain was that she wasn't going to think about it as Joe carried in her bags and she dropped the box with her work in it on the table.

She turned on more lights while Joe crossed the family room and flipped the switch on the gas fireplace. With flames leaping over the faux logs to take the chill from the room, she scooped up Magellan as the little silver tabby walked toward her and crouched down to pet Columbus who'd come to rub against her leg.

Joe had said she had friends waiting to hear from her. Thinking these two were who he'd meant, since other than him and Molly she had no real friends there, she found herself smiling at the tops of their furry little heads. It relieved her greatly to see that the cats had survived their night on their own. Not that they seemed to have missed her all that much. Independent as they tended to be, now that they'd had their pat, they were far more interested in curling up in the heat coming from the fireplace.

Joe remained crouched in front of the fire himself. Watching him run his hands over the cats' fur, she couldn't deny how grateful she was that he was with her. He never had said why he'd come after her. She hadn't asked. Once he'd pulled her from Cindy's sofa, they hadn't talked about anything that didn't involve getting her ready to go and getting her things back to her car.

With her cell phone dead, they hadn't been able to communicate during the long drive back, either.

Thinking of the phone in the bottom of her purse reminded her that she needed to call her mother. She had started to call her from the car. That had been when she'd discovered that her phone's battery was even lower than she'd thought when she'd turned it off yesterday to conserve its power. She'd forgotten to take her charger.

"Do you need to leave soon?"

Magellan had practically turned to putty by Joe's booted feet. Flipped over on his back, he'd all but curled his little body around Joe's hand while his vet's fingers massaged his narrow chest.

Watching Joe look up, she saw his half smile for the ball of gray-striped fur fade as his glance skimmed the weary lines of her face.

"I have to get home to let Bailey and Rex out, but I thought I'd stick around awhile…unless you want me to go."

"No! No," she repeated, forcing the urgency from her tone. She had come back because being alone in a friend's apartment with only her thoughts for company had felt so awful. Now that she was there, back in the place she'd felt so desperate to escape, the thought of being alone again was almost more than she could bear.

She didn't want him to know that, though. Considering the way she'd so abruptly disappeared—and the pathetic shape he'd found her in—he already had to think her one of the larger emotional messes he'd ever encountered. The last thing she wanted was to strengthen that conviction by throwing herself back in his arms and begging him not to go.

The need she felt to do just that was huge.

Doing her best to ignore that desire, along with the fatigue now clawing at her, she slipped off her coat. "I need to call Mom," she explained. "I just thought I'd wait to do it if you were leaving."

"Not for a while," he assured her, back to playing with Magellan. "Go ahead and call."

"You said she had plans for tomorrow, but you never said what they were."

He kept his focus on the cat. "It didn't sound like they were solidified yet."

She and her mom hadn't always spent Thanksgiving together. They each usually knew what the other was doing for the day, though. Thinking her mom might be getting together with work associates who didn't have the time or the inclination to join their own families, Rebecca headed for the phone at the far end of the breakfast bar.

Thinking about her mom's plans was infinitely preferable to dwelling on the misplaced feeling that threatened to get the better of her even now. Certain that fatigue was only making the sensation worse, she was trying to ignore it when she noticed the blinking light on the answering machine.

"Maybe she already left a message," she murmured.

"I left you one," she heard Joe say. "I imagine Molly called, too."

With a mental wince, Rebecca punched the play bar on the machine. The hurried message she'd left Molly yesterday probably hadn't made a whole lot of sense.

According to the LED on the machine, the first call had come within minutes of her leaving Tuesday afternoon.

A tone beeped.

"Rebecca, it's Angela. I just want you to know that you don't have to bring a thing for dinner on Thursday. Unless you want to bring olives." A quick laugh came through the speaker. *"With all the kids we'll have here, we can't have too many of those. I figured we'd eat about four, but everyone's coming early to watch the games, so make it two or so if you can. And bring Joe if he can make it. I hear you've been seeing a lot of him."*

Rebecca closed her eyes, rubbed the faint ache brewing behind her forehead. She couldn't believe she'd forgotten Angela's invitation to Thanksgiving dinner. The whole neighborhood would be there.

The tone for the next call sounded.

"Rebecca, it's Marti Vincent," came the recorded voice of her next-door neighbor and owner of Entrée. *"Ed saw you getting gas at the Minit Mart a while ago. He said you looked really upset. I just want to make sure you're all right. Let me know if there's anything I can do for you. We're at the restaurant until midnight. After that you can get me at home."*

From the corner of her eye she saw Joe plant one hand on his thigh. Rising from where he'd remained on the other side of the room, he tossed his jacket over the arm of the sofa and walked toward her as another tone sounded.

"Rebecca, it's Molly. If you're checking messages call me back. I tried your cell phone but you're not answering. Of course, I'll watch the cats, but where have you gone? You sounded awful. I'm worried about you."

Another tone beeped, this one followed by a hang-up, a long dial tone and another message.

"Rebecca, pick up if you're there." Joe's recorded voice held both unease and command. *"Rebecca?"* A moment of silence was followed by what sounded suspiciously like a terse oath. *"You must have already left. I'll try your cell."*

Hearing the open concern in the messages, she looked to where Joe had stopped beside her. He said nothing. He just watched the confusion in her face as another message started to play.

"Hello, Rebecca? I always feel so silly talking to these machines. It's Sylvia Fulton. Across the street. That nice young man you've been seeing? Well, he was over earlier this evening asking if anyone knew where you'd gone. I was just calling to see if you got back. I don't see your

lights on," the voice continued, making it sound as if Sylvia might have been peeking out her curtains, *"so maybe you haven't. Call me when you do, will you, dear? Horace and I just want to make sure you're okay."*

Another tone. Two more hang-ups. Then came an electronic voice that said "End of Messages."

For a moment, the only sounds Rebecca heard were the beat of rain on the windows and the low rush of warm air coming through the heater vents. In that relative silence, she waited for what she'd just heard to sink in.

"I told you you had friends here waiting to hear from you."

She knew he had. But she'd thought he meant the cats. From the moment she'd moved to Danbury Way, it had been apparent that she'd been the neighborhood curiosity. She'd been the girl from the big city who didn't fit in, the novelty—or oddity—who didn't know a Crock-Pot from a cookie exchange and who had been included in her neighbors' functions simply because the people who lived on the little cul-de-sac were too polite to exclude her.

It had never occurred to her that any of them might actually have been watching out for her, or cared about what happened to her when she wasn't there.

"I should call Molly."

"I already called her from my truck to tell her you were on your way back. She said she'd call everyone else and let them know you're all right. The people around here were pretty anxious to make sure you were okay."

Joe had been anxious himself, but not because he'd feared he wouldn't be able to find her. Once it had become clear that she hadn't told anyone where she'd gone, he'd had a strong hunch that her mom would have some idea of where she was staying. His fear had been that she might have lumped him in with all the other men who'd let her down lately and been running from him, too.

The way she'd flown into his arms had pretty much cured that thought. She was holding herself back from him now, though, and looking very much the way she did when she didn't want anyone to know she didn't have everything under control.

The effort would have been a lot more effective had the strain of the past thirty hours not been so evident in her tired features. He had the feeling she hadn't slept much. He knew for a fact that he hadn't.

Needing to touch her, he tucked his hand beneath her hair and curved it around the back of her neck. Once her mom talked to her, things would be better. At least, he hoped they would. Something about Lillian's phrasing when she'd said she needed to explain Russell to Rebecca told him that the matter of Rebecca's father might not be as straightforward as Rebecca seemed to think. He just hoped that whatever it was her mom intended to tell her wouldn't hurt her more.

"She did ask that you call her tomorrow, though," he added, speaking of Molly. "So did Angela."

Drawn by his touch, needing it in ways she didn't care to define, Rebecca moved closer.

It amazed her to know that her neighbors really cared about her. Yet, the thought that had the firmer grip at the moment filled her with a growing sense of unease.

"Did you tell Molly what happened? About Russell, I mean? And Jack?" she added, because she couldn't escape the embarrassment of what had happened with him, too.

Jack not only knew that her ulterior motive for being there had been to find her father, he had been a firsthand witness to how soundly she'd been rejected by him. Even more mortifying was that when Russell had denied being her father, he had made her sound like a gold digger.

Though Jack had sounded terribly sympathetic on the phone, she had to admit it was entirely possible Jack might think her that, too—especially since, from all appearances, she'd gone after him first.

"Stop worrying," Joe said, as if he'd known she was doing just that. "I never mentioned either of them." Looking as protective of her as he sounded just then, he coaxed her forward. "All I told her is that you were having family problems. I figured you could fill in the blanks if you wanted her to know anything else."

Needing that sense of protection he offered, too weary to worry about how badly she craved it just then, she rested her forehead against the soft flannel of his shirt. "Thank you, Joe."

"I figured it wasn't my story to tell."

"Not just for that."

She felt his fingers skim over her hair. "For what, then?"

Rebecca couldn't help the long sigh that escaped when she felt his arms finally come around her. She had always tried hard to never be a clingy, needy, dependent female. She had made it a point to do everything she could to stand on her own, lead with her chin and not let the world know how badly it hurt when she didn't duck fast enough and she wound up with her heart and her self-confidence in shreds.

She hadn't ducked fast enough with Jason.

With her father, it seemed she hadn't ducked at all, and had been knocked totally flat.

She would figure out how to pick herself up somehow. In the meantime, she would let herself lean on this man who'd cared enough to go to her neighbors and her mom when he'd sensed she was in trouble, simply because he made leaning on him so terribly easy to do. She would worry later about whether or not that caring meant to him what it did to her, and about how very much he meant to her himself.

She simply didn't have the energy to do it now.

Swallowing against the tightness in her throat, she finally said, "For bringing me back."

The huskiness that had entered her voice had him tipping up her chin. The moment he did, she ducked her head to hide the brightness of her eyes.

Joe had seen it anyway.

"Hey," he murmured, much as he had when she'd clung to him hours ago. "You don't need to do that."

He was right. She didn't need to cry. All crying would do was plug up her nose and make it red and make her headache even worse.

"Do you know what you do need?" he asked against the top of her head.

"A good shrink?"

A chuckle rumbled low in his chest. "I was thinking more along the lines of sleep."

"Sleep would be good."

"If I leave, you could go to bed."

He felt her go still.

She wanted him to stay. There wasn't a single doubt in his mind. He wanted that himself. He wanted her. Badly. But he couldn't stay and hold her, and she needed that more than she needed for him to take her to bed, make love with her then bolt out the door as if sex was all he'd wanted from her to begin with. And he would have to go. His dogs needed out, he was practically dead on his feet and he had to be up at dawn for the two hour-drive to his parents'.

"I'll see you at Angela's tomorrow."

Confusion shadowed her expression as she finally lifted her head.

"She invited me to dinner, remember? I have to run up to the farm in the morning," he told her, because he wanted her to know where he'd be. "My family always has Thanksgiving dinner around one." He'd thought about taking her with him. But considering all that she was dealing with right now, the last thing she needed was to be thrust into a group of strangers intent on knowing his intentions toward her. Since he was only now suspecting where those intentions were headed and since it was far too soon to act on them, he figured she'd be better off here in Rosewood with friends.

He kissed the spot on her forehead he'd seen her rub a while ago. "I would have driven up this afternoon," he explained, "but I had something else I needed to do."

He'd needed to come after me, she thought.

The realization that he had totally changed his plans for her collided with the disappointment she felt knowing he was leaving. She knew he had to go, though. Bailey and Rex were probably spinning circles at his back door by now. Still, she would have been more grateful for the comfort of his arms when he pulled her to him had she not known that he was about to take that comfort away.

Or so she was thinking when his head lowered to hers.

He kissed her with the ease of an old lover, thoroughly, completely, systematically altering her heart rate and her breathing before robbing most of the strength from her legs. When he had her leaning against him for support, he cupped her face in his hands and drew back his head.

Opening her eyes, she drew a shuddery breath. Her hands had flattened on the hard wall of his chest. Beneath soft flannel, she could feel the strong, steady beat of his heart.

As he eased her back, it helped enormously to know she would see him tomorrow.

"Don't let your mother get you engaged to anyone," she said.

He brushed another kiss to the spot between her eyes. But his only response was a smile before he told her to go to bed, that he would see her at Angela's in time for dinner and headed for the door.

By morning, rain had turned to light snow. A skiff of the fluffy white stuff dusted the streets, lawns and rooftops. According to the weatherman who'd just interrupted Macy's Thanksgiving Day Parade with a weather bulletin, the pristine dusting of white was considerably deeper upstate.

Rebecca loved snow. The first few hours of it, anyway. In the city, that was about how long it took to turn into a mess of gray slush along the edges of the streets and sidewalks. But even though she understood it stayed fresh considerably longer in the suburbs, she prayed the flakes would stop falling.

Joe was headed in that direction himself. He was probably even at his parents' home by now. Considering the snowfall amounts being predicted where he was, it was possible that he wouldn't make it back that day.

She had no business letting herself count on him the way she was beginning to. Just because he'd rescued her from what would undoubtedly have been one of the more miserable weekends of her life, didn't mean that he would want her to think she could always count on him in the future. As she'd reminded herself once before, helping things with a heartbeat was simply what he did. Both for a living and in his spare time. Still, she really wanted him to be with her at Angela's that afternoon. She knew he hadn't said anything to anyone about Russell. But she had no idea what Jack had told Zooey. Or, in turn, what Zooey might have said to anyone else.

The more she thought about seeing Jack that afternoon, the more uneasy she became. Being a lawyer, if Jack considered the bare facts, it was entirely possible for his legal mind to conclude that she was, indeed, the gold digger Russell had concluded her to be. She'd shown up on Danbury Way out of nowhere, and promptly started asking questions about Jack. When she'd gotten nowhere with him, rich, successful attorney that he was, she'd then approached him claiming to be the daughter of his rich, successful stepfather and wanting him to set up a meeting with the man.

She remembered the murmurings that had flown when she'd first moved there, about Zooey having designs on Jack. On its face, her own case looked even more condemning.

Not caring to drive herself crazy wondering what sort of talk could be going around at that very moment, she picked up the phone to do what she'd planned to do in another minute anyway. She needed to return her neighbors' calls.

She would start with Molly. If there was gossip, she would have heard. Aside from that, she needed to let her know she hadn't meant to cause her concern.

"It's just me," Rebecca said the moment her friend answered her phone. "I'm so sorry, Molly. I didn't mean to worry anyone. I guess I didn't think anyone would be worried," she admitted, only to hurry past that. "Everything's okay. Sort of. I mean it will be when I figure some stuff out. But in the meantime," she continued, hurrying past that, too, "thanks for looking in on the cats. I owe you."

"No, you don't. And you're welcome. Joe said you left

because of a family problem." A smile entered her voice. "I know all about those if you need an ear."

"Maybe later…"

"Well, keep me in mind if you need another female's perspective. I know you have Joe for the guys' point of view. By the way, that man is flat-out crazy about you."

"He said that?"

"He didn't have to. You could hear it in his voice. Is he coming with you to Angela's? She said she invited him."

Rebecca's smile faltered as quickly as it had formed. "That depends on the weather. He went to his parents' place upstate for their dinner. I just heard on the news that the snow is coming down pretty hard there."

It seemed Molly heard the disappointment in her voice. Her own turned sympathetic. "It's hard not to be with the people we care about on holidays, isn't it?"

Days ago Rebecca would have done what she always did with Molly and responded by denying that she cared in that sort of way for Joe. She would have insisted that they were friends and let it go at that. Now, already missing him, she heard herself murmur, "Yeah. It is."

She wouldn't be with her mom, either.

The thoughts had her taking a deep breath.

"Well, you know what?" Molly's tone brightened. "You have me and Adam. And Carly and Bo," she added, speaking of the McMansion's residents. "Carly called just a while ago to see what kind of pies I was bringing and asked if I'd talked to you yet. Everyone's looking forward to seeing you this afternoon."

Two things were immediately evident to Rebecca. There didn't appear to be any untoward gossip flying around about her—and she needed to get herself in gear and come up with her contribution to Thanksgiving dinner.

"You baked pies?"

"I just finished. I made pumpkin. Carly's bringing apple and mince."

"Do you know what everyone else is bringing?"

"I think the Vincents are bringing that fabulous mushroom tart they serve at Entrée. And Sylvia said something about a cranberry, orange, raisin chutney. Zooey is baking homemade yeast rolls. I'm not sure what the Abernathys are bringing. Champagne, maybe. But Angela and Megan are doing the turkey and pretty much everything else."

There wasn't a doubt in Rebecca's mind that everyone's contribution would be wonderfully prepared. It also seemed pretty clear from what she'd been asked to bring that her lack of culinary skill had been accepted as fact.

That didn't mean she couldn't bring it nicely presented, though.

Molly suddenly muttered, "Oh, shoot."

"What?"

"I forgot whipping cream."

"Not a problem," Rebecca informed her. Glad to be thinking of something productive, she told her she would pick up some for her since she was on her way to the store herself. The sign in the supermarket's window last week indicated it would be open on Thanksgiving until three o'clock.

She had barely hung up and was wondering how hard it would be to make a pie herself when the electronic ring of the phone cut off the thoroughly uncharacteristic thought.

The caller ID indicated that it was Joe.

"You just saved the neighborhood," she said by way of greeting. "I was actually thinking of baking."

His deep chuckle made her smile.

"You sound better." More like yourself, he might have said. "I just want to make sure you're still going to Angela's."

She felt her smile fade. She hated how automatic it had become to brace herself for disappointment, but she had the feeling she knew what was coming next. He was going to tell her he wouldn't be able to make it back today because of the snow and wanted to make sure she wasn't spending the day alone.

"Rebecca?"

"I'm going," she murmured, knowing she could always leave if it seemed there was awkward talk going around.

"Good. What time?"

"About two." She wandered to the kitchen window. Snow still fell in fits and starts. "How is everything at your parents'?" She couldn't hear any background noise. None of the sounds of loud conversation and laughter she would have expected to hear from the big, boisterous family he had described. Figuring he'd found a place to talk away from the family, she asked, "Did you take Bailey and Rex with you?"

"They're right here."

"Pat them for me?"

"Consider it done."

"You must be getting ready to sit down to dinner pretty soon."

"Actually, they're in there sitting down now. I'm leaving as soon as we're done. I just needed to know for sure where you'd be," he said, explaining the reason for his call. "There's someone who has to talk to you."

"Someone—?"

"I can't tell you anything more than that. It'll all make

sense later. I promise. Look," he said, noise bursting over the line as if a door had been opened. "I have to make another call. I'll see you this afternoon. If you have any change in plans before that, call me."

The connection clicked off. Moving the phone from her ear, Rebecca stood staring at the small instrument, torn between trying to figure out what she'd just heard coming through it and relief that he still planned to be there.

Someone had to talk to her, he'd said. Who? And about what? And who did he have to call so quickly that he couldn't have taken a minute to explain what was going on?

The questions stayed with her. But she was still at a loss for answers when she started down the snow-dusted sidewalk for Angela's house a couple of hours later.

As embarrassing as it would have been to admit it, Rebecca truly had forgotten about Thanksgiving dinner while in the midst of her little mental meltdown. She had, however, had the foresight last week to buy a hostess gift for the occasion. Carrying the large, tissue-wrapped cinnamon-scented candle in a gift bag in one hand, she balanced a cellophane-covered serving dish in the other. The crystal bowl she'd borrowed from the Turners' china cabinet held four cans of drained black olives circled with parsley sprigs and tiny orange kumquats. She'd thought about using the little grape tomatoes she'd seen in the produce department but had decided the red would look too Christmassy. The orange fruit was better for Thanksgiving. She might not be much of a cook, but she wouldn't think of bringing anything that hadn't been properly accessorized.

Glancing down at her chocolate-brown boots, she knocked a bit of snow off their three-inch heels. The odd mix of anxiety and anticipation she'd felt since Joe called had yet to go away.

She'd barely elbowed the doorbell when the front door of Angela's neat New England Colonial swung open. A cacophony of voices and children's laughter greeted her even before Angela's blond-haired, green-eyed sister, Megan, gave her a welcoming smile and tugged her inside.

"Rebecca's here!" she called. "How great this looks," she said, her artist's eye on the olives as she took them and the gift so Rebecca could take off her coat. "The colors will look wonderful on the table."

"Oh, good, you made it." Angela, looking perfect as always, brushed her hands on her apron as she hurried into the entry to give her a hug. "I was so glad when you called this morning to say you were coming.

"Come on back," she continued, hanging Rebecca's coat among the others filling the guest closet. "Everyone who isn't watching the football game in there," she said with a broad motion to the crowd filling her family room, "is in the kitchen." A giggle and a shriek sounded from somewhere upstairs. "The kids," she added drily, "are everywhere. Isn't Joe with you?"

Breathing in the tantalizing aroma of roasting turkey, Rebecca told her he would be there later and followed her past the stairs toward the kitchen. They'd barely rounded the corner into the busy space with its spruce-green and wine-colored wallpaper and birch cabinetry when Sylvia Fulton caught sight of her.

Beneath her gray pouf, her soft wrinkles deepened as her eyes narrowed.

"There you are." Arms outstretched, she looked her over as carefully as she might have her roses for bugs.

"You sounded fine on the phone when you called, but it's good to see that for myself."

Rebecca bent to return the woman's lavender-scented hug. Sylvia was as short and round as her husband, Horace, was tall and thin. The top of her head barely reached Rebecca's chin. "Thanks again for the call the other night. I'm sorry I worried you."

"Well, it just seemed to me that it had to be something awful for you to leave in such a hurry." Keeping one hand on her arm, she stepped back and lowered her voice. "I hope no one died."

"Oh, no," Rebecca rushed to assure her. "It wasn't anything like that."

"Well, that's a relief," came the grandmotherly woman's reply. "I just hate it when that happens around the holidays."

"So do I." Marti Vincent, the trim, redheaded co-owner of Entrée and mom of two of the children who'd just pounded upstairs from the basement, moved in for a hug, too. "But I'll confess it was my first thought when Ed told me about seeing you. He said he knew it had to be something bad because you'd been crying. We heard it was a family problem," she confided as she stepped back. "I hope everything's okay. My sister separated from her husband over Thanksgiving a few years ago and it made it hard for everybody.

"By the way," she continued, making it clear she didn't intend to pry into personal matters as she stepped back to admire her outfit, "that is great." Her approving glance skimmed Rebecca's cocoa jersey turtleneck and calf-length, subtle plaid skirt that picked up the brown of her boots. A wide leather belt and gold earrings were her only accessories. "Ralph?"

Rebecca smiled at the woman who always looked so stylish herself. "Good eye."

"She brought olives! Mommy, can we have some?"

Angela's seven-year-old daughter had spotted the bowl her Aunt Megan had set on the kitchen island. Having heard her announcement, Jack's little Emily and his two-year-old son rushed to join her. Right behind them were the Vincents' kids and Angela's Michael and Anthony.

"You just had carrots and ranch dip. You'll ruin your dinner."

Rebecca wasn't sure which of the women in the room had replied. It was hard to tell over the whoops and cheers that had just gone up in the living room. It seemed everyone was watching out for everyone else's children anyway as Molly shooed the kids from the kitchen and Adam wandered in to replenish empty drinks.

Molly's husband squeezed Rebecca's shoulder on the way by, then walked up behind his wife to slip his arms around her ever-expanding belly. Whatever he murmured in her ear had Molly smiling as she slipped away to hand him four cans from the fridge. Reaching back in, she then handed Rebecca a relish tray with the request that she deliver it to the football fans in the packed family room.

She'd barely glimpsed the comfortably appointed space when she'd been escorted back to the kitchen. Now, with the volume on the television competing with the voices of the armchair coaches filling the inviting space, she noticed that Justin and Sarah Abernathy, who lived next door to Jack and Zooey, were there. She didn't know the thirty-something doctor and nurse well at all, but their smiles were quick. So was Ed Vincent's.

Next to Ed, who was Marti's husband and the other half of Entrée, Sylvia's long, lanky, gray-haired Horace sat grumbling at one of the game's referees. Joining Horace in his disapproval of the call was Carly's hunky new husband, Bo. Carly herself, perched on the arm of Bo's chair with her hand tucked in his, was chatting quite amiably with Greg, her ex-husband, and with Megan, the pretty graphic artist everyone just knew he would soon ask to marry him. Megan had rejoined them after letting Rebecca in.

Angela's little sister had clearly blossomed in her deepening relationship with Greg and it was good to see Carly and Megan speaking again. But Rebecca wasn't allowed long to marvel at their sophisticated civility with each other. She had no sooner received everyone's quick thanks for the snacks and quicker smiles to see her there, than Molly reappeared to tug her back into the kitchen and the conversation that had resumed about what all had gone into Sylvia's chutney.

Standing in the midst of the women gathered between the sink and the island, having been welcomed and worried over as if she'd been one of them forever, she realized that these ladies really were her friends. Their lives with their clubs and their kids were still a little mysterious to her, and she couldn't imagine ever getting as concerned as some of them did over the health of their holly bushes, but they cared about her. Pulling over a stool for Sylvia to sit on, since she knew her knees occasionally bothered her, she realized she really cared about them, too.

That was why it felt so important to approach the one person who had hung back from her ever since she'd arrived.

She'd seen Zooey the moment she'd entered the bustling kitchen with its bubbling pots and food-laden counters. But Jack's willowy, auburn-haired nanny had said nothing to her. She'd just given her a quick, almost guarded smile before taking the smaller children and slipping into the dining room. She had come with Jack's kids, but Rebecca hadn't seen Jack anywhere.

Slipping into the dining room herself, Rebecca spotted her, kneeling by a child-sized, pastel pink table set apart from the beautifully laid long one, coloring with the girls and Jack Jr.

"Hi," she murmured, lowering herself to one of the children's short chairs.

Zooey barely met her eyes before looking back to the coloring book. "Hi," was all she said.

Zooey was a few years younger than Rebecca, softer edged, definitely more domestic. But Rebecca strongly suspected she possessed a definite mind of her own. It seemed to her, too, that Zooey had always been a little wary of her. But, then, a woman tended to be that way with someone she thought had designs on the man she'd fallen in love with herself.

"I noticed that Jack isn't here." She picked up a crayon, set it back down. Uncomfortable herself with discussing what she'd only talked about with Joe, she offered a small smile. "Did he tell you I went to see him at his office the other day?"

"He did," she quietly replied.

When nothing else helpful was forthcoming, Rebecca took a deep breath and tried again. The little girls giggled about the glitter pen hearts they'd just put on the backs of their hands.

"He told you about why I came here?"

"And about what Russell said," she offered, her voice low, her tone confidential. "I haven't said anything to anyone else, though. He asked me not to yet."

Yet? Rebecca thought, as Zooey's glance shifted away once more.

Jack's girlfriend couldn't seem to maintain eye contact with her. Uneasy about why that might be, but appreciating her discretion nonetheless, she pressed on.

"Is that why he's not here? Because I make him uncomfortable?"

Zooey's smile came softly as the little boy beside her nudged her back to snuggle into her lap. Threading her fingers through his silky brown hair, she kept her focus on him. "He's not here because he's picking up someone from the train station. He'll be here in a while."

That didn't exactly answer all of her questions, but it would have to do, Rebecca supposed. The pretty woman the kids clearly adored sounded kind enough, but she couldn't have been more evasive had she tried.

Emily glanced up from her coloring. Shoving her blond hair back from her eyes, she offered her nanny a look of pure hope. "Can I have an olive now?"

Beside her, Olivia's head popped up. "Me, too?"

"And me?" asked little Jack.

Seeming grateful for the interruption, Zooey grinned. "I think we can probably manage a few. But Rebecca brought them. I think she should help."

"Help?" Rebecca asked.

"With the olives. You know how kids like to eat them, don't you?"

At a loss, Rebecca could only shake her head.

Looking at her in disbelief, or maybe it was sympathy, Zooey whipped the two-year old up into her arms as she rose.

"Come on, girls. Bring Rebecca."

Rebecca didn't know what confused her more just then. That help of some sort was required with an olive, or that

Zooey, as reserved and reticent as she'd just so clearly been, had just graciously included her in whatever it was she was about to do.

Emily grabbed one of her hands. A beaming Olivia took the other.

Two minutes later, the two little girls were walking through the house, eating olives off the tips of all ten of their fingers. Having been informed that the little ones did better with only one at time, Rebecca was crouched on the kitchen floor with Jack Jr. sticking another olive on his outstretched index finger when she looked up to see Joe smiling at her.

Someone had already taken his jacket. Above the collar of his deep blue sweater, deeper blue eyes held hers.

His husky voice held a smile. "You look good doing that."

Chapter Eleven

Joe's glance shifted from Jack Jr. back to where Rebecca knelt in front of the attentive toddler. His expression was totally unfamiliar to her. In his undeniably handsome features, she saw what looked like affection—and acceptance. Yet, the combination was one she didn't understand at all. She just knew without a doubt that she'd never seen that particular look on a man's face before. At least, not a man looking at her.

With her heart beating a little too fast, she stuck one last olive on the little boy's other index finger, smoothed back his soft hair and rose beside the bowl on the island.

Behind her, pots clattered and an electric mixer whirred. The game roared on in the other room.

With all the noise, she hadn't heard him come in. For a few precious seconds, neither had the other women chattering away behind her.

"You're earlier than I thought you'd be," she said when what she wanted to say was how terribly glad she was that he was there. As accepted as she had been beginning to feel with her neighbors, even with Zooey acting so oddly, she hadn't felt anything resembling true ease until she saw him.

"The plows were out."

Still smiling, he stepped closer and touched his hand to her waist.

Her breath stalled. But just when she thought he was actually going to kiss her right there in front of everyone, she heard Molly say, "Joe! You made it!"

Angela whirled around from her spot by the corner sink. "Good to see you, Joe. Glad you're here." Her glance bounced past the women busy at the counters to the oven and the pots on the stove. "Everything is just about ready. As soon as Jack gets here, we'll put dinner on the table."

Apparently knowing better than to enter the kitchen during the final preparation stage, Adam poked his head around the corner. "Hey, Joe. Last down and ten seconds to go."

Joe's broad hand slid from her waist. "I'm on my way."

"Wait!" Grabbing his wrist, Rebecca tugged him back. With her head inches from his, breathing in the scents of fresh air and spice clinging to him, she dropped her tone to a whisper. "When you called you said someone wanted to talk to me." Her eyes searched his. "Who?"

"Not now," he murmured, moving toward the doorway.

"Why not now?" she whispered, moving right with him.

Clearly evading her, he followed his basketball buddy around the corner. "Because there's only ten seconds left in the game."

"You weren't even watching it!"

He gave her his heart-stopping grin.

"Send Megan back in here, will you?" Angela called after the men.

"Will do," came Adam's reply.

Rebecca opened her mouth, promptly closed it again. Her need to know what was going on with him had just lost out to a football game. She hadn't even had a chance to ask where this person who wanted to talk to her was, or if they were there even now.

Zooey didn't seem to be the only one acting oddly. With the strangely certain feeling that Joe had been as interested in avoiding her question as he was watching the end of a game he hadn't even seen, she turned around to see Angela with her head in the fridge.

"It's like a chase scene in a movie," Marti explained from where she pulled a casserole of yams from the oven. "Certain males don't have to have a clue what a show is about to turn into a pillar of salt at the sight of speeding cars on a television. It's the same principle with sports."

"So it doesn't matter that he's missed three hours of the game?"

Angela turned from the fridge. "Not in the least. And by the way," she said, her voice dropping to nearly a whisper. "I don't blame you for changing your mind."

"Changing my mind?" she asked as Sylvia handed Marti another pot holder.

"About swearing off of men." She nodded toward the doorway. "That one anyway." She clearly remembered their conversation at the park the afternoon Joe had drawn out her still-unhappy son. Giving her an approving smile, she held out a bunch of parsley. "How about garnishing the cranberry sauce? And the mashed potatoes when they're ready?"

Garnishing was easier to handle than the fact that she had so obviously neglected her oath to herself. Yet, she couldn't make herself worry just then about how completely Joe had slipped past her guard. As she put her curiosity about who needed to talk to her on simmer and joined the preparations, what struck her most was how his arrival had only added to the wonderful chaos surrounding her.

Listening to his deep voice mingle with the other men's, she could still feel the warmth with which he'd been welcomed. That warmth seemed to infuse the house right along with the wonderful aromas that had the kids wandering in and out wanting to know how long it would be before they could eat.

She felt a tug on her skirt. Glancing down from where she washed parsley at the sink, she saw Jack Jr. smile at her as he held up his index finger.

Knowing what he wanted, she called over her shoulder as she turned off the water, "Can he have one more, Zooey?"

"One," came the reply from across the room.

Bending down, she tucked an olive into place, received a grin in return, and watched the child wander over to show his nanny.

This must be what real family feels like, she thought, returning to her task. This must be what "home" feels like.

The thought brought a smile. Two days ago, she never would have imagined feeling what she did at the moment. And at that moment, she could almost imagine that she actually was home. That these friends were her family. That this was where she belonged.

If Joe hadn't brought her back, she would never have experienced that rich, incredibly foreign feeling. It didn't even matter just then that she would wake up in the morning and the feeling could be gone. For now, it was real. No matter what else happened between her and Joe, she needed to thank him for allowing her that.

"Jack is here!"

The announcement from the foyer had Zooey excusing herself to hurry off with Jack Jr., still chewing, to greet him. It also resurrected a hint of the unease Rebecca had arrived with. At the very least, she needed to take Jack aside and thank him in person for talking to his stepfather for her, though thinking about what had happened with Russell was the last thing she wanted to do just then.

His arrival also put last-minute preparations into overdrive.

To accommodate the two dozen people there, another long table was set up in the foyer for the children and quickly laid with a tablecloth, flowers and plates that Angela had put aside in the laundry room.

Cold dishes were carried in and placed on the buffet in the dining room. The hot dishes followed. With the game over, the volume on the television went down, but the decibel level in the dining room and the foyer that opened to it rose considerably as chairs were pulled back and everyone gathered around the heavily laden tables.

Angela, as usual, had outdone herself. Silver and crystal sparkled. Her centerpiece of fall flowers and candles was a work of art. The golden-brown turkey looked like something off a magazine cover.

Unable to imagine how the woman managed to do everything she did so well, Rebecca watched her carry in the turkey on its nicely garnished platter to a chorus of compliments and appreciative murmurs. With her own tasks complete, she took the chair Joe held for her beside his at the far end of the table. Jack and Zooey were on the other side at the opposite end. As busy as she'd been, she hadn't talked to Jack at all since he'd arrived. Now, he just gave her a strange little smile, gave Joe a short nod and turned to the conversation across from him.

She barely had a chance to wonder at that odd little exchange before Angela straightened at the head of the table and lifted her glass of champagne to propose a toast.

With the little girls trying not to fidget and the little boys eyeing the drumsticks, she thanked them for being such great neighbors, thanked everyone for contributing to the celebration and wished them all blessings, health and happiness.

Murmurs rose as the wishes were returned and glasses of champagne, sparkling cider and milk clinked around the tables. The bright sound was joined by young male laughter as the boys clinked a little too hard and the scrape of chair legs as Greg stood up and cleared his throat.

"As long as we're toasting," he began, with a smile for the pretty blond woman at his side, "Megan and I have an announcement." Without taking his eyes off of her he said, "We're getting married."

For a split second, it seemed as if all the adults went still. Everyone had suspected this engagement was coming, and the divorced Greg and Carly had been beyond civil lately in social situations. Yet, as Carly leaned forward it seemed as if everyone held a collective breath.

Looking from her wealthy and handsome ex-husband to the formerly plain-looking woman who had once been her good friend, she lifted her glass. With the good-hearted and gorgeous love of her life beside her, her eyes sparkled with what looked like genuine understanding.

"Congratulations. Both of you. I hope you'll be happy forever."

Smiles broke out. "So do we," said Molly as the ring of crystal sounded once more.

"Us, too," echoed the Abernathys.

"Well done," said Ed even as everyone started talking over each other.

"Have you set a date?"

"Where's the wedding going to be?"

"New Year's Eve," Megan replied. "And we're not sure yet."

"Oh, that's so perfect. What a way to start the New Year."

"Your ring," Sylvia said. "Let us see your ring, dear."

Megan curled her fingers in her lap. "We haven't picked one out yet."

Greg covered his hand with hers. "We've been too busy to really look. Maybe this weekend."

"Then here's to finding a ring," Adam said, and glasses clinked all over again as more congratulations flowed.

Rebecca joined in, but as pleased as she was for Megan, she couldn't help the tug of empathy she felt for the woman's sister. Angela sat smiling and toasting right along with everyone else. Rebecca didn't doubt for a moment that the single mom of three was truly pleased that her sister had found someone to love who loved her back. But there was resignation in her smile, the sort of unwanted acceptance a woman feels when everyone around her is finding that special someone—except her.

Intimately familiar with the feeling, Rebecca glanced from all that brave strength to the man quietly watching her.

As odd as it seemed, she didn't feel that awful resignation herself just then. With Joe there, it was almost as if she could truly appreciate what it was that Megan felt with Greg, what Molly must feel with Adam, Carly with Bo, and Zooey with her Jack.

Like Angela, those women could cope well enough on their own, but with the guys they loved, they were just more…complete.

Complete was how she felt sitting there with Joe. It was how she'd felt when he'd arrived and she'd looked up to see him smiling at her.

The realization had her going stock-still. She had never felt that way with another man in her entire life.

She also realized that she needed to pay attention to what she was doing as someone handed her a bowl of fruit salad.

She had no idea what Joe had seen in her expression, but a faint frown creased his forehead as she hurriedly looked away and he leaned toward her.

"Are you okay?" he whispered.

Keeping her focus on the salad, she took a spoonful and passed it to him. "Of course," she murmured, though her smile was for Horace as he passed her a vegetable.

She was falling in love with Joe. She felt fairly certain that wasn't the sort of thing a woman tended to realize between fruit salad and creamed onions, but she knew without a doubt that what she felt for this man went light-years beyond physical attraction and friendship.

As the mashed potatoes came toward her, it seemed the most important thing just then was to keep smiling and passing dishes. He didn't have to know. If she played it cool he didn't even have to suspect. The last thing she wanted was to scare him off. Or, herself, for that matter. Backing away before she could get burned had been part of what she'd been doing when she'd run back to Manhattan the other day.

She handed over the dressing, accepted the basket of hot rolls. Her biggest problem at the moment was that Joe could read her better than anyone else she knew—which was why she spent a good portion of the fabulous meal visiting with Horace about his new snowblower, a conversation Joe understood, but she really didn't, and why she insisted he join the men for the other football game someone had turned on while she helped cut pie.

She'd had enough upheaval in the past couple of days. All she wanted was to enjoy the rest of the lovely day without another emotional complication. In the overall scheme of things, it didn't seem like that was too much to ask.

Or so she was thinking when the doorbell chimed.

"Rebecca?" she heard Angela call from the foyer. "Someone's here to see you."

If her mom had planned to surprise her, Rebecca thought, she had certainly succeeded. Lillian rarely showed up unannounced. She was also not at all the sort to indulge in spontaneous visits to her only child.

Hurrying from the kitchen, Rebecca saw her with Angela by the closed front door. Her mom looked terrific as always. Her short bob with its intricate weave of caramels and browns to hide the gray looked perfect. The belted camel-hair coat she wore over her black sweater and slacks made her waist look impossibly tiny. One look at her mother's oddly uncertain smile, though, and she knew her mother hadn't arrived simply to share the holiday.

"You won't be imposing," she heard Angela say as she joined them. "It's Thanksgiving. Please, come have dessert with us."

Lillian spoke with apology in her tone. "I really don't

want to intrude. I know my timing is terrible, but I just need a few minutes to talk with my daughter. Rebecca," her mother said, seeming as relieved as she did excited to see her. Leaning forward, she gave her a quick hug. "I hate to take you away from your friends, but would you come with me, please?"

"Where?"

"Across the street," she replied, motioning vaguely behind her. "To Jack's house."

Though Angela now looked curious herself, she continued to be the perfect hostess. "Come back when you're through. And tell your mother she won't be imposing," she graciously insisted, reaching into the closet. "We have more than enough for everyone."

Rebecca nodded even as she looked back to her mom. "To Jack's?" Suddenly uneasy, not totally sure why, she waited for her mom to answer as Angela headed back to her preparations. "What's going on?"

Her mom didn't reply. Instead her glance shifted over Rebecca's shoulder.

"Hello, Joe."

As Angela headed back to the kitchen, Rebecca felt Joe's hand touch the small of her back. "Hi, Lillian. Good to see you again. Just go," Rebecca heard him quietly coax her, helping her with the coat Angela had just handed him. He turned her to face him. After tugging her lapels together, he jammed his hands into his pockets. "I'll see you in a while."

Rebecca had no idea what to make of the encouraging look he gave her. Or of the odd combination of discomfort and anticipation in her mother's expression as Lillian opened the door and freezing air rushed inside.

Before Rebecca could say another word, Joe had

nudged her out the door. Her mom was already off the porch and down the single step to the curving walkway.

"Mother." Her unease increased by the instant. Her breath came in white puffs. "How do you know Jack?"

"I'll explain everything in a minute."

"Can't you start now?"

"I think you'll want to sit down," she said, picking her way across the tire tracks cut through the scant inch of snow.

Rebecca picked her way right behind her. "I don't need to sit down."

The anticipation she'd seen in her mother's expression was no longer there. Catching up with her, all that she saw now was the anxiety.

"Maybe I do," Lillian said and gave her a look that begged for a little patience as she moved up the walkway of the house directly across the street from Angela's.

She knew Jack and Zooey weren't home. She'd left Zooey cutting pie. On her way from the kitchen herself, she'd glimpsed Jack with his son on his shoulders in the living room watching the game. Because of that, she was wondering who would answer the door even as her mom reached for the latch and opened it herself.

Without a word, Lillian walked in, motioned her in behind her and closed the door to take off her wrap.

"You can leave your coat here," she said, laying her own beside a man's overcoat on the parson's bench.

Rebecca hadn't bothered to button her coat. She didn't bother to take it off now, either.

Her mom had already entered the tidy, expensively furnished living room off the entry. Rebecca barely noticed the nicely appointed surroundings, though. Her attention was on the woman who'd stopped in the middle of the room.

Following as far as the sofa, Rebecca watched her mom

cross her arms protectively over the thin bronze-colored stripes in her black sweater.

"I had no idea you were still looking for your father," she began, sounding very much as if she'd needed to get this over with. "I'm not sure why I thought that," she continued, with a nervous little smile. "Until these past months when your drive seemed to disappear, I'd never known you to give up easily on much of anything. I guess it just had been so long since you'd asked about him that I thought you'd forgotten about wanting to know who he is."

Regarding Rebecca carefully, she moved straight to her point. "I understand you found Russell Lever."

Her mom was right. She did need to sit. Since she was standing by the sofa, she sank onto its nearest cushion.

"Joe told me you'd found my diary. Don't be upset with him," her mom hurried to insist. "When he came looking for you the other day, I wouldn't tell him where you were until he told me why it was so important that he find you. He mentioned some of what happened with you and Russell, and I got the expanded version out of Jack. But, Rebecca…"

She paused as she walked over to where Rebecca sat all but holding her breath. Sitting down beside her, seeming uncharacteristically hesitant, Lillian pushed back Rebecca's hair much the way she had when her daughter had been a little girl.

"…Russell Lever isn't your father."

The air seemed to stick in Rebecca's lungs before it escaped in a rush of disbelief and confusion. For a moment, all she could do was stare at the woman who slowly pulled her hands back to clasp them tightly in her lap. She had been so certain of who Russell was. So certain that he had been lying when he'd denied the possibility of being her father.

"But in your diary," she began, searching her mother's dark eyes. "You sounded so…so in love with him."

"I was," she said simply. "At least I thought so at the time. He was one of those guys every girl was nuts about," she explained, her focus now on the diamond right-hand ring she'd bought herself. "He was the cliché. Literally, tall, dark and handsome. It's been a long time, but I guess I ate up his attention because I wanted so badly to believe I was different from all his other girl-friends. He didn't treat his women very well, though," she mused. "Looking back, that's easy to see. At the time, I probably just took his on-again, off-again interest as more of a challenge."

Russell wasn't her father.

The words seemed to echo inside Rebecca's head even as her mom spoke. After all these months of believing with such conviction that he was, even after having him deny it himself, even hearing her mother deny it now, the reality didn't seem to want to sink in.

"But Jack even said I look like him."

She didn't know if Jack had mentioned that to her mother or not. Her mother, however, didn't appear to think the observation particularly extraordinary.

With a quick glance from Rebecca's blue eyes to the small cleft in her chin, she went back to twisting her ring.

"There's a reason for that," she hurried on before Rebecca could even begin to imagine what that reason might be. "I was supposed to meet Russ at a party. He didn't show up, but I ran into his younger brother there. He was a student at Columbia, too," she explained. "Anyway, Randall didn't know I was dating his brother and I didn't tell him because I was feeling so lousy about having been stood up. We had a nice time, though. He even asked to walk me home. He asked me out the next night, too." She gave a small shrug. "I went because he was nice and because I liked the way he treated me, I guess. I can't honestly tell you what I was thinking then," she admitted, as if the years had erased that part of her memory. "All I know is that one thing led to another...."

"It was one night," she finally said, not looking terribly comfortable describing such details to her daughter. "But when Randall found out I had a thing for Russell, he said he wasn't about to be a substitute for his brother and broke off with me. As Joe says, 'long story short,' a few weeks later I discovered I was pregnant.

"I wasn't seeing either of them by then," she admitted, still twisting her fingers, "but I was so torn between my feelings for both of them that I didn't say anything to Randall. When he left at the end of the term, I decided I'd just keep you and raise you by myself."

She let her words trail off as she slowly shook her short bob. Even as she did, what she was saying slowly sank into Rebecca's head.

"Then Russell's brother is my father?"

"Randall. He is." Looking hugely relieved to have all that out, she finally smiled. "I'd never told him about you until last night. Joe gave me Jack's number and Jack gave me Randall's," she hurried to explain. "He's an attorney in New Haven. Corporate." Animation crept into her tone. "He was married for years, but never had any children with his ex-wife. She didn't...well, we don't need to go into that," she said, with a quick wave of her hand. "The thing is that we talked for hours."

Her father knew about her.

The thought had barely registered when her mom's smile turned cautious. "Would you like to meet him?"

"Of course, I would."

"Good," she said, letting out a breath. "He wants to meet you, too." Giving her daughter's hand a pat, she rose smoothing the front of her slacks. "Stay right here."

"Where are you going?"

"To get him."

"He's here?"

"He's waiting in Jack's den. We wanted us to see each other before I talked to you, so he met me this morning and we came up on the train together. Jack picked us up at the station a while ago."

She hesitated, turned back. "I know Thanksgiving probably wasn't the best time to tell you all this, but I knew you were upset about what happened with Russell. I couldn't let you think what you were thinking," she explained. "That's why I wanted to clear things up as soon as possible." Her smile begged forgiveness on a number of levels. "I called Joe to find out where you'd be this afternoon. Since he said you'd be right across the street from Jack's house, this seemed like the most logical place for his uncle to meet you. We didn't want to interrupt the dinner, so he called after you'd all finished eating."

"Joe did?"

"Jack. They both seem like awfully nice young men." A knowing light entered her eyes. "But I think I'm rather partial to Joe. I like the way he worried about you."

Randall Lever was actually Jack's stepuncle, but Rebecca didn't much care about technicalities just then. As she listened to the fading tap of her mom's heels on the entry floor and caught the murmurings of a quick, quiet conversation moments later, she was too busy thinking she'd waited all her life for this moment—and that Joe had made it happen. If he hadn't gone after her. If he hadn't talked to Jack and to her mother…

Her thoughts trailed off like smoke in a breeze. Her mom had just walked back in, a step behind a tall, dark-haired gentleman with gray at his temples and a look of guarded anticipation in his distinguished-looking features. The cleft in his chin was pronounced. So were the vertical lines bracketing his mouth and the character lines that deepened around his blue eyes as he smiled.

"You're as beautiful as your mother."

All Rebecca could think to say was, "Thank you," as she stared at the man whose genes she shared.

He made no effort to reach for her. It was almost as if he didn't know if his hug would be welcome or, maybe, as if he didn't want to invade her space. As it was, Rebecca didn't move herself. Her visions of her reunion with her father had changed drastically in the past few months. But she had been preparing herself to meet a totally different man.

Now, she didn't have any idea what to expect, or what feelings should have taken hold right about then. If she felt anything, it was slightly…numb.

This man was a stranger to her. He was as good as a stranger to the woman beside him, too. It seemed clear, though, as Lillian moved to form a triangle of the three of them that her father and her mother had, indeed, spent some time discovering what had transpired in all their lives over the past twenty-nine years.

"I understand you wanted to play the violin."

As icebreakers went, that one caught her totally off guard. She hadn't thought of that fleeting obsession since she was thirteen years old. One of the Souder girls had taken lessons for years and she'd ached to be anywhere near as good. "I did. But I'm tone-deaf."

"I am, too," he admitted, trying not to be too obvious about studying her. "Only what I wanted to play was the electric guitar. I'm sorry about that," he confided, as if apologizing for passing on that particular trait. Her mom had perfect pitch. "I understand you're quite the artist, though."

"I wouldn't go that far."

"You're brilliant," her mom insisted. "You should see her sketches from her old design classes," she said to the man beside her. "I told you her professors thought she should try couture, but she loved writing."

"My sister...your aunt," he clarified, "shows her work in several galleries. You might enjoy meeting her sometime."

She had an aunt who was an artist. Randall dabbled a bit himself, he admitted, though she had the feeling he was far more talented than he let on. It seemed he hadn't known that her mom's drawing abilities were limited to stick figures, but it was clear as he moved the conversation from Rebecca's childhood to what she was doing with her life now that he was the most at ease of the three of them.

Since she wasn't totally sure what she was doing with her life at the moment, beyond remaining in her career field, she was about to turn the question back on him to find out what his life was like when the front door opened and Jack stepped inside.

He stopped the moment he saw them all standing just inside his living room. In the space of a second, his glance had bounced to all three of them.

"I'm sorry." The way he grimaced made it clear he hadn't expected them to be standing right there. "Little Jack spilled milk down the front of his shirt. I just need to grab another one."

"Not a problem," his uncle informed him, his smile quick and easygoing.

Jack's curiosity seemed to get the better of him. "Is everything okay?"

"Never better."

"In that case," he said, looking relieved, "Angela wanted me to remind you that you're all welcome for dessert. For what it's worth, all anyone over there knows is that Rebecca's mom arrived a while ago and that my uncle is here."

Having assured them that the Schumacher house wasn't buzzing about them—and that no one need know anything more than that today—Jack looked straight at Lillian.

"She wants you to know you will not be imposing," he told her. To his uncle he said, "The people there are friends from the neighborhood. I think you'll like them."

Though he appeared at ease, Randall seemed quite willing to give them all a little more breathing room. "If you're sure it wouldn't be a problem, then, by all means," he said. "What do you think, Lillian? Do you feel like celebrating what's left of Thanksgiving?"

Her mother's smile seemed to be answer enough.

"Rebecca?" Randall asked her. "Do you mind if we come?"

Having her mom and dad with her on Thanksgiving felt a little surreal. But no more so, she supposed, than the thoroughly unsettling knowledge that she was in love with the man who had made that circumstance possible.

"Heavens no." It was no wonder Joe had been so evasive. And Zooey. She'd undoubtedly known what was going on, too. "I'll get your coats."

"Just FYI," Jack whispered to her as they followed Lillian and Randall through the snow and tire tracks two minutes later. "Russell would never have asked anyone else what they wanted to do. He'd have just done whatever it was he wanted. Randall is a great guy. You definitely got the better deal."

Chapter Twelve

Rebecca stood with her arms crossed over her sweater at one of the windows in Joe's family room. The light snow that had fallen Thanksgiving weekend had disappeared, but the heavy slate-gray sky held the promise of a more serious dusting as she watched her mom and Randall in the distance.

The two of them were walking past the skeletal trees at the back of Joe's property. Her mom carried a bag in one hand, presumably the pinecones they'd gone to collect from the pine grove. Randall carried fir boughs for the fireplace mantel. They weren't touching, but they weren't walking very far apart, either.

In the week since she had met her father, she had talked to him twice on the phone. Once when he had called to ask if he could come to Rosewood to take her to dinner so they could get to know each other a little better. And a second time when he called yesterday to mention that her mom was coming, too, and asked that she be added to the dinner reservation.

They had come up a couple of hours ago on the train—and immediately become part of her date with Joe. It hadn't been planned that way. It had just happened when her mom had learned that Joe had asked her a couple of days ago to help him pick out a tree that morning. Lillian had insisted that they not change their plans just because she and Randall had arrived early. But when Joe had come to pick up Rebecca and her mom had rather shamelessly mentioned that she hadn't picked out a Christmas tree in years, he'd seemed to think nothing of asking them to come with them. He had even agreed to go to dinner that evening when Randall had asked him to join them, which meant Rebecca had called Entrée again to change the reservation to a party of four.

She smiled to herself. She was looking forward to that. She'd wanted to get him to Entrée for weeks.

Behind her, the fire leaping in the fireplace radiated warmth. The scent of pine from the tree they had all picked out at the Community Center's tree lot filled the room. Beside her, Bailey stood with his paws on the windowsill, looking outside with her as she skimmed her hand over his head. Bouncy little Rex was off with Joe trying to find tree ornaments in the garage.

She loved being with them all again. With Joe especially.

Until a couple of hours ago, she hadn't seen him since he had walked her back to her house with her mom and Randall Thanksgiving evening. He'd told her when she'd asked him to come in with them that she didn't need him around right now, that she should spend the time with her dad and her mom, and that he would catch up with her later.

She'd wanted to believe he was just being his usual, thoughtful self. But, considering that she hadn't heard from him until a couple of days ago, she wasn't really sure if he'd been giving her space, or if he'd needed space himself.

Something was set on the floor, the sound muffled by the carpet. A heartbeat later, she felt Joe move toward her.

Taking Bailey's place when the big German shepherd headed off to sniff the boxes he'd brought in, Joe stopped beside her.

"They look comfortable together," he said, his hands in his pockets, his eyes on her parents.

"They do, don't they?" Randall and her mom seemed to be laughing together now. "I get the feeling they really like each other."

She had never seen her mom look as happy as she had when she'd arrived a while ago. Something actually seemed to be happening between her and the man she'd once known so briefly. Something…special. And after all this time.

"I can't thank you enough for what you did," she murmured, still marveling that she had actually, finally, met her birth father. She couldn't believe she'd spent all that time looking for the wrong man, or that her father actually wanted to be part of her life, or that he was there, with her mom, at that very moment.

"You don't have to thank me at all."

"Of course, I do. If it weren't for you, we wouldn't all be here right now."

From the corner of her eye, she saw him lift his hand. Catching her chin, he turned her face to his.

In his beautifully carved features, she saw the same quiet watchfulness that had been there for the past couple of hours.

"How are you doing with all of this?"

She gave him a nod, added a smile. It was so like him

to cut to the heart of what mattered. "I think it's all finally started to sink in."

"You're okay with him then?"

She didn't need to ask what he meant. This man whose calming touch she'd ached for all week knew how she worried about the sort of person Russell seemed to be. Randall, though, appeared to be exactly what Jack had said he was. A genuinely nice guy.

"I'm okay with him," she confirmed.

"What about with him and your mom?" As his hand fell, he nodded toward the couple beyond the window. Lillian and Randall were now holding hands. "How do you feel about that?"

"I don't know," she admitted, wishing Joe would slip his arm around her. It felt like forever since he'd held her. "It would be incredibly romantic if they got together, but only if that's what's best for my mom."

"That's very adult."

"After last week, I'm trying to be." She met the teasing in his eyes with a wry smile. "I'd hate for you to think I melt down that way on a regular basis."

She mentally winced. She hadn't meant to bring that up. She had, in fact, hoped he'd forgotten about the shape he'd found her in at Cindy's apartment.

It appeared that he had not.

"That brings me to my next question." With his hands in his pockets once more, he looked almost as casual as he sounded. Almost. "Have you thought any more about what you want to do? About whether you want to stay here," he clarified, "or go back?"

The feeling of calm she'd had simply standing beside him slowly slid into oblivion. Of all the things he might have mentioned, she really hated that he'd chosen to bring that up. Especially now.

She took a step back, turned toward the room with its sophisticated electronics, green sofa and blank white walls.

Until that moment, she had been doing what Joe had once told her animals do. The creatures he tended and cared for didn't know *future*. They only knew the *past* and *now*. So ever since Thanksgiving when she'd stood in Angela's kitchen and felt the sense of belonging and family that had so eluded her, when she'd realized she was totally, completely in love with Joe, when she'd met her birth father, she had been living minute to minute and letting herself absorb all the new and unfamiliar feelings the past week had brought.

She'd hope to hold on to that for just a little longer.

"I thought we were going to decorate your tree."

"We will when Randall and Lillian get back. Right now," he said, looking far too serious for her, "I think we need to talk."

She didn't care for the sound of that at all. She especially didn't care for the sense of foreboding the ominous phrase brought. It had been her experience that, *We need to talk,* rarely led to anything good.

"Joe, please. Let's not do this right now. It's a nice day. Let's not ruin it."

He'd put the decorations they'd bought for his pets' photo shoot into a cardboard box. That box now sat with another a few yards from the fireplace beside the bare Christmas tree. The faux wreath with its bright red bow listed off to one side.

Heading for the wreath, she lifted it, only to put it right back down again.

The silence behind her fairly echoed off the walls.

Joe's features were guarded when she turned back around. That same unfamiliar caution laced the deep tones of his voice. "Why will talking ruin anything?"

"Joe, please."

"Please what? What would I say or what could we talk about that would wreck things right now?"

Her only response was an uncooperative shake of her head.

As if unwilling to settle for that, he stepped closer. "I only want to know if you'd thought about staying in Rosewood," he told her. "Your lease is up the end of the year. I don't know if you have an option to renew or what your situation is there, but the end of the year is only four weeks away."

She was well aware of how far away it was. Rather, how close.

Her breath escaped in a rush, and a barely audible, "Oh."

An odd sort of tension radiated from him as his eyes narrowed.

"What did you think I wanted?"

"I was afraid…"

Realizing what she was about to admit, she cut herself off and jammed her fingers through her hair. In the space of seconds, the fear had set in that he was going to say something she really couldn't bear to hear just yet. She'd been afraid that having her parents invite themselves along on what was supposed to be a quiet date had made things seem a little too serious for him. Or maybe that he'd invited her out today because he'd picked up that she had gotten completely serious about him herself and he'd intended to let her down easily somehow.

Even as her thoughts hurriedly jumbled over themselves, she'd known it didn't make sense that he'd do something like that while decorating a tree, but being blindsided wasn't exactly unfamiliar to her. Jason had broken up with her after what she'd thought was a perfectly lovely evening. Jack had done it while she'd been blissfully picking out what to wear for their date.

Neither of those men meant anywhere near what this man did to her.

She realized now that she hadn't even begun to prepare herself to lose him, either. She knew that particular failure was totally impractical, too. If she'd learned anything from Joe it was that being practical probably saved a lot of grief and heartache, but losing him wasn't something she wanted to think about at all.

"I wasn't going to push you," Joe said. "I just wanted to know how much time I had."

Her mind seemed to go blank. Push me? "Time?" she echoed.

"For us." A muscle in his jaw jerked. "If you were thinking of staying and can't renew your lease, I was going to offer to help you find a place." A muscle in his jaw jumped. "If you were leaning toward going, I wanted to try to talk you out of it."

Incomprehension shadowed her face. "You weren't thinking about breaking up with me?"

The phenomenon was interesting, Joe thought. He could actually feel the tension drain from the muscles in his neck.

For a few very long seconds, he'd had the grim feeling that her day would be ruined if he admitted how he felt about her.

This woman had been in his thoughts nearly every waking hour for the past week. He knew she'd been a mess after Russell. He'd been fairly certain she'd be dealing with another set of emotions entirely once she learned about Randall. But when she'd started acting strangely around him at Thanksgiving dinner, barely making eye contact with him most of the time, he'd decided then that he had to back off, or he might lose her completely.

He'd fallen in love with her. He wasn't sure when. It could have been any of a hundred different moments. It might have been when she'd confided in him about her father. It could have been the moment she'd thrown herself into his arms when he'd found her at her friend's apartment. For all he knew it might have been the moment he'd first seen her. It didn't matter that a wife or marriage wasn't in his plans right now. As he'd told himself before, a guy couldn't plan for a woman like Rebecca. What did matter was that he hadn't wanted to add to the emotional load he'd known she'd been carrying.

So he'd stayed away, given her breathing room. If he'd had any idea that she'd interpreted his absence as not caring, he would have been on her doorstep in a heartbeat.

He'd never had a clue how her mind worked. As he closed the space between them, he wondered if he ever would.

With her eyes nearly even with his, his glance searched her face. Her skin looked flawless, her makeup perfect, her mouth glossed and ripe. But her features, beautiful as they were, held the same awful caution he'd felt himself.

"Why would you think I wanted to break up with you?" he asked.

"Because I thought I'd scared you off."

The need to touch tugged hard. Lifting his hand, he curved it at the side of her neck. The cashmere of her charcoal sweater felt soft. Her skin felt softer still. "How?"

"You need the list?"

"I'd settle for whatever is at the top of it."

"I can't tell you that."

"Why not?"

"Because then I would scare you away," she admitted. Her voice dropped. "That's the last thing I want to do."

"You want me around?"

The smile in his eyes gave her an odd sort of courage. Or maybe it was the reassurance she felt in his touch that made the admission come so easily. "Definitely."

"In that case…" he murmured, sliding his free hand around her waist, "how about I promise that I'm not going anywhere, and you tell me what you did that is so awful you thought I'd bolt."

Her heart knocked wildly as he pulled her body next to his.

"It isn't awful." It was wonderful. And painful. Thrilling and frightening. "It's just…scary."

He chuckled, the sound deep and oddly soothing as he brushed his lips over hers.

"So what did you do?" he asked, carrying that forgiving kiss to her cheek, her temple. His breath felt warm against her skin, his lips amazingly gentle. He had a way of touching her that made her feel as if she were utterly precious to him. She'd missed that. Missed being with him. Missed the way he had of making her feel cared for.

Held in his arms, surrounded by his quiet strength, she murmured, "I fell in love with you."

It seemed as if every muscle in his hard body went still. For a moment, she didn't think he even breathed. She knew she didn't.

"I don't expect you to love me back," she hurried to explain to the front of his shirt. He said he wouldn't bolt. Undoubtedly, the only thing keeping him there was his word. "And I won't ask anything from you. You've become so special to me, Joe, and I couldn't help it. It just…happened. Well, not just," she amended, wanting to make light of the admission if she could. "I think I probably fought the idea from—"

"I love you, too."

She went suddenly still. Keeping her eyes on plaid flannel, she shook her head. "That's one of the things I won't ask of you," she assured him. "You don't have to say that just because I did."

"I'm not."

"Come on, Joe."

Taking her by the shoulders, he ducked his head to catch her eyes. "Why can't you believe that I love you, too?"

Because it was too easy, she thought. Because guys said what they thought a woman wanted to hear. Because she wanted it too much.

He let her go, stepped back. "Stay right there," he said, holding his hand out to make sure she would. "Just…don't move."

Since she didn't know what else to do, she did as he asked and watched him back out of the room. She was slowly shaking her head while rubbing a spot between her eyes when he walked back in less than a minute.

"One of the reasons I wanted to go to the farm Thanksgiving was to pick up this," he said as he crossed toward her. "It's also the only reason I didn't get a lot of grief for coming back so early."

He held a small blue velvet pouch in his hand. Pulling the worn-looking ribbon at its neck as he stopped in front of her, he spilled something that glinted of gold and diamonds into his palm.

"This was my great-grandmother's. I didn't know when the time would be right to ask you to marry me," he explained while she stared at the beautiful old-fashioned engagement ring. "I just wanted to have it when that time came."

Disbelief kept her frozen where she stood.

It was so seldom that she was at a loss for words, but

she couldn't seem to speak at all. The ring was lovely, intricate and antique. The stones, the largest in the full carat range, winked and sparkled in the overhead lights.

"I know it's old, but the stones can be reset."

She wouldn't dream of changing it. The ring was an heirloom. It had history behind it. Family.

Her chest felt just a little too tight. He really did love her.

"Like I said before, Rebecca. I don't want to push you." Thumbing the ring onto his little finger, he curled the pouch in his palm. "But I do love you." The certainty in his tone was mirrored in his eyes as he tucked back her hair. "I don't ever want you to doubt that." He edged closer. "Okay?"

The tightness in her throat robbed the strength from her voice. "Okay."

"Just so we understand each other."

She'd barely nodded before he eased her to him, capturing her mouth with his. She felt relief in his kiss, her own as well as his, but there was promise there, too. And reassurance. Then possessiveness slipped in as his hand roamed down her back, pulling her closer still.

Pure need had her knees feeling weak and her heart beating a little too fast when he finally lifted his head.

His eyes dark on hers, he brushed his moisture from her mouth with his thumb. She rather liked that his breathing didn't sound all that even, either.

"I think we're clear," he murmured.

She thought so, too. She understood the need she felt in him perfectly. There was only one thing she hadn't quite grasped.

"Just one question," she said.

"What's that?"

"When do you think you'll ask?"

He didn't even hesitate.

"Anytime you're ready."

Encouraged by the glint in his eyes, or maybe it was the heat, Rebecca took a deep breath. "I feel really ready right now."

"Oh, yeah?"

"Yeah," she echoed.

He said nothing else. With his arms back around her, she felt his hands move at the small of her back. Seconds later, her heart bumped in her chest when she realized he'd taken the ring from his little finger.

Edging back, he lifted her left hand and nodded toward the dogs playing tug with the Santa hat they'd pulled from the box.

"You understand they come with the deal, don't you?"

"They'd better."

"And that we'll probably acquire new pets along the way. For the kids, of course."

Her heart squeezed. She'd told him the day she'd met him she wanted children. "How many?"

"Two."

"Pets?"

"Kids."

"I'd like three."

"Numbers are negotiable."

"Absolutely."

"Is that it?"

She gave a nod.

"In that case…" His tone went oddly husky. "Rebecca. Will you marry me?"

"Absolutely," she whispered, and watched him slip the ring onto her finger.

For a moment, she did nothing but stare at it, then at him. The feeling that had just hit wasn't one she had expected at all. But even as she threw her arms around his neck and met his kiss, she knew for certain that she was home.

She couldn't have imagined it before Joe had brought her back, but this place truly was her home. She belonged right here in Rosewood. With her friends. With Joe. Most especially with him.

She would have told him that, too, had he not just carried his kiss to her ear to whisper, "We're not alone."

He must have heard something she hadn't. As he turned her in front of the bare Christmas tree, the light catching the diamonds in her ring, she saw her mom and her newly discovered father on the far side of the room. Randall had his arm around her mother's shoulder. Both were smiling.

She couldn't help but smile back as they walked in with her mom reaching to see what Joe had given her and Randall heading for him to shake his hand. She had imagined all her life what family must feel like. Yet, as she stood with Joe's arm around her, surrounded by her parents and his pets, she realized that nothing compared to reality with the man she'd once thought was her polar opposite.

The man who'd turned out to be her perfect match.

* * * * *

*What happens when suburban supermum
Angela Schumacher gets romance as a
Christmas gift? Find out in* The Super Mum
*by Karen Rose Smith,
the next book in the new
Special Edition continuity,*
TALK OF THE NEIGHBOURHOOD.
On sale December 2007.

Special
moments

We hope that the Special Edition novel you have just
finished has given you plenty of romantic
reading pleasure.

We are thrilled to have put together a section of
special free bonus features, which we hope will add to
the entertainment in each Special Edition novel from
now on.

There will be puzzles for you to do, exciting
horoscopes glimpsing what's in your future, author
information and sneak previews of books in
the pipeline!

Do let us know what you think of these
special extras by emailing
specialmoments@hmb.co.uk

For you, from us…
Relax and enjoy…

fun Star *signs*
puzzles

Dear Reader,

I have a confession to make. I am a hopeless holiday junkie. In mid-September I decorate parts of our home with autumn leaves, pumpkins and little scarecrows. In October I add Halloween. On 1st November the jack-o'-lantern tea-light holders and cutesy witches (I'm not into "scary") give way to pilgrims. And for Thanksgiving weekend "autumn" gets packed up and the snowmen, pine boughs and tiny white lights come out.

I suppose I crave things autumn and winter because we don't have a change of those seasons where we live in the Southwest. (Those autumn leaves come from craft stores.) But I suspect the deeper reason is that part of me still delights in things I loved as a child. As adults we all have our responsibilities of home, work and family, but I truly hope you find moments of something a little magical in all the holidays, too!

Best wishes,

Christine Flynn

Author *Biography*

CHRISTINE FLYNN

admits to being interested in just about everything, which is why she considers herself fortunate to have turned her interest in writing into a career. She feels that a writer gets to explore it all and, to her, exploring relationships – especially the intense, bittersweet or even lighthearted relationships between men and women – is fascinating.

Menu Words
Copyright ©2007 PuzzleJunction.com

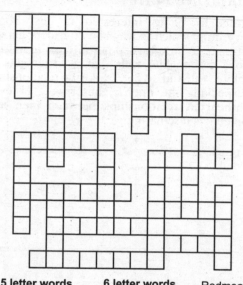

5 letter words

Anise

Bacon

Chips

Clams

Honey

Mango

Roast

Rolls

6 letter words

Apples

Carrot

Cheese

Endive

Millet

Oyster

Salmon

7 letter words

Limeade

Rarebit

Redmeat

Seafood

Sherbet

Waffles

8 letter words

Escargot

Meatloaf

Scallops

Special *moments*

Sudoku

To solve the Sudoku puzzle, each row, column and box must contain the numbers 1 to 9.

				4			3	
3						2		
		7				1		8
	5	6		8	1	7		
		1	4		5			
					6			
			3	9				
			8		7		9	5
	3			5	4	6		7

Copyright ©2007 PuzzleJunction.com

Horo*scopes*

Dadhichi is a renowned astrologer and is frequently seen on TV and in the media. He has the unique ability to draw from complex astrological theory to provide clear, easily understandable advice and insights for people who want to know what their future may hold.

In the twenty-five years that Dadhichi has been practising astrology, face reading and other esoteric studies, he has conducted over 8,500 consultations. His clients include celebrities, political and diplomatic figures and media and corporate identities from all over the world.

Aries
21 March - 20 April

You're deeply interested in investigating the possibilities for your life during November. Your mind is focused, deliberate and less prone to superficial involvements. On the 13th, 18th and the 24th and 25th you could uncover some valuable information which will help you achieve some new success in the coming months.

Taurus
21 April - 21 May

The Sun and Mars will de-stabilise your relationships this month so it's important to be less reactive. By the 11th, you'll observe extreme mood changes in your spouse and this requires more understanding. Relationships with children on the 21st are touchy so your test this month is to remain peaceful and non-reactive.

Special *moments*

Gemini
22 May - 22 June

This is a romantic month but don't be compulsive. On the 14th be less possessive if someone wants more independence. The 14th to the 22nd is an excellent time to pursue a new hobby and discover the hidden talents you've overlooked. The health of a relative on the 25th may concern you but should clear up quickly.

Cancer
23 June - 23 July

Outdoor activities and physical exertion are necessary to relieve you of stress this month. On the 20th, make a greater effort to do your exercise or yoga class. You'll feel so much better for it. Balance your physical and emotional appetites on the 25th so that you have enough energy for social interaction and a fun night out on the 29th.

Leo
24 July - 23 August

Don't let the past haunt you. Let go of unsavoury experiences that you have no control over. Your mind will be dwelling on someone or some situation. Make that phone call, speak your mind and then put the matter to bed. The 10th, 16th and 25th would be ideal days to do that.

Virgo
24 August - 22 September

This month shows just how capable you are of achieving so much with so little. Industriousness and resourcefulness will be evident on the 12th, but you mustn't push others to their limits. On the 13th and 14th changes in your professional environment will be welcomed and offer you centre stage.

Libra

23 September - 23 October

Arguments over money must be avoided this month. You are in a spending mood and this is probably because it's nearing Christmas. On the 12th, study your credit card statements and don't live beyond your means. A profitable period is forecast from the 18th but on the 20th turn down that attractive bargain when shopping.

Scorpio

24 October - 22 November

Your words of kindness and compassion will have the desired effect on the 8th when sparks of romance will fly. An unexpected meeting with a stranger or someone you're introduced to could pave the way for a new love affair. The 11th and the 21st should be put aside to deepen your affection for them.

Sagittarius

23 November - 21 December

Your monetary concerns should be all but cleared up now. Additional income, unearned commissions and interest from savings should be better than expected. An oversight on the 14th might create a glitch in your bank balance, but don't let this deter you from moving forward to bigger and better things.

Special *moments*

Capricorn
22 December - 20 January

A long-lost lover may return or you will be reminiscing about someone you haven't seen in a while. On the 8th, re-connect with those people who just happen to be popping up in your mind. Extending your knowledge of electronic devices and communication is likely after the 8th. Romance flourishes between the 15th and the 24th.

Aquarius
21 January - 18 February

A new social group is what you need. Connecting with a bunch of fresh new faces will lift your spirits and broaden your view of the world. Watch your health on the 6th when your lower energy levels will be telling you something. You will feel refreshed by the 14th and can expect a stroke of good luck around the 23rd.

Pisces
19 February - 20 March

You're restless in love but should count your blessings and be grateful for what you have. You could experience some stresses around the 19th and 20th but if you look at the upside, you will start to feel much better by the 23rd. The attitude of gratitude seems to be the moral of the Piscean story in November.

Gone Swimming

```
G  N  I  H  T  A  B  A  F  B  L  C  M
W  K  C  D  N  Z  N  M  U  W  V  R  M
S  M  H  X  O  A  Y  T  H  C  A  E  B
Y  C  Y  V  B  G  T  D  Z  Q  S  D  Q
F  V  I  A  L  E  P  L  T  I  D  N  E
L  L  C  T  R  M  W  A  D  G  E  A  T
H  P  O  F  A  A  E  E  D  K  G  E  P
S  T  L  A  V  U  S  V  O  D  L  C  I
A  Y  H  E  T  T  Q  R  I  O  L  O  D
L  K  S  F  R  G  T  A  O  D  B  E  Y
P  K  I  O  Q  S  Z  P  L  T  I  T  N
S  B  K  C  P  A  D  D  L  E  K  J  N
M  E  K  R  K  M  C  F  L  V  I  F  I
N  A  T  A  N  T  R  T  D  Z  N  S  K
L  I  F  E  G  U  A  R  D  B  I  U  S
F  W  A  T  E  R  W  I  N  G  S  I  N
H  K  Q  M  C  W  L  T  Q  Q  N  T  D
```

©2007 PuzzleJunction.com

AQUATICS	DOG PADDLE	SIDESTROKE
BATHING	FLOAT	SKINNY DIP
BEACH	KICK	SPLASH
BIKINI	LIFE GUARD	STROKE
BUTTERFLY	NATANT	SUIT
CABANA	OCEAN	WADE
CRAWL	PADDLE	WATER WINGS
DIVE	POOL	WAVES

Special moments

Connect-*it*

From the Spice Rack

Copyright ©2007 PuzzleJunction.com

Each line in the puzzle below has three clues and three
answers. The last letter in the first answer on each line is the
first letter of the second answer, and so on. The connecting
letter is outlined, giving you the correct number of letters for
each answer (the answers in line 1 are 4, 6 and 6 letters).
The clues are numbered 1 to 8, with each number containing
3 clues for the 3 answers on the line. But here's the catch!
The clues are not in order - so the first clue in the line is not
necessarily for the first answer. Good luck!

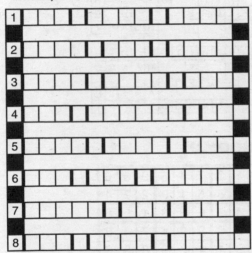

Clues:

1. Foreign. Mature. Spice buds.
2. East Indian spice. Pour. Cede.
3. Allow. Chubby. Minty spice.
4. Grey-green spice. Rant. Teacher.
5. Out of practice. Root spice. Affair.
6. Pimiento spice. Go by. Slough.
7. Melancholy. Wall painting. Eggnog spice.
8. Pickling spice. Sod. Madness.

KRISSKROSS

```
C H I P S       S A L M O N
        C       E       I
L   W   A       E A P P L E S
M E A T L O A F     L       H
S   F   L       O   E       E
    F   O       O Y S T E R
    L   P       D         B
C H E E S E           B   E
A       N       R O A S T
R       D       E   C
R A R E B I T   D   O     H
O           V     M A N G O
T   L I M E A D E         N
    L           A N I S E
  E S C A R G O T         Y
```

SUDOKU

5	1	2	7	4	8	9	3	6
3	6	8	5	1	9	2	7	4
9	4	7	6	2	3	1	5	8
2	5	6	9	8	1	7	4	3
7	9	1	4	3	5	8	6	2
4	8	3	2	7	6	5	1	9
6	7	5	3	9	2	4	8	1
1	2	4	8	6	7	3	9	5
8	3	9	1	5	4	6	2	7

387

Special moments

WORDSEARCH

```
G N I H T A B A F B L C M
W K C D N Z N M U W V R M
S M H X O A Y T H C A E B
Y C Y V B G T D Z Q S D Q
F V I A L E P L T I D N E
L L C T R M W A D G E A T
H P O F A A E E D K G E P
S T L A V U S V O D L C I
A Y H E T T Q R I O L O D
L K S F R G T A O D B E N
P K I O Q S Z P L T I T N
S B K C P A D D L E K J I
M E K R K M C F L V I F I
N A T A N T R T D Z N S K
L I F E G U A R D B I U S
F W A T E R W I N G S I N
H K Q M C W L T Q Q N T D
```

CONNECT-IT

```
1  R I P E X O T I C L O V E S
2  C U R R Y I E L D E C A N T
3  P L U M P E R M I T H Y M E
4  S A G E D U C A T O R A V E
5  F L I N G I N G E R U S T Y
6  P A S S W A M P A P R I K A
7  N U T M E G L O O M U R A L
8  T U R F E N N E L U N A C Y
```

Enjoy this sneak preview of

Sierra's Homecoming
by New York Times bestselling author
Linda Lael Miller

Available in December 2007

Sierra's Homecoming

by

Linda Lael Miller

Soft, smoky music poured into the room.

The next thing she knew, Sierra was in Travis's arms, close against that chest she'd admired earlier, and they were slow dancing.

Why didn't she pull away?

"Relax," he said. His breath was warm in her hair.

She giggled, more nervous than amused. What was the matter with her? She was attracted to Travis, had been from the first, and he was clearly attracted to her. They were both adults. Why not enjoy a little slow dancing in a ranch-house kitchen?

Because slow dancing led to other things. She took a step back and felt the counter flush against her lower back. Travis naturally came with her, since they were holding hands and he had one arm around her waist.

Simple physics.

Then he kissed her.

Physics again—this time, not so simple.

"Yikes," she said, when their mouths parted.

He grinned. "Nobody's ever said that after I kissed them."

She felt the heat and substance of his body pressed against hers. "It's going to happen, isn't it?" she heard herself whisper.

"Yep," Travis answered.

"But not tonight," Sierra said on a sigh.

"Probably not," Travis agreed.

"When, then?"

He chuckled, gave her a slow, nibbling kiss. "Tomorrow morning," he said. "After you drop Liam off at school."

"Isn't that…a little…soon?"

"Not soon enough," Travis answered, his voice husky. "Not nearly soon enough."

* * *

Don't forget
Sierra's Homecoming
is available next month!

BRIDES OF PENHALLY BAY

Medical™ is proud to welcome you to Penhally
Bay Surgery where you can meet the team led by
caring and commanding Dr Nick Tremayne.
For the next twelve months we will bring
you an emotional, tempting romance – devoted
doctors, single fathers, a sheikh surgeon,
royalty, blushing brides and miracle babies
will warm your heart…

*Let us whisk you away to this Cornish coastal
town – to a place where hearts are made whole.*

Turn the page for a sneak preview from
Christmas Eve Baby
by Caroline Anderson
– the first book in the
BRIDES OF PENHALLY BAY series.

CHRSTMAS EVE BABY
by
Caroline Anderson

Ben crossed the room, standing by the window, looking out. It was a pleasant room, and from the window he could see across the boatyard to the lifeboat station and beyond it the sea.

He didn't notice, though, not really. Didn't take it in, couldn't have described the colour of the walls or the furniture, because there was only one thing he'd really seen, only one thing he'd been aware of since Lucy had got out of her car.

Lucy met his eyes, but only with a huge effort, and he could see the emotions racing through their wary, soft brown depths. God only knows what his own expression was, but he held her gaze for a long moment before she coloured and looked away.

'Um – can I make you some tea?' she offered, and he gave a short, disbelieving cough of laughter.

'Don't you think there's something we should talk about first?' he suggested, and she hesitated, her hand on the kettle, catching her lip between those neat, even teeth and nibbling it unconsciously.

'I intend to,' she began, and he laughed and propped his hips on the edge of the desk, his hands each side gripping the thick, solid wood as if his life depended on it.

'When, exactly? Assuming, as I am, perhaps a little rashly, that unless that's a beachball you've got up your jumper it has something to do with me?'

She put the kettle down with a little thump and turned towards him, her eyes flashing fire. 'Rashly? *Rashly?* Is that what you think of me? That I'd sleep with you and then go and fall into bed with another man?'

He shrugged, ignoring the crazy, irrational flicker of hope that it was, indeed, his child. 'I don't know. I would hope not, but I don't know anything about your private life. Not any more,' he added with a tinge of regret.

'Well, you should know enough about me to know that isn't the way I do things.'

'So how do you do things, Lucy?' he asked, trying to stop the anger from creeping into his voice. 'Like your father? You don't like it, so you just pretend it hasn't happened?'

'And what was I supposed to do?' she asked, her eyes flashing sparks again. 'We weren't seeing each other. We'd agreed.'

'But this, surely, changes things? Or should have. Unless you just weren't going to tell me? It must have made it simpler for you.'

She turned away again, but not before he saw her eyes fill, and guilt gnawed at him. 'Simpler?'

she said. 'That's not how I'd describe it.'

'So why not tell me, then?' he said, his voice softening. 'Why, in all these months, didn't you tell me that I'm going to be a father?'

'I was going to,' she said, her voice little more than a whisper. 'But after everything – I didn't know how to. It's just all so difficult –'

'But it *is* mine.'

She nodded, her hair falling over her face and obscuring it from him. 'Yes. Yes, it's yours.'

His heart soared, and for a ridiculous moment he felt like punching the air, but then he pulled himself together. Plenty of time for that later, once he'd got all the facts. Down to the nitty-gritty, he thought, and asked the question that came to the top of the heap.

'Does your father know it's mine…?'

She shook her head, and he winced.

'Have you had lunch?' she said suddenly.

'*Lunch?*' he said, his tone disbelieving. 'No. I got held up in Resus. There wasn't time.'

'Fancy coming back to my house and having something to eat? Only I'm starving, and I'm trying to eat properly, and biscuits and cakes and rubbish like that just won't cut the mustard.'

'Sounds good,' he said, not in the least bit hungry but desperate to be away from there and somewhere private while he assimilated this stunning bit of news.

She opened the door, grabbed her coat out of the staff room as they passed it and led him down the stairs.

They walked to her flat, along Harbour Road and up Bridge Street, the road that ran alongside the river and up out of the old town towards St Piran, the road he'd come in on. It was over a gift shop, in a steep little terrace typical of Cornish coastal towns and villages, and he wondered how she'd manage when she'd had the baby.

Not here, was the answer, especially when she led him through a door into a narrow little hallway and up the precipitous stairs to her flat. 'Make yourself at home, I'll find some food,' she said, a little breathless after her climb, and left him in the small living room. If he got close to the window he could see the sea, but apart from that it had no real charm. It was homely, though, and comfortable, and he wandered round it, picking up things and putting them down, measuring her life.

A book on pregnancy, a mother-and-baby magazine, a book of names, lying in a neat pile on the end of an old leather trunk in front of the sofa. More books in a bookcase, a cosy fleece blanket draped over the arm of the sofa, some flowers in a vase lending a little cheer.

He could see her through the kitchen door, pottering about and making sandwiches, and he went and propped himself in the doorway and watched her.

'I'd offer to help, but the room's too small for three of us,' he murmured, and she gave him a slightly nervous smile.

Why nervous? he wondered, and then realised that of course she was nervous. She had no idea what his attitude would be, whether he'd be pleased or angry, if he'd want to be involved in his child's life – any of it.

When he'd worked it out himself, he'd tell her. The only thing he did know, absolutely with total certainty, was that if, as she had said, this baby was his, he was going to be a part of its life for ever.

And that was non-negotiable.

* * * *

Brides of Penhally Bay
Bachelor doctors become husbands and fathers – in a place where hearts are made whole.

Snuggle up this festive season with
Christmas Eve Baby
by Caroline Anderson
– out in December 2007!

MILLS & BOON
Special Edition

On sale 16th November 2007

IT TAKES A FAMILY
by *Victoria Pade*

Penniless and raising an infant niece after her sister's death, Karis Pratt's only hope was to go to Montana, and find the baby's father, Luke Walker. Did this small-town cop hold the key to renewed family ties and a bright new future for Karis?

CALL ME COWBOY
by *Judy Duarte*

When children's book editor Priscilla Richards uncovered evidence that her father had long ago changed her name, she hired sexy PI 'Cowboy' Whittaker to find out why. Soon they discovered that her mother was alive – and that Cowboy wanted to mend prim-and-proper Priscilla's broken heart.

UNDER THE MISTLETOE
by *Kristin Hardy*

No-nonsense businesswoman Hadley Stone had a job to do – modernise the Hotel Mount Eisenhower. But the manager Gabe Trask stood in her way, guarding the landmark's legacy. Would the beautiful Vermont Christmas – and meetings under the mistletoe – soften these adversaries' hearts?

FREE

4 BOOKS AND A SURPRISE GIFT!

We would like to take this opportunity to thank you for reading this Mills & Boon® book by offering you the chance to take FOUR more specially selected titles from the Special Edition series absolutely FREE! We're also making this offer to introduce you to the benefits of the Mills & Boon® Reader Service™—

* ★ **FREE home delivery**
* ★ **FREE gifts and competitions**
* ★ **FREE monthly Newsletter**
* ★ **Books available before they're in the shops**
* ★ **Exclusive Reader Service offers**

Accepting these FREE books and gift places you under no obligation to buy; you may cancel at any time, even after receiving your free shipment. Simply complete your details below and return the entire page to the address below. You don't even need a stamp!

YES! Please send me 4 free Special Edition books and a surprise gift. I understand that unless you hear from me, I will receive 6 superb new titles every month for just £3.10 each, postage and packing free. I am under no obligation to purchase any books and may cancel my subscription at any time. The free books and gift will be mine to keep in any case.

E7ZEE

Ms/Mrs/Miss/Mr...Initials ....
BLOCK CAPITALS PLEASE

Surname ....

Address ....

....

....Postcode ....

Send this whole page to:

The Reader Service, FREEPOST CN81, Croydon, CR9 3WZ